COLD CANADIAN CRIME

A CRIME WRITERS OF CANADA ANTHOLOGY

Edited by TAIJA MORGAN

Introduction by WILLIAM DEVERELL

Foreword by LINWOOD BARCLAY

Crime Writers
of Canada

FEATURING

K.L. ABRAHAMSON
PAM BARNSLEY
THOM BENNETT
SUSAN CALDER
MELODIE CAMPBELL
BRENDA CHAPMAN
LISA DE NIKOLITS
ELIZABETH ELWOOD
ALICE FITZPATRICK
DELEE FROMM
R.M. GREENAWAY
BLAIR KEETCH
SYLVIA MAULTASH WARSH
ROSEMARY MCCRACKEN
DONALEE MOULTON
LYNNE MURPHY
C.S. O'CINNEIDE
LORNA POPLAK
DAVID A. POULSEN
GABRIELLE ST. GEORGE
HOPE THOMSON

PRAISE FOR COLD CANADIAN CRIME
A CRIME WRITERS OF CANADA ANTHOLOGY

"The Canadian crime writing community has never been stronger, more creative, more diverse, richer in talent and daring. This anthology, to celebrate 40 years of the CWC, is a reflection of that. I have never been more proud to be a member of the CWC, and of this community. Congratulations to all who have contributed to this anthology and to the canon of Canadian crime writing." —*Louise Penny, award winning author.*

"A delight for lovers of short crime stories. A veritable buffet of intrigue, menace, and mystery."—*Rick Mofina, bestselling author of* Her Last Goodbye.

"This year's *Cold Canadian Crime* anthology celebrating Crime Writers of Canada's 40 years of excellence raises the bar on Canadian crime writing with the turn of every unsettling, delightfully disturbing page. Each story in this memorable collection is shrouded in a cool mist of mystery, murder and mayhem that pulls in the reader, demands attention, and dares us to turn away, knowing we can't."—*Anthony Bidulka, author of the Russell Quant mystery series and novels* Set Free *and* Going to Beautiful.

"The breadth and imagination displayed by the wide variety of storytelling in this collection prove that the future of Canadian crime writing is bright indeed."—*Vicki Delany, Recipient of the 2019 Derrick Murdoch Award for Contributions to Canadian Crime Writing.*

"This gang of Canadian crime writers has pulled off one clever caper. From mad trappers to angry actors to larcenous ladies, every one of these tales will offer the crime afficionado someone to love." —*Giles Blunt, author of* Forty Words for Sorrow.

"The line 'murder will out' appears three times in Geoffrey Chaucer's late 14th-century work *The Canterbury Tales*. The settings of the 21 stories that make up *Cold Canadian Crime* are as disparate as Iqaluit, Quebec City, Toronto, Calgary, and Victoria, but each reveals the distinct desire for justice that we see in Chaucer. Some of the stories are light-hearted, some are dark, but all explore the human need to redress an imbalance in the scales of justice. *Cold Canadian Crime* offers readers meticulously drawn characters who live in very different worlds, compelling plots, and the comforting reassurance that, as Launcelot Gobbo says in *The Merchant of Venice*, "Murder will come to light/Murder cannot be hid long.'"—*Gail Bowen, author of the Joanne Kilbourn Shreve mystery series.*

"Writers from across the nation serve up twisty, punchy, and murderously engaging stories. This anthology will bring a smile to the faces of those who like their crime fiction short and deadly and are eager to discover new voices in Canadian crime fiction."—*Cathy Ace, award-winning author of the Cait Morgan mystery series.*

"What a wonderful banquet of delights. Different styles, different moods, all excellent."—*Maureen Jennings, author of Murdoch Mysteries and Paradise Cafe series.*

COPYRIGHT

David A. Poulsen

Anita Sachanska

Gabrielle St. George

Hope Thompson

Managing Editor: Ludvica Boota

Anthology Committee: Alice Bienia, Susan Daly, Zana Gordon, Winona Kent, Judy Penz Sheluk, Lorna Poplak

Administrative Support: Alison Bruce

Edited by Taija Morgan

Proofread by Alexandra Zych

Formatted by Karen Abrahamson

Cover Design by Tuhin Giri

Published by Crime Writers of Canada

ISBN Trade Paperback: 978-0-9696825-7-8

ISBN e-Book: 978-0-9696825-6-1

First Edition: May 2022

CONTENTS

R.M. GREENAWAY

THOM BENNETT

DELEE FROMM

ELIZABETH ELWOOD

HOPE THOMPSON

ROSEMARY MCCRACKEN

BRENDA CHAPMAN

INTRODUCTION

WILLIAM DEVERELL

Canadian crime writers have come a long way since the early 1980s, when our numbers were sparse and the genre was considered by the literary elite as uncouth and vaguely vulgar.

That's doubtless because of the strict Victorian mindset that dominated Canadian culture in the mid-twentieth century. Crime fiction was then considered by public libraries to be déclassé, and such novels were not allowed to foul their shelves. And even when the libraries, faced with public demand, began to buy mysteries and thrillers, works by British and American authors dwarfed the meagre output of Canucks.

Matters were far worse in the nineteenth century. When Canada's first home-grown murder mystery saw print in 1876, the author, Mary Leslie, had to use a male pseudonym, then was forced to withdraw all copies because of an uproar in the Ontario town where her story seemed (too accurately) to be set.

A prurient attitude has continued to seduce academic libraries and graduate English courses, where students are made to believe that Hugo and Dostoevsky, Maugham and Conrad had not written crime novels. The virus still flourishes in our schools and cultural institutions, as genre writers rarely make the literary tea guest lists.

She writes mysteries, my dear, she'll show up reeking of gin. Or you get: *He writes thrillers? How crass. It's so American.*

I felt that sting in 1979, when I opened the *Vancouver Sun* to a censorial review of my first novel: "A decade ago, before decency was outmoded, his book would have risked prosecution under Canada's obscenity laws. Today, in our permissive society, the book wins a literary prize." (Sales in Vancouver jumped, however, a pleasant irony.)

The late Marian Engle once confessed to me that she occasionally enjoyed the "guilty pleasure" of reading a mystery. I grappled with that—why should that pleasure cause guilt? Thankfully, over the years, Canada has hosted an ever-increasing number of crime writers whose work is of such high quality that book lovers no longer have to be wracked with guilt as they take their reading fix. Much of our crime writing now matches or beats the literary qualities demanded by our self-appointed guardians of culture.

And we are not copycatting our American brothers and sisters. Essayist David Skene-Melvin wrote in his bibliography, *Canadian Crime Fiction*: "Canadians today are telling their own stories, no longer feeling obliged to hide their nationality nor pretending to be British or American."

Our protagonists also tend to be more thoughtful, introspective, cerebral. Skene-Melvin also believes Canadian crime writing is "more subtle, more psychological, more caring" than in the U.S., "where the gun is forged into the collective soul, where the gunslingers of the wild west became the hardboiled private eyes in the cities." A case in point: the late Eric Wright constructed his protagonist, Inspector Salter, "according to what I like about Canadians—he has a gentleness and a fundamental sense of decency."

It was due to the efforts of Eric Wright and a small club of Toronto-based authors that Canadian book lovers woke up to the reality that they no longer had to rely on Dame Agatha or Rex Stout to satisfy their hunger for an enjoyable read. These pioneers, some of whom are, sadly, no longer with us, also included Howard

Engel, Larry Morse, Tony Aspler, and book reviewer Derrick Murdoch, and they regularly gathered in the early 1980s in Dooley's bar.

They were the architects of the Crime Writers of Canada, now celebrating its fortieth birthday with this masterful collection of short pieces. Many took trailblazing shifts serving as the CWC's presidents in the 1980s.

Admittedly, one could sense an all-boys-clubiness here, but the CWC has been enriched by a tsunami of talented women. (They clearly outnumber male contributors to this celebratory collection. I hasten to add that the twenty-one pieces in the following pages were selected by judges clueless as to the authors' names and gender.)

The theme is "Cold Canadian Crime," and the stories contain not just chills but some wintry humour—so you're guaranteed to enjoy either shivers of delight or rollicks in the snow. Guiltlessly.

William Deverell

FOREWORD

LINWOOD BARCLAY

I almost never write short stories. They're too hard.

You wouldn't think so, right? I mean, it's clear enough from the description. They're *short*. When someone says "Make short work of this" they're suggesting it's no big deal. So a short story ought to be something any half-decent writer can produce in a few hours. Come up with a dynamite first sentence in the morning, take a break for lunch at noon, get back to the computer at one, and by three o'clock you've typed "The End" and are off to the pub to tell your friends you knocked off another Hitchcockian gem without breaking a sweat.

If only.

Back in another life, I was a newspaper columnist. I wrote three pieces a week. Some people seemed to think that was a real grind, basically doing a column every other day. Wouldn't one article a week be easier? No. When you do one a week, it's really got to be good. When you do three, if you write a clunker, well, there'll be another one day after tomorrow. If it's moderately acceptable (now there's a great blurb for you: "A moderately acceptable read!") your audience will forget that weaker effort that's now lining a birdcage. (Note to kids: newspapers were once made of actual paper.)

In a short story, every word counts. In a novel, you can take your time, wax poetic, go off on irrelevant tangents. Like that thriller writer (bless him, no longer with us) who, when he had some bad guy pull a gun, he'd write three pages on what kind of gun it was. Just shoot the bastard, for crying out loud.

Writing a good short story is an art. It's distilling an idea down to its essence. You've got to set your scene, introduce your characters, present your dilemma, and wrap it up with a flourish, all in a few thousand words. It's a high-wire act on a page. No thank you. I'll just blather on in a 100,000-word novel.

In this anthology—aptly named *Cold Canadian Crime*—you have twenty-one perfect examples of that approach, and what distinguishes this anthology from others is its distinctive "We The North" flavour. (And if I may digress, how do a bunch of Canadian writers crank out nasty stories like these when we're supposedly such a nice people? Someone once asked me whether there were any differences between the Canadian and American editions of my novels. I said that in the Canadian ones, after the killers off someone, they always say, "Sorry.")

Take David A. Poulsen's 'The Day Peter Gzowski Died' (you can't get any more Canadian than that) in which a private detective is engaged to track down a serial killer on the very same day the legendary broadcaster passes on. The murders are inspired by a university course called Murder in the Classics, and in true, classical detective fiction form, our P.I. learns he may be the killer's next victim.

Melodie Campbell, whose stories can usually be counted on for a laugh or five, takes a turn down a very dark street in 'Death of a Ghost' when a Toronto woman, after the death of her much-reviled father, receives a visit from the mother she thought had died years earlier. There are more than a few unresolved mother-daughter issues here, and in a story like this, they must be settled—one way or another.

We find ourselves in St. Catharines in Brenda Chapman's 'The Final Hit.' A professional killer struggling to distance himself from his past faces a reckoning when his latest assignment involves inflicting more harm on innocent lives than he'd signed up for.

Gabrielle St. George takes on domestic violence when she describes the lengths an 82-year-old mother in Ontario will go to save her two daughters from their abusive husbands. This tale is a perfect example of how crime fiction— in novels and short stories— can use the conventions of a mystery novel to tackle big, societal issues.

These are but a sampling of the suspenseful tales you're about to encounter. And as you're reading them, keep this in mind. It's not as easy as it looks. In fact, it's likely the authors of these stories found that, to hit all the right notes, to keep you on the edge of your seat, to keep you guessing to the end, it nearly killed them.

And we couldn't be more grateful.

Linwood Barclay

MELODIE CAMPBELL

Called the "Queen of Comedy" by the *Toronto Sun*, Melodie Campbell has also been named the "Canadian literary heir to Donald Westlake" by *Ellery Queen Mystery Magazine*. Winner of ten awards, including The Derringer (US) and the Crime Writers of Canada Award of Excellence, she has multiple bestsellers, and was featured on *USA Today*. Her publications include over 100 comedy credits, sixteen novels and sixty short stories, but she's best known for The Goddaughter mob caper series. Melodie's website is www.melodiecampbell.com

DEATH OF A GHOST

MELODIE CAMPBELL

MY FATHER WAS DEAD. Dead a week, and no doubt on his way to hell.

Flowers had been arriving at a great pace; absurdly cheerful arrangements of carnations, roses and lilies littered the front room of my small Victorian two-storey. Stupid custom for such a grim event. Who decided that flowers should be associated with death? Probably the same moron who declared hell would be hot, whereas every Canadian knows it will be endless winter with blizzards vicious enough to freeze your soul.

It was cold enough to do that tonight, clear crisp evidence of the recent ice storm that had taken Toronto by surprise.

Someone was knocking at the door. Strange, for this time of night, but I crossed the room to answer it, expecting more sympathy deliveries. All these flowers were a travesty under the circumstances, and I'd laugh about it later. Really, I would.

The door creaked as I opened it. A blast of air whooshed in; the hairs in my nose froze almost instantly.

No flowers this time, but a middle-aged woman, shivering on the porch.

She wore no hat and the brown serge coat she clutched around her seemed pitifully thin for this time of year. I stared at her for several moments, trying to get a grip. The similarity set my heart racing. Like looking through the door into a distant mirror...

Unusual auburn hair like mine, light eyes, pointed chin, slight build, same height. Worried expression. Deep creases forming horizontal ridges across her forehead. If I could take my face and project it decades into the future...

"Mom?" I whispered, tentatively. *Ridiculous. My mother had died twenty years ago.*

Her thin mouth broke to a smile. "It's cold out here. May I come in?" Her voice brought every jagged memory to the forefront of my mind.

I opened the door wide.

S he talked. We sat on the worn leather sectional sofa, kitty-corner from each other. I didn't offer coffee and I didn't take her coat.

She talked for at least ten minutes straight. About the flight from Australia, the Covid-19 restrictions, the taxi from the airport. How she had planned this trip for years, waiting for the right time. How, after so many years in the Southern Hemisphere, she'd forgotten how cold January in Canada could be.

All the while, I stared at her trying to conjure up feelings.

"You're all grown up," she said. Her eyes never left my face. "I always remember you as seven."

"I was eight," I said flatly.

The room felt cloying. Damned flowers. I hate the smell of lilies.

"I kept track of you both, all these years. I knew you had moved back to Toronto from New York. I even knew you had become an accountant, like I am." There was something like pride in her voice.

She continued to clutch the russet-brown coat around her and tried for a smile. "As soon as I heard your father had died, I booked a plane ticket to come home and find you."

No boots, I noticed. At least my brain was registering something.

"You have no idea how much I wanted to see you. All these years…"

All these years… Still, I couldn't muster up any feelings. What was wrong with me? Had the cold penetrated my heart?

She continued to talk in that soft, shaky voice. "I know it was wrong of me. But you have to understand: your father was brutal to me. More than once, he'd put me in hospital. I had to get away, and then when I was presented with this perfect opportunity…" Her eyes glazed over in memory. "I could just disappear, and no one would be any the wiser. It was too good to pass up."

The clock on the wall ticked away the seconds. I tried not to think of the years gone by.

She'd been saving money for months, she told me. Thousands, stored along with her passport in a secret safety deposit box that she could empty and use to find her way out of the country. Disappear without a trace.

But this was the kicker: she wasn't in the office that morning. She'd had a breakfast meeting with a client at his place, and was making her way back on foot. A mere two blocks away, she was, when it happened.

I stared at her with dead eyes.

"So you went to Australia and made yourself a new family. How nice for you." The words almost froze my lips, leaving my mouth. "I probably have brothers and sisters I don't even know about."

"Just one sister," she said, perking up. "Jas, short for Jasmine. Younger than you, of course."

Of course. She would have to be. A little girl to replace me. I wanted to laugh but no sound came out.

"Here, let me show you a picture." She reached for her purse, but the volume of my voice took her by surprise.

"Did you ever think once about the daughter you left behind?"

She stopped, paused, and put the purse down beside her. "Oh sweetie, certainly I did! Every day that first year, I ached for you. Every birthday and holiday since then, I've grieved for you. You have no idea. I had to give up so much for my safety."

Safety. She gave up so much for her safety. I could feel the rage rise in me. Finally, an emotion.

The woman leaned forward. She tried to take my hand, but I snatched it away. "Surely you understand. Of course I wanted you with me. But if I took you, if I came back for you, he would know. The only way to do it was to disappear completely with all the others, and then I would be safe." She nodded earnestly.

Anger is hot. Rage, I discovered, can be ice cold. The air around me froze.

"So you disappeared to save yourself."

"Yes," she said, her voice brightening. "But now that he's dead, we can get to know each other."

She prattled on with words that didn't manage to penetrate my brain. I simply glared at her with eyes of stone until she saw my face and stopped talking abruptly.

"You saved yourself," I repeated.

"Yes. I told you why I had to." I'm sure she thought I was simple.

"And left me with a monster," I said coldly. "Your own daughter."

She stared at me, mouth gaping.

"If he'd treated you badly, what did you think he'd do to me?" I felt my hands go to fists. "Oh, you didn't think, did you? You didn't think at all about me being left with that—that—"

All the fury that had accumulated over the past twenty years came to a crescendo. I leapt to my feet.

"First the beatings. You weren't there to run interference, so when you died, NO, excuse me, when you LEFT, he turned it all on me."

Her face was a study of horror, but I wasn't finished. Not by a long shot.

"Then—when I wasn't even into my teens—the sexual abuse. Do I need to go into detail?" I stopped pacing and turned. "Years and years of hiding bruises and shame and fear, constant fear, until I could finally leave home and get out of his clutches. You saved yourself and left me with a monster!" I screamed. "How could you? What did you think would happen?"

She stared at me, mouth gaping. A hand groped for her purse. "I shouldn't have come," she said, vaulting up from the sofa. "I didn't think. I had better go."

"I was eleven!" I yelled at her back.

She bolted for the door, turned the handle, and pulled. I followed her out the entrance and grabbed her shoulder. "Look at me!" I screamed. "For God's sake, at least look at me!"

I tried to turn her, but she struggled out of my grip. Every ounce of rage in me coursed through my arms. I shoved her hard across the back. There was a slight oomph, and the body went over, tumbling down the icy concrete steps like a pumpkin with bandy legs. In a moment, all was quiet.

I looked this way and that. No one about. The darkness made a perfect shroud.

I gazed down at her, at the trickle of red beneath her head that was pooling on the ice. That gave me an idea.

I went back into the house. The God-awful lily arrangement in the cheap white ceramic vase would do perfectly. I snatched the card from it, discarded it, carried the rest of the arrangement to the door, and tossed it on the step just above her head. The vase broke into pieces as it hit the icy concrete.

Then I went inside to call the police.

"So you found her like this?" said the heavy-set older cop.

I nodded. We stood on the porch looking down at the body on the sidewalk. "She was carrying flowers," I said. "I guess her hands were full so she couldn't use the railing. My father died this week. Lots of flowers have been arriving." I waved a hand to the other floral arrangements in the house behind us.

"I'm sorry," said the cop. "This must be awful for you."

"It's so cold," I said, with a shiver. "With all this ice—I guess she just tripped and fell." I looked down at the still body and gave another muffled cry, trying to muster up real emotion. Nothing. So I covered my mouth with my hand, hoping this seemed natural.

The old cop just looked sympathetic. "Was she your mother?"

I dropped the hand and shook my head vigorously. "Oh no. My mother died on 9-11. She worked in the Twin Towers."

I didn't kill her. You can't kill a ghost.

DONALEE MOULTON

donalee Moulton is a professional writer based in Halifax. She has written for legal magazines including *The Lawyer's Daily, Canadian Lawyer,* and *The Legal Post.* donalee has won numerous awards including best feature and short article from the Professional Writers Association of Canada. donalee has had short stories and poetry published in journals across the country. She is a former editor of *The Pottersfield Portfolio* and *Atlantic Books Today.* "Swan Song" is her first mystery short story. donalee's Twitter handle is @donaleeMoulton

SWAN SONG

DONALEE MOULTON

THE CALL CAME in at 1:24 p.m. I heard Ahnah answer, "Iqaluit Constabulary," but my attention was focused on the Keurig coffee maker I had brought with me from Humboldt, Saskatchewan. This was only the third day the city's new police force was officially up and running, and the plan was to slowly take over full responsibility from the RCMP. Good coffee would be critical.

As my dark roast continued to drip into a new blue-and-white IC coffee mug, I heard Ahnah's soft voice in the background, but it was the silence that compelled me to turn around.

"Everything okay?" I asked our exec assistant.

"No," she said. "There's a dead body at the Tundra Inn and Suites. It appears to be murder."

Before she could finish, I was reaching for my coat and yelling for the two constables in training, Kallik Redfern and Willie Appaqaq, to follow me. Our office was only five minutes from the hotel (although in Iqaluit, I was learning, you're really only five minutes from anywhere). By the time we arrived, there was a crowd of people. That crowd included David Picco, the government's elected representative for Rankin Inlet and the driving force behind the establishment of the Iqaluit Constabulary, a first for the twelve-year-old territory.

"I was across the street at the legislature," he said. "What's going on?"

"I don't know," I admitted, "but it's not good."

People moved back to let us through, a consideration I was also learning is second nature to Iqalummiut. The hotel manager was waiting for us in the lobby. "Doug Brumal," I said by way of introduction. "I'm the new police chief."

"This is awful, just awful," said the manager, a small, round man who in his distress had forgotten to give us his name. I nodded at Kallik, who moved quietly to the front desk. He would get the names and contact information for everyone in the hotel at the time of the incident.

By now, the unnamed manager was leading us down a long hallway past the dining room and lounge to a series of meeting rooms. The first door on our left was the only one closed. When I opened it, I saw round tables with linen tablecloths positioned throughout the room. Two coffee urns and one teapot were resting on a tilted table. (Floors here often shift because of the ice and permafrost.) There were muffins, fresh fruit, and a cheese plate on the table. A large screen faced a projector, which held centre stage in the room.

Except, of course, for the dead woman on the floor. She was reed thin, about 5'8", silver-grey hair that may have been dyed. She was wearing a black skirt, checkered jacket, and white blouse. Well, now the blouse was white and red. Blood red.

Willie moved forward and started taking pictures. I returned to the hallway and shut the door behind me. The manager was nowhere in sight, but a young, brunette woman was waiting for me. "I'm Elsa Nattaq, assistant manager," she said. "I found the body."

"Is there somewhere quiet we can talk?" I asked. Kallik had joined me, and we followed the assistant manager into an adjacent meeting room. As I was dropping my big butt (at 6'6" most of me is big) into a boardroom chair, I looked up to see Ahnah Friesen standing in the doorway.

"I thought you might want me to take notes," she said, settling into the chair on my left.

Elsa Nattaq didn't wait for our questions. We learned the dead woman was Eira Winter, owner of HR Exemplary, a training firm out of Calgary. Winter was a regular visitor to the hotel, a contractor from the south who flew into Iqaluit several times a year.

"I'll ask Carol Logan to drop by this afternoon to speak with us," Ahnah said as the assistant manager stopped to take a breath. "She's the training coordinator for the GN."

I had learned enough to know GN stood for Government of Nunavut. Apparently, I had not learned quite how sharp our admin support was.

The assistant manager assured us she had not touched anything in the room, including the body, and had locked the door after she backed out of the room. "Do you know who was on room duty over lunch?" Ahnah asked.

I didn't even try to mask my surprise.

"Meeting rooms are cleared over lunch to make way for the afternoon break," Ahnah said, looking me in the eyes. "I used to work here."

"But the room wasn't cleared," I noted, seeing where Ahnah was going. I also noted, to myself, that Ahnah had been in the murder room.

I thanked Nattaq for her help and told her we might have more questions. She agreed to let us use the boardroom for the afternoon. Then the three of us joined Willie in room 101. Another woman was also there. I recognized Kari Frost, the chief coroner.

Frost, a Southerner, was all business. "Dead as a nit," she said. "Stabbed, repeatedly, with what appears to be a steak knife." I looked over at Willie, who was holding up an evidence bag with a small, bloody, serrated knife.

"I'll know cause of death for certain once I do the autopsy. Likely hit a vital organ or two. Nasty business," Frost said, grabbing her crime scene bag and heading out.

I looked at my team, already knee deep in murder. This wasn't what any of us had expected. Were we ready? As if she could read my mind, Ahnah said, "We're all good. I've set up an interview with Carol Logan for 3:30, and Paul Saila is coming in at 4."

"Who the hell is Paul Saila?" I asked.

"The busboy sent to tidy up the training room," said Ahnah. Seeing my confusion at her apparent psychic ability, she added, "Elsa texted me."

Almost as an afterthought, she said, "I also ordered some coffee, juice, and muffins for us in the boardroom. It might be a long day."

Promptly at 3:30 Carol Logan, a big-boned brunette with a warm smile, breezed in. After expressing her distress and her belief that she wouldn't be much help, Logan went on to give us much-needed background on our victim. An HR specialist, Winter had been conducting training sessions in Nunavut for four years. The sixty-three-year-old was mid-way through a lucrative contract with an option to renew for another three years. That contract called on Winter's company to certify GN employees in human resources and payroll services.

"How important is that certification?" I asked.

"Without it, employees cannot continue in their jobs," Logan said simply.

Skilled labour is an ongoing issue for the GN, I knew. The Government of Nunavut had committed to creating a public service that is representative of the population it serves, and qualified Inuit applicants are given priority for all job competitions. It was the word "qualified," however, that posed significant problems. Indeed, it was the reason I was sitting in the police chief's chair.

"How many people fail?" I asked.

"In the last few years, not many. In fact, none," Logan said. "But that may have been about to change. Eira and her partner, Crystal Pele, divide the curriculum. They don't usually come together. You should talk to Crystal." I could see Ahnah reaching for her phone.

"Did you like Eira Winter?" I asked.

"She's very good at her job, and she has helped us advance our HR skills significantly," Logan said. She didn't meet my eyes.

Within seconds of Logan leaving the boardroom, a lanky young man in his late twenties was ushered in. I held out my hand and thanked Paul Saila for coming. He looked at the floor and mumbled something. I wasn't sure if this was respect for an older person, shyness, or something else altogether.

"You know why you're here?" I asked.

Saila nodded.

"I need you to tell me," I said without rancour.

"It's about the dead woman."

"What about her?" I asked.

"I was doing her classroom."

"What exactly were you doing, Paul?"

"I bring the food in and take it out," he answered.

"Did you speak with Ms. Winter or see her over the lunch hour?"

Paul continued to look at the floor. "No," he said. I didn't know if he was telling me the truth.

"Did you like her?" I asked.

Saila shifted in his seat. "Didn't know her."

Crystal Pele was more talkative. The trainer showed up a few minutes after Saila left. (Ahnah's work, I presumed.) She entered checking her watch, hand outstretched. "I can't believe this. Who would want to hurt Eira?"

"We're hoping you can help us with that," I answered. "Why was she here on this trip?"

Pele appeared confused. "It's her job."

"I understand the two of you didn't usually come together."

The Calgary trainer nodded. "Yes. It's more productive for one of us to travel, where possible. But these are the final exams for the group, and we both felt we should be here."

"Why?" I pushed.

"It's about quality control and due diligence," Pele said, sitting a little taller and a little more stiffly. The educator's hat was on, but before she could explain quality control and due diligence to me, I interjected.

"I understand you oversaw exams individually in the past."

The stiffness remained. "We review each class and determine

the schedule accordingly," Pele said. "In this case, we felt it would be beneficial for us both to be here."

"Why?" I persisted.

You could see Crystal Pele deflate. "There is a participant who is struggling. She may not pass. Eira thought we should both be here to break any bad news."

"Do you agree with that decision?" I asked.

"What decision?" Pele countered.

"To remove an employee from their job."

I watched Pele's jaw for a reaction. It clenched ever so slightly. "We work with every person to help them reach the best possible outcome. Some people just don't make the grade. Literally." Before I could speak, Pele continued. I'm not sure whom she was trying to convince. "It's best for everyone. If an employee can't grasp the HR essentials, it makes them feel inadequate, and it makes the government less effective and efficient."

I switched lanes. "When did you last see Ms. Winter?"

"We had dinner together last night at the hotel."

"You didn't see her today?" I asked.

"No, we decided only one of us would be needed in the classroom to oversee the exam itself. Eira drew the short straw. I slept in and ate breakfast in my room."

"Did you like Ms. Winter?" I asked. I could see the surprise on Pele's face. I didn't know if it was the switch in questioning or the question itself.

"She was my colleague. My partner," Pele said. She sounded a little breathless. Defensive, perhaps. Or nervous.

"Not what I asked," I said. I could feel my team looking at me with a similar expression to Pele's. I made a mental note to discuss questioning strategy with them when we debriefed.

Pele sat up straighter. "Of course, I liked Eira. She was a dedicated, skilled professional who put her heart into everything she did."

"So you liked her." It was a question and a statement. And it got me a glare. "Did other people like Eira Winter?" I asked, veering slightly.

I could feel Pele relax—and hesitate. "Eira was a perfectionist, and she could be impatient. People may not have appreciated those qualities."

Now it was my turn to check my watch. I thanked Pele for coming and walked her out. Three sets of eyes were staring at me when I turned back to the boardroom. "What do you want us to do now?" Willie asked.

"Go home," I said. "Enjoy your dinner. Watch some TV. Let's meet tomorrow at 7:30 for a debrief and strategy session. We may have more information by then."

"I'll bring bannock," Kallik said.

My government-provided apartment reminded me I was not home as soon as I pulled in front. Permafrost prevents buildings in Iqaluit being built from the ground up. I was on the first floor, a short walk up a small flight of steps with a clear view of the "stilts" on which the building sat. This was not familiar territory.

Before I had a chance to think about food, my phone rang. It was David Picco. "Have you eaten?" he asked before the word "hello" was fully out of my mouth.

"No," I said.

"Do you want some company? I have char."

"Come right over," I said. I meant it. I really liked and respected David. He was gently and skillfully introducing me to Nunavut, the culture, and the role I would play in life here in Iqaluit. I also really liked Arctic char, a rich, delicate taste somewhere between trout and salmon.

David let me enjoy dinner—we pan fried char with a splash of lemon, boiled potatoes, and zapped some frozen peas. (In a community where a head of lettuce routinely costs $6.99, frozen vegetables are more common than fresh.)

Over coffee and a plate of packaged cookies (brought from Humboldt), we got to the unspoken matter at hand. "Doug, do you have a handle on this?" David asked without any preamble.

"It's been all of six hours," I pointed out.

"Would you like to call in the RCMP for assistance?"

"I'd like to meet with my team tomorrow, review the forensics, and continue interviews," I said. "If I feel we need RCMP support, I will ask for it."

"This is the first test of the new force. Everyone is watching," David said, reminding me of the pressure we were under to succeed. And quickly. "There are opponents, as you know, people who strongly objected to establishing our own constabulary."

"We're untested, and we need to find our footing," I acknowledged, "but the team is trained, I'm experienced, and we're following protocol. Give us a chance to breathe here."

"It's not me you have to worry about," David said.

I arrived at the office at 7 a.m. The team was already there, and the bannock, a deep-fried bread, was warm. I brought molasses, a tradition passed down from my Newfoundland grandmother. Willie, Kallik, and Ahnah thought this was sacrilege but agreed to give it a try. Willie tossed his in the garbage when he thought I wasn't looking, and Ahnah wrapped hers neatly in a paper towel, also when she thought I wasn't looking. Kallik ate everything on his plate and reached for more bannock—and molasses.

After small talk and big bites, we got down to business. We reviewed what forensics we had, the most important being the knife. "Not a typical murder weapon," I pointed out. "It's too small to be guaranteed effective, if murder was what our killer had in mind."

"So do you think this was a crime of passion?" Kallik asked. He'd clearly been reading mystery novels.

"It would appear to be spur of the moment," I agreed. "Perhaps grabbing a weapon close to hand."

Ahnah looked at the ground and shuffled her feet. "It's a steak knife from the dining room," she said.

I nodded.

"Steak is only served on Tuesdays," she noted.

I immediately understood the implication. "So, either someone took this knife from the dining room on Tuesday, the night before the murder, or someone with access to the kitchen grabbed it yesterday. Either way, it looks premeditated."

Now, it was Ahnah's turn to nod.

"So why would someone want Eira Winter dead?" I asked, more to myself than the group.

"She doesn't sound like a nice lady," Willie said. We all agreed, but we all wondered if that was enough for someone to want her dead.

In my experience, it wasn't.

L umi Nakasuk showed up for her interview fifteen minutes after our debrief. I wasn't aware we'd booked an interview, but I wasn't surprised when Ahnah told me Carol Logan had emailed the info last night about Nakasuk, an HR and payroll clerk with the Executive and Intergovernmental Affairs department. And the failing participant in Winter's certificate program. I also wasn't surprised when Ahnah joined us in the interview room.

Nakasuk, a plump, 5'3" woman in her early twenties, would be unlikely to take Winter down in a fist fight, but if she caught the trainer off guard, she'd have no trouble driving a steak knife into human flesh.

The young woman was clearly nervous, but then she had reason to be, even if innocent. There are two options for interrogation: tough cop, gentle cop. If the Iqaluit Constabulary was to be accepted in the community, we had to earn its respect. I opted for gentle cop.

"Thank you for coming in," I said. Nakasuk looked up from the floor for a second.

"I didn't do anything wrong."

"I'm sure you didn't," I responded, "but we understand you were having problems in Ms. Winter's program."

"No reason to kill her," Nakasuk countered quietly. So perhaps all the women in Nunavut would be one step ahead of me.

"Can you tell us where you were yesterday from noon to 1 p.m.?"

Nakasuk stared at me, then the floor. "We have Ms. Winter's calendar. It says she had an appointment with you yesterday over the lunch hour," I said, lying through my teeth. Gently.

"I went to meet her, but she was busy," Nakasuk said softly. I couldn't tell if she was lying.

"Doing what?" I pushed.

"She's not a nice lady," Nakasuk said suddenly and a little loudly. And here it is, the moment when the suspect lets go, says to hell with reticence and caution. "She's mean. She yells. She thinks she's better than everyone."

I waited. Nakasuk hesitated, but the gate was open. There was no going back. "I showed up yesterday, but she was yelling at someone. Really yelling. It was awful. I got the hell out of there."

"Who was she yelling at?" I asked. This was why Nakasuk was holding back—the information she didn't want us to have. But she was in too deep now.

"Paul Saila," Nakasuk said. "She told him she couldn't wait to leave Nunavut, to get away from all this crap, and no little pissant like him was going to stand in her way. She called him a thief. Said he was taking the food from the classroom for himself."

Now she looked at me, defiant. "So, what if he was."

Once Nakasuk left, we gathered to review what we now knew and the implications of that new knowledge. Nakasuk was still a suspect, but she had moved way down the list. There was no duplicity in her. The story about Saila and Winter rang true.

"Is theft an issue at the hotel?" I asked Ahnah.

I could feel her tension. "The hotel has to throw leftovers out. So sometimes employees take home the fruit, muffins, and cheese."

Without pause, she added, "The Southerners do the same. They take the food to their rooms and eat it for breakfast or supper." I could understand why. Chicken fingers here could cost $20 and a clubhouse even more.

"So maybe Saila was taking food home and Winter objected," I said, ignoring Ahnah's tone and the bait. "Are a few muffins and cheese bites worth killing for?"

"They are if you're hungry enough," Ahnah said.

I decided to walk home, about ten minutes. I had been warned about the winter temperatures in Iqaluit, sometimes as low as -50° C. At that temperature, the hair in your nose and the cilia in your lungs can freeze. But this was October. The first snowfall had lightly blanketed the city of roughly 8,000. The air was crisp and dry. Without many of the daytime lights from offices and other buildings, it was dusky. Stars draped the sky. Few people were outside, and the city felt like it was my own. I breathed deeply.

The feeling of contentment lasted throughout the evening. I heated up caribou stew, compliments of Kallik's wife. (I really liked her. Couldn't wait to meet her.) I put Elvis on the stereo and put my feet up on the sofa. This was not laziness, but ritual. It's my way of thinking through things. As "Suspicious Minds" played, I reached the obvious conclusion. I simply didn't know enough to think anything through.

I got up and grabbed my parka, rammed my feet into my Bugaboots, and headed for my Ford F150. There wasn't going to be any more Elvis for me tonight. I'd be settling in with Eira Winter's laptop and the thousands of emails and files she had stored in hundreds of folders. Such a night.

The first drips of coffee were winding their way from pod to cup when Ahnah walked into the office. "You're early," I said. It wasn't even 7 a.m.

"Couldn't sleep," she responded. "And I figured you'd want to speak with Paul Saila first thing this morning."

She was right. I did want to speak with Saila. I also wanted to speak with Crystal Pele. I needed to learn more about the victim to understand why someone would want her dead.

Saila proved to be elusive. He didn't show up for work at the hotel, and he wasn't at home when Willie and Kallik went to look. They continued the search starting with his mother's house. Meanwhile, Pele arrived, simultaneously uneasy and annoyed. Both are common reactions to police requests for an interview.

"I told you everything I know," she said before I could ask a question.

"Yes," I agreed. "Thank you."

That left her a little confused. Point one for the Iqaluit Constabulary. "I want to learn more about Ms. Winter. I was hoping you could help."

"How?" Pele asked. Her tone was not warm.

"We're getting the distinct impression your colleague was not a nice woman."

"So what?" Pele said. You could almost see her body resign itself to the inevitable.

I didn't have time for petulance or reticence. "Ms. Pele, we can do this one of two ways. Your choice. Good cop or bad cop." I saw Ahnah smile into her Dell laptop.

"What do you want to know?" Pele asked. The annoyance was gone.

"Tell me why someone would want to kill Eira Winter."

"She's mean, she's heartless, she's inflexible, she's arrogant...do you want me to continue?" Pele asked. She stared at the floor.

"Please," I said. My tone was not warm, either.

"Look, Eira was not an easy woman. She prided herself on being rigorous, but that left little room for openness or flexibility. Eira defined fairness as treating everybody the same."

"Isn't that a good thing?" I asked.

"It could be, but with Eira it meant no exceptions, ever. For example, she didn't tolerate lateness. Arrive after class started and you weren't allowed in the room. It didn't matter if someone had been up all night with a critically ill baby or the minister of health had called them in for a meeting. No exceptions."

I could see how that would rankle. "How did she treat you?"

"The same as everybody," Pele said. "But I have worked with Eira for more than five years now. I know how to avoid the outbursts, the cold shoulder, and the retribution. I also know what to expect when I've crossed one of her lines. We found a balance that worked for us."

"What happens now?" I asked.

"Happens with what?" She seemed confused.

"With your work in Nunavut?"

"The contract continues," she said. "This course is winding up; the next one will start in another month. If I need help, I'll subcontract work just like Eira did with me."

"I know this is a long shot," I said, "but do you have any idea who might have killed Ms. Winter?"

Pele looked me in the eye. She didn't hesitate. "Anyone who ever met her."

I grabbed a sandwich for lunch at The Snack. When I got back to the station, Willie and Kallik nodded toward the interview room. Paul Saila was waiting for us. Truculent and terrified. "I didn't kill that woman," he said. Defensive and defiant.

"I didn't say you did," I answered. "Want a coffee? Muffin? Piece of fruit?"

"Piss off," Saila said, and deservedly so, but now I had him off balance.

"So you got yelled at," I said.

"No big deal," Saila said, trying to appear nonchalant.

"Not what we heard."

"Okay, so the bitch tore one off me. Big deal."

"It is if you lose your job," I said.

"Then they'd have to fire everyone," Saila snapped. "And I'd have another job five minutes later." I looked at Ahnah. She nodded yes.

"Tell me what happened," I said.

"I was cleaning up the room and taking some of the leftovers when that woman walked in. She screamed at me. Called me a thief. Called me a low life. Nothing I haven't been called before. Said I wasn't going to ruin her reputation."

"And then…" I prodded.

"I got out of there fast. She was alive and foaming at the mouth when I left. Calling me nasty names. Screaming something about me trying to ruin something for her and not letting her go in peace."

Saila was almost out the door when he turned.

"Don't know if it matters," he said, "but she was really upset about some bird that was singing." He grinned at Willie. "Qugjuk."

I looked at Willie in bewilderment. He shrugged. "It's nothing. Guy's an idiot. He's spent so much time down south he doesn't even know his own language anymore."

I told the team I was making a Timmy's run, which they understood but found a little strange. We have coffee in the station. I returned with hot chocolate and doughnuts. That enhanced the understanding significantly. A few minutes later, Carol Logan walked in. She grabbed a Boston cream and said, "I understand you wanted to see me."

I looked at Ahnah. "About the contract," Ahnah said. Apparently we have the most fascinating floors.

Carol followed me to my office. "I brought a copy with me." She handed me a fairly thick wad of paper. "But it may be easier if I walk you through it."

The Government of Nunavut had a four-year contract with HR Exemplary, Winter's company. The contract was worth at least $250,000 a year, and automatically renewable for another three years. There were standard clauses for indemnity, termination, and confidentiality. If something happened to Winter mid-contract, it would be fulfilled by Crystal Pele.

"There's nothing sinister in that," Logan said as if sensing where I was going. "Same clause as in the previous contract, and Winter lived through that."

The remainder of the caribou stew was settling nicely in my stomach and Elvis was mid-way through "Don't be Cruel" when I sat upright. I needed to get my hands on three things: Eira Winter's contract, her laptop, and an Inuit dictionary. The first two were at the station; the other was on the Internet.

I texted the team. Thirty minutes later, everyone was sitting in my small living room. Willie had made a Timmy's run.

"Let's go through what we know so far," I said. "We're close." I could feel the pride. I could also feel the surprise.

Willie and Kallik thought Paul Saila the most likely suspect for obvious reasons. I thought the murderer was Crystal Pele. Ahnah agreed, but she was uncertain of the motive.

"Pele stood to lose a very lucrative contract," I pointed out.

Ahnah frowned. "But she wasn't losing the contract."

"Yes," I said. "She was."

"How do you know?" Willie asked.

"Paul Saila told us."

Now everyone looked at me in bewilderment. "What's a qugjuk?" I asked.

"It's a big white bird," Willie said, still puzzled.

"Yellow around the eyes," Kallik added.

"It's a swan," I said. "That's the bird that was singing for Eira Winter." Three pairs of eyes looked at me blankly.

The phrase "swan song" may have mystified the team, but the termination clause in the contract was crystal clear. If Eira Winter chose to terminate the contract, Crystal Pele was out of a job. And nestled in her laptop under a file called, aptly, "Swan Song," was Winter's letter bringing her contract with the GN to an official end.

Crystal Pele was arrested at the Tundra Inn before she finished her Caesar salad. It took less than an hour for her to confess. Actually, it was more of a declaration than a confession. Winter was retiring, closing her company's doors, and Pele was out. This final trip to Iqaluit was Winter's swan song. Pele wanted to make sure it wasn't hers.

Ahnah beat me in to work the next morning. Coffee was on, and there were fruit, cheese, and muffin trays, compliments of the Tundra Inn and Suites.

"You know you don't have to come in early every morning," I said with a smile.

"I have a question," Ahnah said without a single glance at the floor. "Pele has money, a job, a career. She likely has a house, a car, a vacation every year. So why kill Winter?"

"She was hungry," I explained.

"She had plenty of food," Ahnah said.

"Not that kind of hunger."

I'm not sure Ahnah understood, but she would, especially when she became the first female constable of the Iqaluit Constabulary. But that was a path yet taken.

Ahnah turned to go to her desk but stopped after a few steps. "I forgot to tell you. Carol Logan texted. All the participants in the current course passed their exam."

C.S. O'CINNEIDE

C.S. O'Cinneide (oh-ki-nay-da) is an Edgar nominated author of thriller and noir. Her debut novel, *Petra's Ghost*, was a semi-finalist in the 2019 Goodreads Choice Awards. The second book in her Candace Starr Crime Series, *Starr Sign* was nominated for Best Paperback Original by the Mystery Writers of America in 2022. She blogs on She Kills Lit, where she features women writers of thriller and noir. C.S. O'Cinneide's website is www.shekillslit.com

COOL CUSTOMER

C.S. O'CINNEIDE

"What's with the stiff?"

"It's a body."

"I can see that. My question is how it came to appear on your living room floor?"

"It's a long story."

"I've got some time."

"Can we get into this later?"

"No."

"Why?"

"The blood is staining the sectional."

"I see."

"And the cat's fallen asleep on his face."

"Oh."

"It's undignified."

"I get that."

I guess no one really starts off the day believing they're going to kill someone, at least no one in my corner of the world, a small-town satellite of a much larger urban planet called Waterloo. All of us circle around for work, or entertainment, or maybe just for the gravitational pull that will keep us from flinging ourselves out into the universe in a mad fit of boredom and regret. Murder is for mob bosses and former playboy bunnies with an axe to grind, not for dignified wives of software executives living in Elora, Ontario.

But here I find myself, with a bottle of bleach and a collection of garbage bags, trying to clean up the mess of my own transgressions. The matter of disposal poses the greatest issue. I cannot very well leave him here. Choosing to bash his head in with the heel of my new Jimmy Choos was a poetic yet poorly conceived choice. I will surely be blamed, if only for my ostentatious choice in footwear.

"You should have used a clog," my mother says. "Then they would never know it was you."

I could have been a clog girl. If I hadn't quit my job to keep the home fires burning while my husband went out and lit fires of his own. I could have donned sensible shoes while I went about my sensible life with my own sensible achievements; like a real person, instead of a paper cut-out piece of origami gracing the windows of my lovely home.

But I digress. Here I am talking about myself and I haven't even got rid of the body yet. Burying it in the back yard is not an option. My azaleas wouldn't live through it.

"We'll have to throw him in the river," I tell my mother.

"Great," she says. "I always wanted to throw him in there anyway."

My mother is a cool customer. More like a mentor than a mother. Children were a social experiment she conducted as an unbiased observer. I believe she expected us to prove the null hypothesis. That is, that children really aren't worth it all in the end, and there are, in fact, lots of things like a mother's love. For instance, the love I felt for my first dog, Rocky. Who was so stupid, he ran into the sliding door to the deck at least once a day. Or the love one feels for chocolate, or a nice peppery Shiraz, both of which beat hands down spending even one day of a vacation with a surly teenage girl. Thankfully, my two daughters are at boarding school right now, waiting out the years of their adolescent angst.

In any case, she's always been in my corner, my mother, despite not being the most maternal type. When I had my first child, my mother-in-law sent word she would come stay with me; my mother sent a Filipino nanny. The nanny ended up sleeping on the pull-out couch. Eventually she would end up sleeping with my husband. That was the beginning, but certainly not the end of my humiliation. The day I found out, I bought my first pair of $800 shoes.

"He won't fit in the car."

"What do you mean he won't fit in the car?"

"I only have the two-seater."

"The Smart car?"

"The ozone's depleting."

"No it isn't."

"In any case, he won't fit in the trunk. So what do we do?"

"Perhaps we can use him to plug the ozone."

It gets easier after a while, trading trust and fidelity for clothes and credit cards. You can convince yourself of anything if your cleavage is low enough and your Botox is never allowed to wear off. Although I was never quite sure if the inability to appear surprised anymore by my husband's affairs had less to do with my increasingly callous attitude and more to do with the loss of the use of my facial muscles. But regardless, I found it easier and easier to look the other way. That is, until today.

"I don't see why we couldn't have put him in the trunk," I complain. My mother is driving. I am too nervous.

"We would have had to cut him in half."

"Would that have been so bad?"

"Maybe not for him."

"It's creepy like this. He keeps falling on me when you take a sharp turn and I can feel his Blackberry poking at me through the garbage bag."

"He hasn't got his Blackberry. I put it on the hall table."

"Then what is that...? Oh God, that's just gross."

"Those things are expensive."

"God help me."

I don't usually drop by unannounced. It's not done where I come from. My mother divorced her first husband for dropping by unannounced. You think I'm joking, but I'm not. Today was different though. Today I had on a Vivienne Westwood wrap and a pair of gorgeous Jimmy Choos with killer stiletto heels. Dramatic foreshadowing in fashion is my forte.

I wanted to show off to my new best friend, Janelle. She lives one block over, in the new subdivision where family values in the form of a huge mortgage and a postage stamp lawn can be had for $1.5 million and the removal of your soul. Janelle is younger and fitter than me, looking great in anything, which makes her a prime target for my undying admiration and sincere need to destroy her. Janelle is "house poor" as we say out here in the suburbs. Meaning she and her husband put more stock in having an impressive home than other less pressing issues such as sending their kids to college, or having enough to eat. She has always been jealous of my fabulous wardrobe and I couldn't resist a chance to drop by for a cup of java with a side order of jealousy.

"You're standing on my foot, Mom."

"I'm sorry."

"I thought he'd float more."

"I filled his pockets with stones when you were throwing up."

"I wasn't throwing up. I had a coughing fit."

"You have vomit in your hair."

"No I don't."

The door standing ajar should have been my first tip. No one leaves their door open in our neighbourhood unless they're crazy or having an affair. I don't know why. It's just the way it is. Perhaps people are too busy to shut the door in the mad dash to get to the bedroom. Perhaps their lovemaking blows the door off its hinges. I don't question these things. What I did question was what over two dozen shopping bags from Yorkdale were doing in Janelle's living room when I knew she couldn't afford so much as a sock from Juicy Couture. That's when I heard them. The moaning, the clawing, the screaming. It was disgusting.

Actually, the screaming and clawing were coming from me. I couldn't help but attack those bags and yank out the contents. Shoes and handbags sailed into the air, dresses and blouses were torn from their tasteful tissue wrap. When the two of them came running down the stairs, I had a Holt Renfrew bustier in my hands as I tore at the bodice with my perfectly veneered teeth.

"I came for coffee," I said, my mouth full of black lace. Then I ran home.

I could tell you the rest of the story, but I think you can fill in the blanks. Woman runs home. Man runs after her. Woman pierces man's skull with stiletto heel. Over and over again. Until the sole comes away from the creamy blood-soaked leather and grey matter embeds daintily into the saucy peekaboo toe.

I won't bore you with details. Suffice it to say, I called my mother immediately afterwards and she came and helped me herself. No hired illegals this time. I've got to give her credit for that. She was always coldly calm in a crisis, or really in any situation for that matter. Heartbreak, disenchantment, murder; none of it fazed her. I think she had her feelings removed along with her appendix at twelve.

"It wasn't about the sex," I sobbed when we were back home and done.

"I know, dear."

"He bought her all those things."

"Yes, dear."

"What will I do now?"

"Well, first, you're going to have to replace the sectional. That stain is never coming out."

"I'll get on it."

"I knew you would, dear."

Money can't buy you love, but it can buy you time. Years of it, actually, spent with a veil pulled over your eyes of the finest fabrics, as you walk through the fog of your existence in your glossy black boots. Only don't pull the veil back, even for a second, or you might see the true cost of your shiny bright life.

"I knew you would, dear. I knew you would."

ALICE FITZPATRICK

Alice Fitzpatrick has contributed short stories to literary magazines as well as the Sisters in Crime anthology *The Whole She-Bang 3*. The second novel in her Meredith Island Mysteries, set on an island off the coast of Wales, was a finalist for the Killer Nashville Claymore Award. A member of both Crime Writers of Canada and Sisters in Crime, Alice has a masters degree in women's history and has taught writing, high school English, and ESL. Alice's website is www.alicefitzpatrick.com

THE CLIENT

ALICE FITZPATRICK

The Haworth Street Café, Victoria, BC, February 5, 8:09 a.m.

Henry stood in line, breathing in the warmth of coffee and sweet pastry. All around him, people were bent over their phones, their fingers and thumbs tapping out messages and racking up scores on games. Rain ran from their boots and formed dirty puddles on the floor.

A wooden bench in the park across the street was his usual observation spot, providing him with a clear view of Ally preparing the coffees. Henry would spend his mornings making notes, taking photographs, and eating cold bacon sandwiches from a plastic container.

But today was different. Today he was inside.

It was Henry's turn at the counter.

"Would you like to try one of our fresh cheese croissants?" An older woman with frizzy blond hair pointed to a pile on display in the glass cabinet. Her nametag identified her as Joan.

Croissants were messy. You couldn't eat them without getting crumbs everywhere. He ordered a butter tart.

Joan smiled. "Can't go wrong with a butter tart. Bag or plate?"

"Plate, please."

She handed over a gooey tart. "There you go, sweetie."

He moved along to where Ally made the coffees. Her thick ponytail bounced as she worked the hissing machines. She was wearing the drab café uniform—green smock and loose black pants. It wasn't at all flattering, not like her short summer dresses or the spandex leggings she wore on her morning runs. Those show off her toned calves and thighs. But the winter weather had forced her to cover up.

Ally stared at him quizzically. "You look familiar. Do we have a class together?"

Henry felt a flutter of panic. Had she seen him outside the café, the pub, the lecture hall, her apartment? He was always so careful.

"No."

He'd never been this close to her. Her eyes were a lovely blue-green like the ocean on a warm summer day.

She continued to stare. Was she waiting for him to introduce himself? He couldn't use his real name. After all, he was undercover. Truth be told, he hated his name. He wanted to be called Hank. Hank was a PI in an American thriller who roamed the seedy underbelly of 1950s Chicago. Men called Henry collected Princess Diana memorabilia and drank sherry with their nans.

"What can I get you?" Ally asked.

"Plain coffee."

Despite his regular observation of the café, he didn't understand the attraction of fancy coffees, the need for whipped cream or sprinkles, or the purpose of shots or hot milk.

"Will you be having this in or taking it out?" she asked.

"I'll sit in the corner and do some writing." Henry purposely mentioned the writing. The only other customer sitting at a table was a middle-aged man with greasy hair and a stained jacket who looked like he had nowhere else to be. Henry didn't want Ally to think of him that way.

"What are you writing?" She seemed interested.

"A novel." He was glad he'd taken the time to develop a backstory. A good investigator has to be prepared.

Her beautiful eyes widened. "A novel! I wish I could do that."

He blushed. He was flattered by her attention, even though the person Ally admired wasn't him.

She handed over his coffee. "Good luck with your book."

"Thank you."

Henry paid for his food, added some milk and two packets of sugar to his mug, and settled himself at a table where he could watch for DE.

He was the man Ally was seeing. Henry had named him for the double espresso he ordered every morning. He always had a smug smile plastered on his face. Henry wasn't supposed to get emotionally involved with his subjects, but DE made him angry. Ally was in second year university, and this man was at least ten years older.

Ally and DE had gone on four dates over the past three weeks. The first was at a trendy gastro pub with tiny portions of food. Henry couldn't imagine Ally felt comfortable in a place like that. From what he'd observed, she was never happier than in the university pub, drinking draft beer and eating fries with her fingers. At the end of the evening, DE received a dismissive kiss at the door.

Henry was surprised when Ally agreed to a second date. This time it was at an Italian restaurant, which suited her better. They shared a bottle of red wine. Ally ordered lasagna and a green salad while DE gorged himself on two servings of gnocchi. He insisted they order dessert. She had one bite.

After the meal, she invited him back to her apartment. Ally lived on the second floor and her living room window faced the street. Through his binoculars, Henry watched them sitting side by side on the sofa while they chatted and drank coffee for seventeen minutes. When DE put his hand on her thigh, she scooped up their mugs and took refuge in the kitchen. Henry could tell that DE was upset at not being invited to spend the night.

The third and fourth dates—a film and Chinese food—ended much the same.

This gave Henry hope their relationship was doomed. He was in the coffee shop to observe them first-hand. But most importantly, he was hoping to learn DE's identity. After all, the job of an investigator is to investigate. That's what the Client paid him for.

DE strode through the door at 8:23. Henry recorded the event in his notebook.

The women behind the counter suddenly stood taller, straightening their green smocks and smoothing their hair. Several of the women waiting in line gave him inviting smiles.

"Good morning, ladies." He lifted a hand in greeting, but his gaze was focused on Ally steaming milk.

He stood in front of the food counter. "How's my favourite girl this morning?"

Joan giggled. Henry's mother would never giggle at a man. She had more self-respect.

"The usual, Mr. Smith?"

Smith! Did he really expect people to believe that was his name?

"You know me so well, Joan."

Slimy bastard, Henry thought. Henry wanted to write this in his notes, but the Client expected him to remain neutral. On the other hand, it might provide valuable insight into Smith's character.

Joan slipped a cheese croissant into a takeout bag and handed it across the counter.

Under his open coat, Smith was wearing the same navy suit as last week. He obviously worked in an office, but his suit didn't look expensive, nor did it appear to be cleaned or pressed on a regular basis. Therefore, not an executive or a salesman where appearance was important. Still, the women in the coffee shop seemed taken by him.

Henry didn't understand the attraction. Smith wasn't what Henry would call good-looking. His nose was sharp and his hair needed a trim, but he had large brown eyes like Scruffy, a dog Henry once had as a boy.

Smith was standing in front of Ally. She gave him a smile that said she was pleased to see him. Maybe she once had a dog.

"Saturday still free?" he asked in a low voice.

Henry leaned forward to listen.

Ally's left hand pushed a stray piece of dark hair behind her ear. "Yes."

"How about a weekend away? I know a nice out-of-the-way hotel. On me, of course, Alison."

Her name tag said Alison, but Henry knew all her friends called her Ally, so she obviously preferred it. *You could make the effort to learn that*, Henry wanted to shout at him.

Ally looked down at the counter, hesitant. *Good*, Henry thought. It was too soon for a weekend away. Just what sort of a woman did Smith think she was?

"Separate rooms," he added in an effort to reassure her. "Great food, romantic walks in the woods, curled up in front of a roaring fire."

"I've got an essay due on Monday."

"Bring your laptop. I promise not to monopolize all your time. What do you say?" He had a big, stupid grin plastered on his face, as if certain of a positive response.

With his phone, Henry zoomed onto Smith's left hand. There appeared to be no swelling or indentation, no white band on his finger. But then not all married men wear rings, especially those in the habit of seducing vulnerable young women.

Henry quickly took a few shots of the two of them as well as a close-up of Smith.

"Yes, all right," Ally finally said. "I'd love to go."

Henry couldn't believe she'd agreed.

Smith flashed that stupid grin again, reached into his pocket, and passed her a brochure folded in half. "Pick you up after class on Friday."

He grabbed her hand, pulled her forward, and planted a quick kiss on her cheek. "Call you."

He left with his coffee and croissant.

Even though Smith had said separate rooms, Henry doubted he was planning to stay in his. It was imperative Henry be there. That would involve renting a car, possibly staying the weekend. Surely the Client would be willing to cover the expense.

When there was a pause in the morning rush, Ally took the opportunity to show Joan the brochure.

Henry approached and managed to get a glimpse of the name on the front: The Shore Pine Lodge.

Joan looked up. "Can I help you?"

"Another butter tart, please."

"Sure thing." Joan passed over another plate. She didn't giggle at Henry.

"The man you were speaking with earlier—dark hair, grey coat, striped tie," Henry addressed Ally. "I think he might have been at school with my brother. What's his name?"

"Mr. Smith, you mean?"

"Yes, Smith. His first name isn't Tom, is it?"

"No." Ally blushed. "Not Tom."

But she didn't volunteer any further information. It would appear suspicious if Henry continued to ask questions, so he just shrugged. "Not the same guy. He sure looks like him though."

Henry paid, took the plate back to his table, and pulled out his laptop to search for the hotel.

Shore Pine Lodge, February 8

Henry had been preparing for this trip for the past three days. Upon completing his undercover surveillance in the café, he'd emailed the Client explaining the situation had escalated and Ally was in danger. Was he prepared for Henry to take the next step? There would be no additional charge. Henry gave him twenty-four hours to respond. If he didn't hear back, he'd assume the Client had given his consent.

There was no reply.

Henry rose early Friday morning and packed a bag with two changes of underwear and socks, an extra sweater, his first and second favourite shirts, laptop, toiletries in a plastic bag, and his grandfather's Luger.

He picked up his rental car and drove through the rain to the hotel. He checked in, left his bag in his room, and went back down to the lobby. He found a chair by some tall plants in a corner and waited. More than once he wished he had his box of bacon sandwiches. He treated himself to a bar of chocolate.

It was almost six-thirty when Smith and Ally arrived.

Henry moved closer to hear the young woman behind the shiny reception desk announce their room numbers. Ally was in 202 and Smith in 305. Smith demanded a room next to Ally, but the receptionist said it was as close as she could get him.

Ally looked embarrassed and offered the woman an apologetic smile. Smith grabbed his key. He'd parked by the front door, so the woman gave directions to the parking lot.

Smith grunted. "Let's take our cases to our rooms. Then I'll move the car, and we can have dinner."

Henry returned to his spot in the corner.

Seven minutes later, Smith walked out of the hotel. Henry took the elevator up to the third floor and found Ally's room. He knocked and heard soft footsteps approaching. "Have you parked already?" she inquired from inside the room.

She opened the door.

She had already changed into a red dress that clung to her body. No doubt Smith expected her to be ready when he returned. Henry hadn't seen the dress before. He hoped she hadn't bought it especially for this weekend.

Henry walked in. They didn't have time for niceties.

She looked surprised. "You're the writer from the café. What are you doing here?"

Henry was pleased she remembered him. "The Client sent me."

"What are you talking about?"

"Ally, he's not right for you."

"Who?" She looked genuinely confused.

"Smith, if that's even his name. You must come with me." Henry offered his hand, but Ally stepped back out of his reach.

"I'm not going anywhere with you. You have to leave now." She looked frightened.

Smith obviously intimidated her. Was that why she was here? She was afraid of what he'd do if she'd said no?

More than ever, Henry was convinced he must fulfill his mission. "I've been watching you. Does he threaten you?"

"You've been watching me?"

"To keep you safe." Henry took a step toward her, but she backed away.

"Is that why you were in the café asking questions?"

"The Client told me to look after you."

"Get away from her," Smith barked from behind him. "And drop the act. There is no client."

Henry should have heard him approach. He'd been too focused on Ally. He wouldn't make that mistake again.

Henry took the gun from his pocket. He swung around to face Smith.

Ally gasped.

"Of course, there's a client," Henry insisted.

Smith's eyes were on the Luger. "No, there isn't, Henry."

How did he know Henry's name?

"I send him reports every week. He sends me money." Henry was thinking of offering to show Smith the emails on his phone, but why should he have to? Smith was obviously trying to throw suspicion off himself by making wild accusations.

Smith took a step toward him. He was staring directly into Henry's face. "The money is an allowance from your mother, and you send the emails to yourself. We searched your flat. We found pictures of Alison, hundreds of them."

"The Client expects to see photographs. It's my job to protect her." But Henry was wasting his breath. Smith was determined to make him look foolish.

"No, that's my job."

Smith pulled what looked like a black wallet from his jacket pocket and flipped it open. It was a badge. "I'm Detective Sergeant

Darryl Smith. Now put down the gun before it goes off and hurts someone. You don't want Alison to get hurt, do you?"

He took another step forward and held out his hand as if expecting Henry to hand over the gun.

"Her name is Ally, not Alison." Henry waved the Luger back and forth as if he might pull the trigger at any moment.

But Smith wouldn't back off. "You're a grubby little man who gets his kicks spying on women."

Smith looked like he was about to punch Henry. But Henry wasn't afraid.

"Do you watch her get undressed? Is that what you like to do?" Smith sneered at him.

"I'd never do that." Henry looked at Ally, who'd turned away from him. "Ally, please. It isn't like that."

How could he make her understand?

"I won't tell you again. Give me the gun."

Henry shook his head. "It belonged to my grandfather. He was a war hero."

He heard someone behind him. His breath exploded out of him as he was knocked to the floor. The gun fell from his hand. His arms were jerked back and locked together with something that hurt his wrists.

Ally looked down at him with soft, watery eyes. It was obvious she knew this was wrong.

Two men pulled him to his feet. Smith came close, the faint smell of coffee on his breath. "Henry Dibley, I'm arresting you for criminal harassment, unlawful possession…"

But Henry didn't hear the rest of it. He was watching Ally's face. She obviously knew the police had made a mistake. Why wasn't she saying anything?

"I'd never hurt you, Ally. The gun isn't even loaded."

Something shiny on the floor—something gold—caught Henry's attention. Smith looked down where Henry was staring, scooped it up, and slipped it into his pocket. He flashed a smug grin at Henry.

"Ally," Henry shouted as he was dragged toward the door. "He has a ring. It's in his pocket. Ally, he's married."

Ally stood with her head against Smith's shoulder, his arm about her.

"I'm sorry you had to go through that, Alison, but you're safe now," he heard Smith say. "The kid is obviously delusional. We'll see he gets the help he needs."

If only she'd look in Smith's pocket, she'd realize Henry was telling the truth.

All he'd ever wanted was to protect her.

The Client was not going to be pleased.

LISA DE NIKOLITS

Lisa de Nikolits has been hailed as "the Queen of Canadian speculative fiction" and is an international award-winning author. Her short fiction and poetry have been published in various international anthologies and journals. Other works include *The Hungry Mirror, West of Wawa, A Glittering Chaos, Witchdoctor's Bones, Between The Cracks She Fell, The Nearly Girl, No Fury Like That, Rotten Peaches, The Occult Persuasion and the Anarchist's Solution* and *The Rage Room* (all Inanna Publications). Lisa's website is www.lisawriter.com

SOMEWHERE NEAR SUDBURY

LISA DE NIKOLITS

PEACE AT LAST! I shut the front door and waved to my kids through the glass. They climbed on the yellow school bus without a backward glance, and I turned away with a sigh of relief. I loved the little munchkins more than life itself but that didn't mean I wasn't down for some solo time.

This was my favourite moment of the day. Sunshine poured through the bay window and my domain was my own except for Snoodles, our French poodle, and Popsicle, our ginger cat. Popsicle was nowhere to be seen and Snoodles was napping in her basket, worn out from barking during breakfast and begging for scraps. I really needed to get that dog some training but, what with Kayley's hockey and Ian's trumpet-playing, who had time for anything?

I started by cleaning the kitchen. I tuned into SiriusXM, Classic Rock, and danced and sang tunelessly at the top of my lungs while I cleaned.

I was humming along happily to "If You Could Read My Mind" with my yellow rubber gloves immersed in hot soapy water when Snoodles woke up and had a barking fit. I swung around and, from the kitchen window, I saw a police car parked at the end of our driveway. Oh, my word! A police car!

I dived onto the floor and hid behind the kitchen island. Snoodles was going crazy, but I could make out the "Für Elise" doorbell, although my heart was pounding so hard in my ears that it sounded like a fire alarm.

I crept around the kitchen island on my hands and knees. Snoodles licked my face but didn't pause in her yapping. "Sssh!" I hissed at her. "Be quiet." She wagged her tail and barked louder. I inched my way across the floor and peeked into the hallway. Two police officers were at the door. I knew exactly why they were there. I'd been dreading this day for the past fifteen years. I backed away and hid behind the sofa.

"Snoodles! Shut up," I whispered. "Shut up!"

What would happen if I didn't answer the door? Would the police go away? Maybe they thought I wasn't home and I'd left the dog unattended. But what about the music? And my car in the driveway? But, still, I could be in the washroom. I could be in the basement doing the laundry. There was no law that said I had to answer the door, right? The truth was, I could *not* answer that door. I had to stay exactly where I was.

My Timbit Birthday Cake cereal rose in my throat. I swallowed hard to keep it down. My heart was hammering and my clothes were drenched in sweat. I looked down at my yellow gloves, feeling ridiculous. But I held my ground and lay very still. They rang the doorbell a few times and knocked. I heard them chatting, but I couldn't make out what they were saying.

I finally heard the letter box clang open. Their voices dropped in volume as they moved away from the door. I figured the officer must have left his or her card, but I knew it wasn't yet safe to move. For all I knew, they'd gone next-door to ask Mrs. Cruikshank if I was home, then they'd come back. She was such a nosey old busybody, no love lost between us; she'd be sure to tell them I was at home.

Would they break the door down to get in? It probably depended on whether they had a warrant; considering the gravity of my crime, my money was on the warrant. Snoodles finally got tired of licking my face and barking, and went back to her basket and her nap. Thank heavens for that. The music was still playing and its cheery onslaught was an affront. I wanted to turn it off, but I couldn't risk the officers seeing me through the window.

I lay behind the sofa for what felt like an eternity. I finally heard a car start up and I crawled toward the bay window, noticing as I went that the carpet under the sofa needed a good vacuum. I peeked out from behind the lilac flounced drapes and saw the police car driving off.

I was flooded with relief but it didn't last long.

Convinced that they'd swing back at any moment, I scurried to the front door, my hands slimy inside the yellow gloves. I ripped them off, reached for the officer's card. Constable Alicia Train. Yeah, like a freight train coming right at me. There was a note written on the back. *Please call at soonest convenience. We'll try you again later.*

I rushed into the living room and closed the drapes. I pulled down the blinds on the front door. I turned off the music. I ran upstairs and pretty soon the whole house was in darkness. I darted into our bedroom, jumped into bed, and pulled the covers over me. I had to figure out what to do.

They had finally come for me. That terrible night of fifteen years before had caught up with me as I knew it would. Hot tears ran down my face. I was going to lose everything. My children would know that I was a criminal and so would my husband. Their lives would be ruined. I was going to prison.

I felt something land on the bed. I screamed but it was just Popsicle, which made me cry even harder. He always knew when I was sad or worried because he'd jump up on the bed and lick my hand. "Oh, Popsicle," I cried, "I've ruined everything. I know what I've got to do but I'm too afraid to do it." The cat headbutted me. I nodded, blew my nose, reached for my phone.

Joey picked up, sounding distracted. "Honey, why are you calling? Is everything okay? You know I've got that huge presentation in fifteen minutes." Joey was a graphic designer at an ad agency, a super-pressured job. In my panic, I'd totally forgotten about his presentation. I should have told him everything was okay and let him go, but I couldn't.

"Joey," I said, my voice quivering, "I'm sorry but you've got to come home as soon as you can. I'm in big trouble. I wouldn't ask, you know that, but something terrible has happened." I started sobbing.

"Is it the kids?" he asked. I heard the terror in his voice.

"No, no," I replied. "It's me. It's something from before I met you."

"Honey, I can't leave now. The client's already here. I'm the only one who can do this. I'll come home right after. We're in this together. We'll fix whatever it is. I'll be home as soon as I can."

He hung up. I lay in bed, my skin on fire from the stress. I was itching all over. It felt like a thousand samurai were having sword fights behind my eyeballs. I got out of bed, grabbed a couple of Tylenol. I paced up and down. Snoodles was still asleep and the house was quiet in a terrible way. There was always some noise: my music, the kiddies on their phones, chatting or watching TV, or Joey watching his sports. There was always happiness and noise, and now there was this deathly silence. I knew I should clean up the kitchen, do the laundry, but all I could do was wait.

My makeup was a mess and my hair was standing up from hiding under the bed covers. I sat on the sofa and put my head in my hands. Which was how Joey found me.

"Honey!" He ran to me, cursing as he stepped on a piece of Ian's Star Wars Millennium Falcon Lego. "What's going on?"

"How was the presentation?"

"Good, good. I did fine, even though all I could think of was you. Please tell me what's going on." He looked around. "Gee whiz, this house looks like a bomb hit it."

"Looks like this every morning," I said. "I tidy when you all leave." I was procrastinating and he sensed it.

He took my hand. "Honey, what's going on? Come on. You can tell me anything."

Could I though? I pulled my hand away and got up. "There's no easy way to say this." I looked around our cozy living room with the lilac drapes I loved so much. The room was filled with soft chairs and cushions and framed pictures of us and the kids. It was everything I'd ever wanted. Now I was going to lose it.

"Remember when you met me?" I asked. "I told you that I'd had a bad patch?"

"Yeah, sure, I remember." Joey scrunched up his face in that way that I love. We'd met in a really unromantic way. I was working as a medical receptionist, and he came in to see the gastroenterologist for a colonoscopy. We hit it off right away, and I remember our first date at The Keg on Jarvis Street as clear as day. We both had the shrimp cocktail with martini sauce, and then the Sirloin Oscar with béarnaise sauce, then cheesecake with cherry sauce. Joey and I bonded over sauces; we agreed they really made a meal.

Joey wore super thick glasses that made his eyes look bulbous like a goldfish, but I thought it was sexy. He loved wearing houndstooth waistcoats and fancy cufflinks. At our first office Christmas party, I heard people mocking him. I didn't tell Joey what they said, but I did tell him he deserved better and he should resign.

"Who cares what they think?" he'd said. "None of them can create the artwork I do. Besides, I like it there even though Richard is a dick. But most bosses are dicks."

"Riley?" Joey brought me back to the present. "What's going on?" My real name was Marilla because my mom had a thing for *Anne of Green Gables*, but I hated it.

"Honey, we've all got baggage. We agreed on a fresh start when we met, but we also agreed on no secrets. Spill the beans."

Only Joey could actually say spill the beans and not sound corny.

"The beans," I said vaguely and sat down next to him. "Okay. I was about twenty-two, I guess. My dad had just died and I was working a call centre and I hated it. My dad was all I had growing up since my mom skipped out on us when I was little. She gave me a stupid name and left. Married somebody else. So he was all I had, then he was gone. Dad struggled with cancer for a couple of years, and I got a bit too fond of weed when I was looking after him."

I peeked at Joey. I expected him to look shocked because we

were very conservative about drugs, especially in front of the kids, and we hadn't been in favour of legalizing cannabis, no sirree. But he just nodded.

"I lost my job because I had a meltdown with a client, which is a no-no, even though the woman was so rude. It wasn't my fault the coat wasn't the same colour as in the catalogue, but she didn't want to hear that."

Joey patted my shoulder. "Carry on, honey. I know this isn't easy. Revisiting the past is tough. I never told you, but I hacked into the school's computer and adjusted my grades. No one caught me and I've never told anyone. I did the same at college. I never gave myself A's, just B+'s, a good steady student."

"Wow, babe," I said. "Can you hack into CIBC and get rid of our mortgage? Reduce it?"

He shook his head. "Too many firewalls these days. Believe me, I've been tempted. Anyway, carry on."

Hearing about Joey's past transgressions made me feel better. Then I remembered something. "If the police come back, tell them I'm not here, okay?"

He was startled. "Police? Riley, you never mentioned that. Is that why the blinds and drapes are closed?"

I nodded.

"Carry on."

I sighed. "The afternoon I was fired, I went to Value Village to cheer myself up. I figured I'd buy myself a treat. My finances were shot because Dad's cancer ate up everything we had. So I'm wandering around and I see this amazing pineapple lamp. It was like a lava lamp, only in shape of a pineapple. I reached for it and, just as I did, so did someone else." The story was getting harder to tell. "I looked up and there was this guy."

I bit my lip and twisted my wedding ring, a triple row of baguette and pavé diamonds. The centre wheel spun, which was symbolic of Joey and me being together forever. He'd designed it and it was beautiful. I looked at him, my eyes filled with tears.

"Babe," he said gently, "I know you had other relationships, so just tell me what happened."

I nodded. "Have you ever felt completely lost?" I asked. "That was how I felt. And then there was this guy, on one of the worst days of my life, who loved the pineapple lamp as much as I did. I felt like something good had fallen from the sky when I needed it most. I bought the lamp and we went back to my place. I was still staying at Dad's apartment on Roncesvalles Avenue. It turned out that Clive—that was his name—had a lot of connections to good weed, and I just wanted to escape from my life for a while. Before I knew it, Clive had moved in with me. I should have realized he had issues, because he showed up with three black plastic bags filled with his stuff. Who does that? No suitcase or backpack or tote, just three black plastic bags full of clothes and a crocheted coverlet that he said his granny from St. John's had made for him."

I shook my head, full of memories and shame and wonder that I'd ever been that girl who hooked up with that guy.

"It was a crazy time. We watched movies all night and slept all day. Queen Video was close by, and we started at one end of the store and decided we'd work our way through the movies regardless of what they were. Cost me a bunch of money I didn't have. I knew the whole thing was a mess, but I thought things would somehow sort themselves out. Luckily, Dad had paid six months of rent before he died. I think he knew my wheels would fall off after he died, so he wanted me to have that."

I stared off into space. I didn't want to tell Joey about the wild sexual chemistry between Clive and me, but he probably figured it out for himself. Just like I didn't want to hear about Joey's hot and steamy episodes between the sheets, I was pretty sure he didn't want to know about mine. Although, with Clive, it wasn't so much between the sheets as on the floor, in the shower, on the sofa, and on the coffee table—at least until we broke it. Clive was super destructive. He even broke the pineapple lamp, which made me mad as heck, but he was so beautiful, big and strong and wild, like Keanu Reeves, only with ice-blue eyes, and I forgave him anything.

"Clive said he was in construction, but he was living off the pogey and he owed a bunch to Mr. Payday Easy Loans and Money Mart. Another red flag I ignored. Before long, we ran out of booze and drugs, and he got mad and left me. He said he'd fix things, which he did, by coming back with a tote bag full of cash and drugs."

"Riley!"

I nodded and ran my fingers over the arm of the sofa as I tried to decide how to tell Joey the rest of the story.

"And then he kidnapped me."

Joey's jaw dropped. "What do you mean he kidnapped you?"

"I woke up in a van in the middle of the night with my hands tied and my mouth gagged. We were on the highway." I said all this in a rush. "It was snowing like crazy and the van didn't have snow tires. It was pretty scary. At least Clive had the wherewithal to get me into my coat and boots."

"Had he drugged you?" Joey asked.

I nodded. "Roofied me. He said he never would've got me to leave the apartment, so he drugged me and carried me out so we could start a new life. He said we were heading out west, that he had a buddy in Saskatoon we could crash with." I couldn't tell Joey that part of me thought Clive was being romantic.

"Whose van were you in?"

I sighed. "He stole it from the drug dealer."

"Then what happened?"

"We were somewhere near Sudbury. Clive pulled in to get some gas. He went in to pay, then he came out and he just sat there, thinking. My hands were still tied and the gag was in my mouth. I really needed to pee but I couldn't say anything, right? Then he got this really weird look in his eyes and glanced around, like he was trying to see who else was there, or maybe he was looking for cameras. That's what I figured when I thought about it, afterwards. Then he jumped out of the car and ran back into the store. I was totally freaked out, but what could I do? He came out with bags of stuff. It was like he grabbed all the cigarettes and Twinkies and sandwiches and Cokes and Oh Henry bars. He ran in and out about four times, in the end. He didn't even have bags, he just gathered up stuff in his arms and threw it in the van."

"Did he kill the cashier?" Joey's voice was low.

I nodded. "I read about it in the newspaper. He strangled him. There weren't any cameras, and no one saw us."

Joey was pale. When he grabbed my knee, his hand was sweaty. "Go on."

"He took the gag off me and untied me, and he gave me a Coke and a sandwich. But I felt so sick, I couldn't eat anything. He ate a couple of packs of Lune Moon cakes, and he was laughing, like he was a hero or something. But pretty soon, he needed to rest. I offered to drive while he slept, and he said yeah right, right, like he could trust me. We found a motel in the middle of nowhere. It was still snowing like mad. Clive got us a room, but I stayed in the car while he paid for it. He smoked a big fat doobie and drank a bottle of Jack and passed out. I knew what I had to do."

I looked at Joey.

"You'll never love me after this," I said, taking both his hands in mine and hanging on tight. "I've been dreading this moment the whole time we've been together and now it's here." I hesitated, then barrelled ahead. "I tied Clive up with the same rope he had used on me. I put the gag in his mouth. Then I set fire to the room and drove away with the money as fast as I could."

"Holy shit!" The sweat on Joey's hands had turned from warm to ice cold. "Did anyone die?"

I nodded. "Clive died. And the desk clerk died. He was the only other person there. The motel burned to the ground. It was pretty terrifying, white-knuckling it back to Toronto, and I nearly wiped out a dozen times. The heat died just before I got to Toronto. I got a bottle of bleach at a Shoppers Drug Mart and some paper towels and gloves, and wiped the whole van down. I ditched it near the Queensway. The police identified Clive's remains and tied the convenience store robbery to him. He had a record a mile long, from the east coast to the west. He'd been run out of the Alberta oil fields and kicked out of Yellowknife. But they never could find who was with him that night, and they certainly looked, because they knew he hadn't started the fire in the motel since he was on the bed."

I started to cry.

"I used the money to go back to school and became a medical receptionist. I got my life together. A few years later, I met you. And now they're coming for me. Dollars to doughnuts, they had DNA from the motel and when my mother remarried, she may have had kids. If they did the ancestry thing, it could have led to me. I keep reading about stuff like that. Plus I had a record from some shoplifting I did when I was a teenager, so I could be on file. There are a thousand reasons how they could have found me."

Joey shook his head. "Honey, the odds of that seem pretty slim."

"Well, maybe so, but these days they solve cold cases all the time. Maybe the desk clerk's family was bugging them so they looked into it again. I saw on the news that he was just a kid. He had his whole life ahead of him. I wanted to tell the police what I knew but I couldn't. I had to hide it all these years and now it's come home to roost. I'll be sent to prison as an accomplice to murder and robbery. Mrs. Cruikshank will have a field day. The kids will hate me. We'll lose the house."

I started to sob my heart out. Joey bolted upstairs. He was packing a suitcase and kicking me out, who could blame him? He came back downstairs and ran into the kitchen. He handed me a tablet and a glass of water. "It's a mild tranquilizer," he said. "I have to take them sometimes for big presentations. I never told you because I didn't want you to think I was a loser."

"Oh, Joey, you are so not a loser." I swallowed the tablet and blew my nose.

"Honey, here's what you're going to do. You're going to a hotel right now so you won't be here if the police come back today. I'll take care of the kids. And," he said with a grin, "I'll work through the night and use my extensive Photoshop skills to create an alibi for you. All we need is a ticket stub for an event that happened in Toronto on the night the murder took place. Do you remember when it happened?"

"Yeah, I'll never forget. February 10, 2006. I read every newspaper I could for years afterwards, to see if they were onto me. But wouldn't it look weird if I'd kept the stub for that one concert all these years?"

"Don't worry. I'll create stubs for several concerts you went to in 2006 and 2007." He grinned. "Don't worry, honey, creating realistic artwork is my bailiwick."

"Oh, Joey." I was so relieved. "But I killed somebody. Doesn't that freak you out?"

"Clive sounded like a piece of shit who deserved to die. You did what you had to do. If he lived, he'd have come back to Toronto and found you. You didn't know he was going to kill that guy. And he kidnapped you. You were young and scared out of your mind."

"Yeah, I was." That was true, but it was also true that I was hopping mad at Clive. He'd gotten me into all kinds of shit. What did he think, that we were some kind of Bonnie and Clyde, going out together in a romantic hail of bullets?

And what I didn't tell Joey was that Clive woke up, moments before I set the room on fire. He was squirming like a big fish and he looked out of his mind with terror. I was glad I had tied him up nice and tight.

"We had something good," I told him, "and you broke it just like you break everything. You lied to me and now you've got me into this hot mess. Well, no way, buster. You're not taking me down with you." And then I ran, before he could somehow get free.

I couldn't tell Joey any of that, of course.

Joey brought me back to the present. "I'll tell the kids you're having an overnight spa stay," he said. "I'll call you a cab; you can't drive because of the tranq. Go to any hotel you like and book a massage or mani pedi, okay? All moms are entitled to a day off. Order room service and watch a movie."

I grabbed an overnight tote while Joey called a cab, and I did exactly what he said. I went straight to The Windsor Arms, frickin' five hundred dollars for the night, go big or go home, right? They threw in a free massage, real generous of them, and two Manhattans at The Gatsby. I enjoyed every sip, along with a thirty-dollar Wagyu burger with bibb lettuce and the most amazing herb mayo.

The next morning, just before checkout time, I got a call from

Joey. I could come home. I jumped into a cab and raced home as fast as the driver would go.

Whoa! The house was an even bigger mess than when I'd left it, topped off by a layer of Swiss Chalet takeout remains. Snoodles nearly lost her mind with joy when she saw me, and I swear even Popsicle looked relieved that I was back.

Joey proudly showed me a bunch of concert stubs he'd made, and they looked so real. I grabbed him and hugged him. Apparently, I saw Broken Social Scene that terrible night.

"You are my hero," I said. "I'm going to call Constable Train right now."

Joey and I held hands while I dialled. When the constable answered the phone, my heart nearly stopped.

"This is Marilla Bunnings. You came by my home yesterday," I said, speaking as casually as I could. "How can I help you?" I stuck to the script Joey had prepared.

"Yes, ma'am. Thank you for calling back. We've had a noise complaint from your neighbour, Mrs. Cruikshank, about your dog barking. You need to get the situation under control. We can't enforce anything, but we have to let you know."

Snoodles! *Oh my God!* This was all about Snoodles and Mrs. Cruikshank. It wasn't about Clive or the cashier or the desk clerk on that terrible night.

Constable Alicia Train had no idea why I couldn't stop laughing. When I managed to convey the message to Joey, he nearly split a rib too. When I finally could speak, I assured the constable that we'd get Snoodles some training ASAP, and I thanked her for her time.

Joey and I waltzed around the kitchen, yelling like kids.

Of course, Snoodles joined in with gusto and we didn't have the heart to stop her. After all, we had so much to celebrate!

LYNNE MURPHY

Lynne Murphy was born and raised in Saskatchewan, educated at the University of Saskatchewan and Carleton University and worked as a journalist in print and radio. Her short fiction has been published by Sisters in Crime Toronto, the Mesdames of Mayhem, and Carrick Publishing. Selected stories appear in *Potluck and Other Stories*, from Carrick Publishing. Lynne is a member of Sisters in Crime, the Mesdames of Mayhem and Crime Writers of Canada. Lynne's website is www.lynnemurphy.ca

THE LADY-KILLER

LYNNE MURPHY

JULIE WARD and her family flew out to Saskatchewan in January for her grandmother's funeral. Julie was a little ashamed of how she felt. She had loved her grandmother and would miss her, but if Nana had to have a heart attack and die, why couldn't she have done it in June instead of January? No one in their right mind would want to go to Saskatchewan in January.

It was Julie's first time back to her hometown of Clairville in more than five years. That was when the Wards had moved to Ontario and she had started university. Now she was a graduate student, working on her master's degree in history, an adult, teenage crushes behind her. Still, she found herself wondering if she might see Theo Carmody while she was in Clairville.

The summer of 1977, when Julie turned seventeen, she was seduced by an older man. Oh, not physically. Theo Carmody never laid a finger on her, much as she wanted him to. But he cast a spell over her.

He wasn't at all handsome, with a scar down one side of his

face, the result of a recent motorcycle accident. He was built like a wrestler and a bit bow-legged. But she forgot his looks when he talked to her in that confident, teasing way he had. Julie had her first summer job, as a cashier at Clairville's outdoor swimming pool. Theo was the pool manager. He was living with his parents for the summer, recovering from the accident, and needed something to do. There were rumours of problems besides the accident that had brought him home from the Coast.

Julie was looking forward to starting university in Kingston in the fall, but Theo didn't think much of university. "Tried it once, didn't like it," he said. He was proud of being a ski-bum at thirty. He suggested she take a year off, travel a bit, find out what she really wanted to do.

Her mother turned that idea down flat. "Julie, you have your scholarship to Queen's," she said. "If you ask them to delay it, you'll lose it."

Theo drove a yellow Porsche. Julie had never even seen a Porsche until then. Sometimes, when the pool stayed open late, because of a heatwave, Theo would drive her home. She revelled in the glory of it, riding down the main street where anybody could see them together. Actually, the streets were almost empty at 10:30 at night, but it felt as though she and Theo were on display.

The pool staff was a party crowd. Every Saturday night, after the pool closed, they would gather in someone's backyard. It was the '70s so there was a lot of drinking and some pot smoking. No one ever saw Theo take so much as a beer, but he often disappeared into the shadows with some of the other guys and came back smelling of skunk.

Julie was the youngest, so the lifeguards and other cashiers treated her like a little sister. The senior lifeguard, Clara, was especially nice, almost protective. She didn't have much time for Theo, but the other girls swarmed around him. Still, Julie was the one he drove home.

Men didn't seem as keen on Theo as women were. He had Jake, one of the lifeguards, fired because of "insubordination." Julie thought Jake deserved it. He was a mouthy guy, always making crude comments about how the women looked in their bikinis. And one evening, after the pool had closed, he dumped her in the water, fully dressed. It was his idea of a joke. Julie was wearing her mother's good linen jacket, which she had borrowed without permission. Her mother wasn't happy about that.

Most of the time that summer, her mother didn't pay much attention to her. She was busy getting the family ready to move to Toronto. Julie's dad had been transferred there, a promotion, and the family had stayed behind so the kids could finish the school year. Her mother was also impressed by Theo's charm, though she didn't approve of his lifestyle. And Julie's younger brothers, who were taking swimming lessons that summer, idolized him. They tried to walk the way he did, "like a cowboy." Even Julie's grandmother, (who was really old, at least sixty-five) was smitten. She called him "the lady-killer."

One hot night, after a difficult day at the pool, Theo took the Porsche out on the highway and let it out. It was terrifying but exhilarating. Julie held her breath the whole time. Finally, Theo turned the car around and drove back to town at a normal rate of speed.

"Have you ever killed anyone with this car?" she asked when she could speak. She didn't want him to know she'd been scared.

"Not with the car," he said.

Julie waited, shocked, for whatever he was going to say.

"A few years ago, I was night skiing in California. Dolores, my girlfriend, went over a jump ahead of me. I didn't wait long enough. She had fallen and when I landed, my pole went right through her chest."

"Oh, my God!"

"She died instantly."

"It was an accident," she said. "It wasn't your fault." It was all she could think of. They were in front of her house by then. She thanked him for the ride, got out of the car, and watched him drive away.

The next day, she hoped he would acknowledge that their relationship had changed because of what he had told her. But he was just the same, teasing her a little, flirting with the older girls, running the pool like his private kingdom.

Labour Day weekend the pool staff had the party of all parties. One of the guys had brought a keg of beer and even Clara let go and drank too much. When Theo drove Julie home for the last time, she hoped he would kiss her. They got to her house and she didn't get out of the car right away, wanting him to make a move, just this once. She was starting university in Kingston in a week and would probably never see him again. The radio was playing an old, sentimental song called "Unchained Melody." Theo turned it off.

"I hate that song," he said.

"Why? It's a pretty song."

"A few years ago, in B.C., my girlfriend, Emily, and I were on holiday in the mountains. We had a fight. She got in her car and took off. I went after her on the Harley. Well, it was winter and the roads were icy. She was going too fast and went over the side. When I managed to climb down to her, that song was playing on the radio."

"Was she——?"

"She died on the way to hospital." He was quiet for a moment then leaned across and opened the door. "So, I guess this is goodbye. Hope you like Toronto."

Julie got out of the Porsche. She couldn't think of anything to say except, "Goodbye, Theo. I liked working with you."

University was hard at first. Julie was in Kingston and the family was in Toronto, several hours away by car. She felt homesick. She even missed her horrible younger brothers. And she missed Theo. Now there was no chance that he would suddenly realize she was what he had needed all his life. Clara had promised to keep in touch but there was just one short note from her and then she stopped replying to Julie's letters.

The university classes were enormous and Julie didn't know anyone. But gradually she began to make friends. At a frosh party one night, someone asked what she had done that summer and, trying to make herself more interesting, she told them about Theo and the dead girls. The others listened, fascinated, but then one girl said, "Julie, he was bullshitting you. That guy was just trying to make himself look big. Likely so he could get into your pants."

For the first time, she wondered about Theo. Could he have made up those stories to impress her? Wouldn't the police have been involved? Surely someone else in Clairville would have heard about the accidents.

She stopped whining, much to her parents' relief, and joined a few clubs. Boys asked her out. Slowly, she adapted to her new life.

Then, just after the Christmas holidays, her mother phoned. "Julie," she said, "here's something that will interest you. You know your boss at the pool, Theo? The guy you had such a crush on?"

Julie winced.

"Well, your Aunt Vi writes that he's engaged to that nice girl who worked at the pool with you. Clara Whitmore."

"But Clara didn't like him. And he didn't like her. They avoided each other as much as they could."

Was that why Clara had stopped writing? Because she was embarrassed about her change of heart?

Her mother was still talking. "Love can sometimes surprise you," she said. "When I first met your father, I thought he was a real creep. It took a while before I could see his good points."

Now, five years later, Julie was back in Clairville. The first days were busy with her grandmother's funeral and the reception to arrange. She was old enough now to be of some help to her parents and that felt good. Some of her high school friends came to the church but she didn't see Clara.

The day after the service, her father and the two boys flew back to Toronto, but Julie and her mother stayed to help Aunt Vi and Uncle George deal with the will and clearing out her grandmother's apartment.

It was bitter cold that January, even colder than Julie remembered. She sometimes wondered why people believed Hell was hot. For her, Hell was standing on a Clairville street corner in the winter, waiting for buses that never came.

The three women worked hard in the apartment, cleaning and throwing out. Every now and then her mother or aunt would find something that brought back memories and then they would have a good cry together. After several days of this, Julie was itching to get out. When a Chinook blew in overnight and warmed things up, she asked to take some time off.

She decided to go for a walk and visit old haunts. Clairville looked very small and old-fashioned after Toronto and the past five years had not been good to the city. The downtown area seemed to be more rundown than she remembered and many of the nicer stores had closed. She was walking along what had been one of the better shopping streets when a shabbily dressed man approached and said, "Spare some change, lady?"

There was something familiar about his voice. She looked him in the face and then, at the same time, she said, "Jake?" and he said, "Julie?"

They stood there for a long moment until she said, "My God. What happened to you?" As soon as the words were out, she could have bitten off her tongue, but he didn't seem to mind.

"Had some hard luck," he said. "What are you doing back here?"

"My grandmother died. My family came from Toronto for the funeral."

"Sorry to hear that." He looked down at the ground then up again. "You heard Clara died?"

"No! That can't be true."

He stepped back as though she had hit him and she cringed again. Of course he wouldn't make up something like that.

Quickly, she said, "No, I didn't hear. I've been really busy with the funeral and all." She made a decision. "Look, can we go somewhere for coffee? I'll treat. Since I haven't seen you for so long." It wasn't much of a reason, but she didn't want him to feel like she was offering charity.

He thought for a minute. "There's a diner down the street that isn't too picky about how you're dressed. I don't mean you, Julie. You look good."

The café he led her to certainly didn't have any right to be fussy, but she thought coffee was probably safe. She suggested Jake have something to eat and he ordered a BLT without too much persuading. Then they sat back and looked at each other.

"Tell me about Clara. What happened?" she asked.

"It was that son-of-a-bitch, Theo. You know she married the bastard?"

"I heard they got engaged not long after I moved east. What do you mean? What did he do?"

"He said it was an accident. They were up north at her family's cottage. It was cold and the roads were icy. He went off a bridge and the car ended up in the water. He got out but she didn't. He said he dove and dove but he couldn't get her out."

"Oh, my God. Like Ted Kennedy," she said, trying not to imagine what it must have been like for Clara, trapped there in the front seat. She found herself wondering if it had been the Porsche, as if that mattered. Then she said, "That makes three."

"Wha' do you mean, three?"

"Three women's deaths he's been involved in. Three accidents."

"Yeah. Well, some people thought this wasn't an accident. Including me. Only nobody that mattered would listen to me. The dirty bastard."

Their coffee and his sandwich came then, and it was almost frightening to see how he fell on the food. Like a hungry animal. She had to look away.

"I understand you hating him, after what he did, getting you fired," she said, when he took a pause after half the sandwich had disappeared. "I didn't have anything to do with that, Jake. I hope you know that."

"I didn't blame you, Julie. I was out of line. And you know, I really liked you. I wanted to ask you out but I went about things the wrong way."

In the past few years, Julie had learned that some men were like little boys, acting up to get the attention of the girls they liked, so she nodded.

"I really needed that job. I was supposed to start university in the fall. I wanted to teach Phys-Ed. My mother was on her own and she didn't have the money to pay my fees. Then, after I got fired, no one else would hire me. I think Theo had some influence in town. His parents knew everybody that mattered."

He attacked the sandwich again, as though he hated it.

"Clara was such a good person," Julie said, remembering her easy way of letting people know when they made mistakes, her way of showing appreciation when they did well. "She was my brothers' swimming teacher. They really liked her."

"She was—she was special. She tried to help me that summer, but I was such a jerk. I thought I knew everything. Then," he paused, "then I started drinking. I got one crappy job after another. I kept losing them." He gave a little shamefaced laugh. "Well, here I am."

They sat there quietly, drinking the dreadful coffee. Finally she said, "So what happened to Theo? After the accident?"

"He's back in town. He keeps coming back. Like a dog to its vomit. His parents are dead now, but his brother still lives here. Someday he's going to pay for what he did to Clara."

All the time they had been talking, Julie had been thinking about those other young women. And thinking, *Suppose I was wrong, doubting those stories, suppose they were true?* She wanted to keep Jake talking, sorting out her thoughts. The waitress brought him the apple pie she had ordered.

He took a bite and then he said, "What did you mean about the other dead women?"

And Julie did something she shouldn't have done. She said, "Jake, this is what Theo told me that summer when we worked at the pool."

By the time she'd finished, Jake was shivering. She reached across the table and patted his arm.

"Then it wasn't an accident," he said.

"That's what I've been thinking. Three accidents are too many. And, God, Jake,"—this struck her suddenly—"there may have been others we don't know about."

"Somebody has to stop him."

"How? Would the police listen to you?" She looked at him and thought, *I wouldn't believe him, so shabby and smelling of booze.*

"They might if you came with me."

Would the police listen to her? Julie doubted they would think much of stories she had heard five years ago, as a teenager. She might have made them up for some reason. And the police might want her to stay on in Clairville, make statements, meet Theo face to face. "Jake, I don't think I can do it. I'm sorry."

He finished his pie and then he came to a decision.

"Will you do me a favour then? Will you call him and ask if he can meet you for a drink tonight?"

"Jake, I don't want to see him. I might say something stupid." It occurred to her that confronting a man who could have murdered three women was not a sensible thing to do.

"You don't have to be there. I will. I just want him to admit what he did. Come on, Julie. Do it for Clara, if you won't do it for me."

He looked so pathetic in his shabby running shoes and thin windbreaker. She said, "Okay."

There was a payphone outside the diner. Jake had the Carmody phone number memorized.

Julie thought Theo might have forgotten who she was. Or he might not be home. But when she rang him, he answered right away.

"Theo," she said, her voice a little shaky, "this is Julie Ward. Remember I worked at the pool the summer of '77. I'm in town."

She started to say she was sorry about Clara but he cut her off. "Julie! Of course I remember you. Little Julie. It's been a long time." Then he made things easy for her. "Are you here for long? Maybe we could meet up."

"I'm flying back to Toronto tomorrow. My mother and I were here for my grandmother's funeral."

"I remember your grandmother. She was quite a character. Then let's have a drink tonight."

"Make it late," Jake whispered. "After dark. At that bar."

And he pointed across the street.

"A nightcap, maybe?" she said. "Nine o'clock? At the Al Hambra? I remember it."

"Kind of rough area now after dark," Theo said. "But that's okay. I'll drive you home."

"Good work," Jake said, after she hung up. "That's all I need from you."

"Be careful," she said, but he was already scurrying away.

"Theo never even mentioned Clara," Julie whispered to herself.

Back at the apartment, her mother and aunt were busy preparing dinner, trying to make it a bit special for her last night there. They didn't ask about her walk, if she had seen anyone she knew.

It snowed that night. Her flight the next morning was delayed but she finally made it back to Toronto and returned to her classes at Queen's in Kingston. Jake didn't have any way to get in touch with her and she didn't know how to reach him. Maybe it was better not to know what had happened.

A few weeks later, she found out. Her mother was finally home and phoned. Most of their talk concerned heirlooms she thought Julie might want, but at the very end of the conversation she mentioned something she had read in the Clairville paper the day before.

"Remember that fellow, Jake Farmer, who worked at the pool with you that summer? The one who ruined my linen jacket? Apparently he was living rough, panhandling. Well, he's dead. Some city workmen just found his body in a snowbank they were clearing."

"That's awful," Julie said. She found it hard to speak. "Did they say how he died?"

"The paper said it looked like he'd been in a fight. It was in a rough part of town. They're not sure how he died—maybe froze to death. Not something you'd wish on anyone. The police are investigating, wanting to talk to anyone who saw him last. It seems he'd been dead for some time."

"That's horrible. He—he wasn't much older than me."

Her mother remembered then that there was a silver tea-set among Nana's things that needed a home and did Julie want it? She tried to take an interest but all she could think of was Jake, in his skimpy windbreaker, lying there in the snow.

The news affected her studies. She wasn't able to concentrate and one of her profs criticized an important essay, quite severely. She had a fight with her boyfriend about something trivial and they stopped speaking to each other. The winter dragged on. Then it was March. The days grew longer and it began to seem as though spring might come sometime.

Walking home from the library late one evening, she began to feel almost herself again. Maybe Jake hadn't met Theo at all. Or the meeting might have ended with a bit of name calling. Jake had been living rough, drinking a lot. He could have picked a fight with another panhandler and fallen down drunk in the snow. Anything could happen to a person living on the streets, in the winter.

When a man stepped out of the shadows by the front door of her apartment building, she didn't recognize him at first.

"Julie," he said, and she knew that teasing voice, "I finally get to see you again."

"Theo? What are you doing here?"

"You never turned up at the Al Hambra. I'm driving down to Florida and thought I'd stop and see what happened to you." He took hold of her arm.

"How did you find me?" She tried to pull away but he held on.

"I ran into your mother back in Clairville. She didn't tell you, eh? She mentioned you were here in Kingston at the university, and it wasn't too hard after that."

"Theo, I'm sorry but I can't do this now. It's late. I have an eight o'clock class in the morning." She wondered if she should scream.

Someone in the building might hear her. But she would look like such a fool.

He kept talking. "You owe me a drink, kid. What do you say we go have one now?"

And as he talked, he was moving her down the sidewalk toward a parked car.

"I heard about Jake," she said.

He stopped walking. "That guy? I ran into him the night you didn't show up. I have you to thank for being able to fire him that summer. What a loser." He started walking again, moving her along.

"And Clara?" she said. "I'm sorry about Clara."

"Yeah. That was terrible. Ever had hypothermia, Julie? I almost died from it."

He stopped at the black sedan and opened the side door. "Hop in," he said, giving Julie a little push.

Why had she gotten inside? Why hadn't she run? The door closed on her. She groped for the door handle, but there wasn't one. Then he was around to the driver's side, opening the door, sliding in under the wheel, slamming the door shut.

"This isn't the Porsche," she whispered.

"It's not a car for driving in the winter." He started the car and pulled away from the curb. "What say we go for a drive before we have that drink? It'll be just like old times. You and me and the night is young."

PAM BARNSLEY

Pam Barnsley is a former journalist whose work has appeared in *Ellery Queen Mystery Magazine* and *Storyteller Canada*. Her novel, *The River Cage*, was shortlisted for the CWC's Best Unpublished Manuscript (Unhanged Arthur) in 2020. She is a member of Crime Writers of Canada and Sisters in Crime. Pam is also a former snowboard instructor, an award-winning poet and, from her father, she learned the ancient art of training a cat to jump over a stick. Pam's website is www.pambarnsley.com

ALMOST SELF-DEFENCE

PAM BARNSLEY

Rodney, 12:05 p.m.

R odney didn't want to kill his boss, but the way Rodney saw it, it was pretty much self-defence.

Moss stuck his head into Rodney's office. "Meet you in the car park in half an hour. Your turn for bevvies at The Bucket List."

Rodney nodded, his mouth dry. He was afraid if he tried to speak, he'd squeak. His guilt must be plain for his boss to see.

Rodney's therapist was always going on about Rodney's feelings of guilt, his lack of self-esteem, his abandonment issues. Okay, Rodney did feel guilty about everything from drinking milk straight out of the carton, to buying a week's worth of veggies and then letting them turn to compost, to wearing dirty clothes out of the hamper.

But if stealing half a million bucks' worth of gems and cash from your boss doesn't make you feel guilty, maybe you've got the wrong therapist.

Rodney tidied up his desk and took a last look around. He wouldn't be back.

The chill he felt as he waited for Moss in the downtown Vancouver parkade wasn't only from the November cold coming down off the North Shore Mountains. Moss's diamond-and-gems dealership was one of the biggest money launderers in Western Canada for the big criminals, and Rodney was supposed to keep track of it all. Skimming was a death sentence.

Moss and Rodney quit early some Fridays, when Moss was in a fishing mood. They'd make the three-hour drive north, to Moss's cabins along the remote Anderson Lake. Rodney hated it. Rodney's new wife, Keisha, hated it too, but Moss insisted, and Moss was the boss.

Finally, here he came, grinning like he'd copped one last feel off his secretary, Marsha, or pinched a few giggles out of Eleanor, the sales clerk.

"Anchors aweigh," Moss said as he unlocked his car. "I'm a parched man."

Rodney listened to his boss's terrible jokes all the way to Pemberton. At The Bucket List, Moss leaned back in his chair and ran both hands through his hair, as if he were getting himself ready for some event. He had great hair, Rodney gave him that, thick and wavy, even if it was dyed a phony black. Rodney shaved his own head to hide his baldness, though Keisha said she liked him just the way he was.

If she only knew what Rodney had been up to, well. Although he was terrified of getting caught, he also felt a tingle of pride that he wasn't just the dull and boring accountant everyone thought he was. Right now, his inside jacket pockets were stuffed with uncut diamonds and a wad of bills.

Moss waved a server over. "Double rum and cokes, darling. Save the lime wedges for the yuppies. And keep your eyes peeled, we're thirsty."

Rodney sipped carefully; he'd need his wits about him later. Moss might be a podgy old lush, but he was cagey.

Twice recently Moss had questioned Rodney about discrepancies in their cash and illegal diamonds, and Rodney had been able to fudge explanations. But he'd been stealing too much, he could feel it, and Moss wasn't blind.

And Moss's bosses, well, anybody who messed with their money had a short life expectancy. So Rodney had to kill Moss, and throw the blame onto him, before they found out.

His plan was simple. As usual, after Moss was half-drunk, Rodney would drive them the rest of the way up to the cabins. Where the pavement ended, the Highline Road snaked along, far above the north-western shore of Anderson Lake. It was a treacherous old logging road, with switchbacks and drop-offs to the lake hundreds of feet below.

At the highest point of the road, Moss always made them pull over at the lookout for a contest, see who could send their stream farthest into the void. Moss always declared himself the winner. Rodney got vertigo looking hundreds of feet down into the inky lake; it was a wonder he could even piddle at all.

But tonight, this was where Rodney would give Moss a little shove.

There was no guardrail, and a slight misstep by an older, out-of-shape man who'd been known to drink too many rum and cokes could take him down into the lake below. If he didn't smash his head on the rocks on the way down, he'd drown in the black depths. Anderson Lake was a thousand feet deep in places, and this time of year it was cold as ice.

Rodney had rehearsed his story to the police. "I warned him," he'd say, "it's so dangerous, but Moss, he's been stopping there since forever. There's no talking him out of something, he's like that. He was gone before I could save him."

Rodney imagined he might even choke up a little as he relayed the tragic events. "Moss was a good boss, a good man. If only I could've saved him. I'm just gutted."

The police knew nothing of Moss's illegal business, so they'd only be concerned with his accidental death.

Rodney wouldn't be so foolish as to spend any of the cash right away. The stones, those he would hang onto until it was safe to sell them, after he and Keisha moved across the country. Houses were cheaper in the Maritimes; and they could start a little business there.

Moss's bosses would blame Moss for the missing gems and cash. They'd sniff around trying to find their share, but it would be hard with the police involved in his death, and then Moss's kids would probably show up to inherit the business. Messy.

Rodney thought the bosses might talk to him, but he'd claim to know nothing. "Moss didn't tell me any of that. I had no idea. He was a guy kept his cards close to his chest, didn't trust other people, you know?"

Moss sucked back his drink and signalled the server for another. "So, Rodster, tell me, you thinking of starting up your own business? Lots of accountants already, so maybe not that." Moss's eyes glittered. "But perhaps you think you know enough about gems now?"

Rodney's mouth was suddenly dry. He gulped some more of his drink.

"No. No way," he said. He stood up. "I've gotta hit the men's room."

"Again?" Moss grinned. "Save some for the contest at the lookout."

Rodney locked the stall and leaned his head against the door. How had he come to this, killing another man?

How could he claim to be any better than greedy Moss? Moss at least was honest about himself, made no apologies, didn't pretend to be a decent human being. Rodney was a hypocrite.

When he came back from the washroom, Moss was reading their server's palm—he could see an incredibly sexy older guy in her future.

"Hey, watch out for this cheapskate." Moss pointed at Rodney. "I give the guy a great salary, I mean big bonuses too, really big, and he gives me a hard time about buying us drinks. Can you believe it?"

"We really should be getting on before it's too dark," Rodney said. "Keisha will be worrying something's happened."

He stood up and fumbled into his jacket. He slipped his hands into the pockets, just to reassure himself that the diamonds and cash were still there.

They weren't.

Moss, 3:15 p.m.

M oss had never imagined that, of all people, he'd have to kill Rodney. It cheesed him off that Rodney had put him in this position.

Rodney was driving Moss's big Buick, as Moss sat in the passenger seat playing with his switchblade, flicking the blade in and out. The knife had a nice weight to it, heavy for such a small tool, but balanced. He'd have preferred his gun, but it was in his office desk. Oh well, a mimsy little twerp like Rodney, Moss could probably scare him to death, wouldn't even have to shove him over the lookout. But the lookout would be tidier, it would seem like an accident; man couldn't hold his liquor.

"So, did you and Keisha have a plan for how you were going to get away with ripping me and the big bosses off?"

"Keisha doesn't know a thing about this, I swear. I'd never tell her. Never."

Moss believed that part; Rodney seriously under-estimated his luscious wife. If she'd been the one ripping Moss off, she'd have been smarter about it than her dolt of a husband.

Moss had the bag of uncut diamonds in his own pocket now, and a roll of bills he'd liberated from Rodney's jacket. That still left about the same amount that Rodney had been nicking over the past few months. He'd guess upwards of five hundred grand total. Moss needed that back. He had some investments that hadn't worked out lately, and he was over-extended.

Not to mention the big bosses.

"You straighten this out," Alby had told him. "Forty-eight hours." He didn't need to say, *or else we'll crush your dangly bits in a vice,* but it was obvious from the way his whole face looked sad, even just thinking about it. Even Alby's eyebrows looked sad. His frickin' ears.

"Hey, no worries. I got it under control, really," he reassured Alby. "Rodney's going to cough up the stones. I'll straighten out your account."

Alby stared at him.

"Ah, right, I get it," Moss said. "I'll take care of Rodney, too."

So that was it. Either Rodney or Moss was being put underground for this, and it wasn't going to be Moss. Killing Rodney was pretty much self-defence.

But Lord, give him patience, Rodney was the worst driver ever. Not setting up for curves, braking in the corners, jamming the gas, then brake, over-steering. He was liable to kill them both on this deadly road. How the man had ever passed his driver's exam, just shows you how corrupt the licencing department was.

"So," said Moss, "where's my other missing diamonds and cash?"

He tapped the blade against Rodney's arm, Rodney yelped, and the car swerved.

"Dammit, man, hold it together. There's the lookout; pull over."

Rodney parked the car and turned the engine off. His face was grey and there was too much white around his eyes. It was hard not to feel a bit sorry for someone who looked like a nag that didn't know it was headed for the glue factory.

But life wasn't fair. Moss had a job to do. Not everyone got to be in the helping professions, like doctors, escort girls, or dog-walkers.

Rodney said, "I'm sorry—"

"Save it. I don't waste time feeling sorry for anyone."

Moss had survived by being unsentimental, one step ahead of the other guys. His kids didn't talk to him anymore, his three exes were long gone, but hell, you didn't see him feeling sorry for himself, did you? That was life. He had enough bucks to buy his version of happiness, and that's all that counted.

"Moss, can we work this out? Can I pay extra?"

"You idiot, what you think this is, you're in arrears on your TV payment or something?" Moss laughed. "You bit the hand that feeds you. And after all I've done for you."

Moss had some affection for Rod. He was like a nephew, almost. A doofus nephew who irritated the snot out of Moss and made his shoes itch just wanting to give him a kick, but still.

Rodney's wife, she was the smart one. She had that wide-eyed look dialled, but it was an act.

Moss had been working on commitment issues with his therapist lately, and he'd come to see that clever women weren't the best choice for him. Certainly, his smart exes always got tired of his tricks.

He suspected his therapist didn't like him. Maybe it was his jokes; not everyone got his sense of humour.

"Get out of the car," he said to Rodney.

Rodney dragged his feet as they walked over to the edge. Moss indicated they were to step over to their little spot where they'd relieved themselves in the past.

Far below them, the lake lapped at its banks, like a hungry animal waiting to be fed. The black water glittered.

Moss flicked the blade in and out. "Last chance, Hot-Rod, where's my other diamonds and cash?"

Moss was confident Keisha would know exactly where Rodney had hidden the gems and cash anyway. She was a survivor, he could tell.

Still, Rodney should confess, it was good for the soul.

He could see Rodney shaking with fear. It was embarrassing, made Moss feel like a bully.

Rodney reached out a trembling hand and gripped Moss's sleeve. "The gems and cash are in a safe place. Please, if you take me—"

"Shut it." Moss needed to quit feeling sorry for the pathetic dolt. "Tell me now where they are. If you're lying, you're dead, and I'll go take it out on that lovely wife of yours."

Rodney had both hands on Moss's arm now, desperate. "Okay, okay. They're buried behind the mailbox post at the cabin—"

Rodney shoved Moss hard toward the drop-off, and Moss felt a jolt of surprise, that the man would dare. Moss dropped his knife, grabbed Rodney's arm, and saved himself. He swung Rodney around toward the edge, straining to push him over, their crazed eyes inches apart as air and water and blackness awaited them.

Keisha, 5:45 p.m.

K eisha pressed the record button on her cellphone. "Help me, please! There are burglars! They're going to kill us! Help!"

She dropped the cell and gave a shriek, which she hoped would sound as though she were being dragged away.

She picked her phone up off the deck of the little cottage where she and Rodney had to stay when Moss wanted a fishing buddy. The deck was cantilevered out over the awful drop to the lake below; some people thought that was cool, but Keisha thought it was creepy. But it was going to come in handy, too.

She listened to her recording. Not bad. She would've liked to really scream, but it was a hard thing to do; she was no Oscar-winning actor.

She erased the recording. She would call Moss's office and leave that same message after Rodney came home, after she killed him. If Moss came too, worse luck for him. Either way, she'd have enough of a head start to get halfway across the country.

"Don't worry, I have a plan," Rodney had said. "Trust me." He wouldn't say more.

Well, she had a better plan.

She didn't want to kill poor Rodney, but it would be kind of self-defence.

If Moss stopped in for dinner tonight, she'd kill him, too. Otherwise, he'd come tomorrow morning and find them both gone, Rodney's blood where he'd been dragged across the deck and tipped into the lake, Keisha presumed murdered as well.

Rodney didn't realize she knew about the stolen gems and cash. As if she wouldn't figure out he'd been hiding the loose stones in a little cloth bag under the deck. The cash was in an old tobacco tin in his shoe-polishing kit. Duh.

As if Moss wouldn't know they'd run away with his illegal stones, as if the higher-ups in Alby's outfit wouldn't track them down and kill them both. Rodney had no experience running away and hiding. Keisha did.

She moved the plastic deck chair under the porch light and unscrewed the bulb. It threw the deck into almost complete darkness, just enough light from the open sky above the lake to make out the shapes of shadows. She couldn't see the switchback path that ran from behind the cottage up to the road, but she knew it had small landscape lights that illuminated the ground, enough to keep a person from tripping.

Keisha pulled the chair back to the railing and sat down to wait. She wished it would just go ahead and snow, instead of tightening down the screws, colder and colder. On the railing, she had her phone, a glass of whisky, a revolver, and the bag of diamonds. The first three were going into the lake when she was finished with them. The last was bankrolling her new life.

She sipped the whisky and checked her phone for messages again. Where was Rodney? He was usually here by now, even if Moss kept them for extra rounds at that cheesy Pemberton bar.

She texted Rodney. *"u on yr way babe? dinnerz reddy."* With two heart emojis.

What was keeping him so long?

Keisha took her gun and walked through the cottage. Spaghetti and meatballs on the stove, turned off, waiting. Salad and dressing in the fridge, waiting. None of it ever to be eaten. Props in a play.

She'd cleaned the cottage, leaving nothing behind that could lead to her. She ran her eyes over the bedroom—tidy, but not too tidy, that might be suspicious. The clothes in her side of the closet, and in her drawers, weren't actually hers. She'd removed all her own clothing that she wasn't taking with her, and dropped them at a thrift store. She'd bought an assortment of clothes, right down to the underwear, in two sizes larger than she was, to replace hers.

Maybe she was over-planning this whole thing, but still, she thought it was a clever touch, throw anyone off the scent. Keisha was a size four; let them be searching for a woman size eight. She'd even done the shoes three sizes larger; she was proud of her dainty feet.

The bathroom was clean, her toiletries replaced with cheap ones she'd opened and partly mucked out. In the mirror, she admired her new look. Blond tresses gone, cropped as short as a boy's, dyed dark brown. She thought it added a good twenty IQ points. No makeup, and the tortoiseshell glasses, she looked like someone running for political office on the environmental ticket, or selling mortgage derivatives to schoolteachers' funds. She lifted the gun and pointed it at the mirror; she could sell them at gunpoint.

She went back to the deck and sipped more whisky.

She would shoot Rodney when he came down the path, as soon as he came around the back corner of the cottage onto the deck. Before he even knew it was her. Before she had to feel sorry for him, the big goof.

Ditto for Moss, if he came.

She would drag their bodies across the deck and tip them into the lake. They might be found, or not. Call the office, leave her tragic plea for help. The assumption would be, her body was in the lake too, but never found. It was a notoriously deep lake.

She would drive through the night, leave Rodney's car with the keys in it, in a part of Vancouver where the vultures would find it. Then she would make her way east in the rental car she'd left in a long-term parking lot. She had a new pay-as-you-go phone, fake ID, and a pre-loaded credit card. Drive across Canada to Toronto, and start over.

She poured herself three more fingers of whisky; it wasn't as bad now that her tastebuds had been beaten into submission.

The alcohol released the sizzle of running into her veins. She'd always told herself it was the guys she was running from. She only needed a decent man and she'd stay. But Rodney was decent. She was running away from a man who promised to cherish her forever, a man who would do anything for her—the schmuck, look at what he'd gone and done for her.

She could just leave the stones and cash behind and run, but no, she was taking them, and killing men for them. She told herself this time she'd be able to set herself up. Not pretend to be dimwitted for some guy's ego. Order what she wanted from the menu and not thank anyone for it.

She gulped the whisky, splashed more in her glass. It wasn't quenching her thirst, or her nerves.

Who was she kidding? All the years of pretending, you become the thing you're pretending to be.

Dear, hopeless Rodney. Rodney wasn't a bad person. She was the bad person. Or maybe she was a good person who kept doing bad things. Well, this was going to be the last bad thing she did.

She would atone for killing him somehow. She would give winter mittens to street kids, tip waiters large, buy her hairdresser dinner at a fancy joint. As soon as she could afford it, she would be a better person.

She knocked back another inch of amber liquid.

It was time; she could feel it coming. Was that a car door slam? She strained to hear, but there was only the sound of the wind in the trees. The diamonds winked at her as she rolled them off her palm, back into their soft bag, promising her everything, creating their own warmth in the bitter night.

Keisha set the bag on the rail and took up her gun.

She pressed deeper into the shadows against the wall of the cottage, waiting to see if it was just Rodney, or Moss too. If it was Moss, he'd be yacking—he was always yacking. She'd have to wait a second longer for them both to get onto the deck, then pop-pop, shoot them both.

It was quiet, only her own heartbeat. No voices. Only a single set of soft footsteps. Only Rodney.

The bulk of him came around the corner and Keisha was terrified by his looming shadow, not a dozen feet away.

Bang-bang-bang!

She shot him three times; had to fight her panic not to keep squeezing the trigger until the gun was empty.

Annie, 6:48 p.m.

"N.O.D.'s are the worst, aren't they?" Annie Wachtel said in a low voice.

Every officer dreaded having to deliver a Notification of Death to an unsuspecting mother, father, lover, friend.

"The worst," agreed her partner, Ben Sidhu. He stopped on the step below her and turned back to her. "I can't even imagine how I'd be able to live if something happened to you."

On the lower step he was the same height as her, and as she looked into his dark eyes, for a moment she forgot everything else.

They leaned together until their foreheads touched. "We'd better go," Annie whispered.

Ben sighed. Annie smiled; she understood that sigh perfectly, their hunger to be in one another's arms, a hunger that was almost pain.

"You have the counsellor services card?" she asked.

"Shoot, no. I'll go back to the cruiser and get it."

"That's okay, I'll get it," she said. "I'll see you down there."

Ben nodded and headed back down the switchback path, while Annie turned and hurried up the trail.

At the police cruiser she found one of the counsellor's cards and tucked it into her uniform shirt pocket. She'd just started down the path again when she heard the three shots. Not Ben's semi-automatic; it sounded more like a revolver.

Adrenaline kicked through her. She pulled her own gun and dropped into a crouch.

She pressed her mic button. "Ben, you clear?"

No answer.

"Ben?"

She switched channels, called the emergency dispatch, requested backup and an ambulance. "Possible officer down."

She ran down the path, her footsteps silent on the packed dirt and snow. The cottage appeared out of the shadows, the path skirting along the rear of it. She could see the end of a deck now, a body lying on it. Just a crumpled silhouette in the darkness.

Please, please, not Ben. She'd do anything, give anything, everything, please.

She crept forward to the corner of the building and looked. The right side of Ben's head was blown away, dark clumps of matter staining the deck.

The howl in Annie's head drowned out the whole world.

She heard a scraping noise from the deck. She angled herself to look around the corner.

A petite woman in black jeans and a hoodie stood on a plastic deck chair, with a revolver in one hand, reaching up to the lightbulb over the entry door. She screwed the bulb in and the deck was washed in light. The woman climbed down from the chair and turned to Ben's body.

The woman recoiled. "Oh, no. No, no, no, no, no."

She'd been expecting someone other than Ben.

The woman turned and stepped to the railing, took the glass sitting there, and drained it. She brought her right arm back, the one with the revolver, winding up for a big throw. The gun was going in the lake.

"Police! Hold it! Put the gun down! Now!"

Annie saw the flinch of shock, followed by a fraction of hesitation.

"Now! Or I'll shoot!"

The woman put the gun down carefully. As she turned around to face Annie, she wobbled, bumped the glass with her elbow, reached back to grab it. She saved the glass but knocked a small cloth bag off the rail. The bag spilled its contents, what looked to Annie like dusty chips of glass, pale aquarium rocks. As the little stones sprinkled through the air, the woman lunged after them. For a moment, it seemed she was going into the lake after them.

"Hands up! Now!" Annie barked. "Where I can see them!"

The woman turned back to Annie, put her hands up. "I panicked. I thought he was a burglar."

"Who else is here?"

"No one, I ... I was waiting for my husband to get home from work ... I thought your partner was a burglar—"

"You're Keisha Milford? Rodney Milford's wife?"

"Yes."

Annie kicked Keisha's revolver away. She flipped out her handcuffs.

"Down on the ground. Hands behind your back."

She cuffed Keisha's hands. She glanced in the window of the little cottage, saw no one in the main room. Two more doors, presumably bedroom and bathroom. Annie went and knelt beside Ben's body.

She put her hand on his throat, not to feel for a pulse, just to feel the last fading warmth of him as he vanished from her.

"I'm so sorry. I thought—"

"No," said Annie, "you didn't."

Keisha's face was turned toward Annie. Her eyes rounded, but calculating.

"We've had break-ins, some of the cottages along here, burglars know—"

"You were going to throw your gun in the lake."

"No! I ... I just wanted to get it away from me. It was all so terrible. I was scared to death."

"You weren't scared at all. Not until you saw it was a police officer you'd shot."

Keisha opened her mouth to speak; closed it.

"And you screwed the lightbulb back in. The one you'd unscrewed earlier—you were planning to shoot your husband, weren't you?"

"No! It wasn't like that. I, uh, I just thought I'd check the lightbulb maybe wasn't burnt out, and it wasn't."

Annie shook her head. With a good lawyer, and her big, soft eyes, this woman was going to give the judge or jury a workout. Any woman alone in the night in a remote cabin would be scared, could accidentally shoot a man.

Annie felt the rage building in her chest. She forced herself to breathe.

"Your husband is dead. Fell off the lookout spot earlier tonight."

"What?! Rodney? No, uh-uh."

"That's why my partner and I were here. To tell you."

Keisha wriggled into a sitting position, with her cuffed wrists behind her, and leaned against the wall of the cottage.

"Rodney and his boss, Michael Moss, both fell to their deaths," Annie said. "A motorist saw them fall. Looked like one of them was trying to save the other, and they both went over."

"Unbelievable...." Keisha coughed, as though trying to cover an ironic laugh. She turned to Annie; her face back under control, tears in her eyes now. "It was obviously an accident. Those two were the best of friends. They loved one another like brothers. They always stopped at the lookout for a tinkle—boys will be boys."

Annie could see how she would play the jury, that quiver in her pouty lips.

The muscles in Annie's arm where she held her service pistol were strung so tight, she'd have to be careful not to accidentally shoot Keisha. And she could shoot this woman, in self-defence, easy as that. Keisha's prints were on the gun that killed Ben, there would be gunshot residue on her hands. Who's to say Annie didn't shoot Keisha in self-defence, when Annie first came down the path and onto the deck?

"Stand up," Annie said.

Keisha looked at her, seemed to register something in Annie's voice. "Why?"

"Do it." She flicked her gun upwards, and Keisha stood.

Annie knew nothing was ever going to make this right. Ben was gone. But the gun in her hand promised its own justice. A simple squeeze of her finger. The self-defence Ben never got.

She could hear the sirens wailing in the distance now.

Beyond the deck, the lake shone black as death as the first snowflakes started to fall.

The gun was heavy in her hand, so heavy.

GABRIELLE ST. GEORGE

Gabrielle St. George is a Canadian screenwriter and story-editor with credits on over 100 produced television shows, both in the USA and Canada. Her feature film scripts have been optioned in Hollywood. Ms. St. George writes humourous mysteries and domestic noir about subjects of which she is an expert—mostly failed relationships, hence her debut soft-boiled series, The Ex-Whisperer Files, which launched with *How to Murder a Marriage* in November 2021, followed by *How to Kill a Kingpin* in July 2022. Gabrielle's website is www.gabriellestgeorge.com

COLD ETHYL

GABRIELLE ST. GEORGE

TAMMY IS PERCHED on a vinyl chair at the end of her dining table, day-old toast crumbs sticking to her forearms, her ice-cold hands wrapped around a lukewarm mug of black coffee. She's spent the morning staring out the kitchen's large bay window at the row of cookie-cutter houses nearly identical to her own that line the other side of the unremarkable suburban street.

The garage doors are different colours and, over the years, some neighbours have sprung for pretty patio pavers and raised flower beds, but the thirty-year-old neighbourhood looks faded and frayed like most of its inhabitants. The children who grew up here fled to Toronto or Ottawa at first chance, leaving lost-looking parents battling mid-life crises and HRT fallout. Signs of life are sporadic. Signs of boredom are everywhere.

Tammy's gaze has been fixed on the house directly across from hers. The one with the too-bright coral-coloured door that sports a cyclical parade of tacky seasonal wreaths woven from plastic spring blooms, fake fall leaves, or glue-gunned pinecones.

When Tammy and Craig moved into this house three decades earlier it was shiny and new and exciting and bursting with potential, just like they were. Now their two children have grown and flown the coop to begin their own shiny new lives and Craig peaced out shortly afterwards. He left Tammy to sort out his messes, including his unpaid income taxes and a second mortgage he'd taken out on their home that she hadn't known about.

Tammy shut down her feelings and closed up camp on her dreams and desires a few years back after she began suspecting that Craig was dipping his wick elsewhere. As a distraction from cavorting Craig and their crumbling marriage, Tammy busied herself with Zumba classes and stained-glass window workshops. It worked. She didn't even notice Craig prepping to leave her and was genuinely surprised when she came home from her book club meet-up to the sauce-stained note he left on this same kitchen table, reprimanding her for ignoring all his needs and blaming her for everything that ever went wrong in his life. He stapled the Dear Jane letter to a hefty credit card bill and asked Tammy to make the payment for him. Tammy couldn't help but notice the charges for expensive dinners at restaurants she'd never been to, and purchases at a lingerie shop and florist she didn't frequent.

A few days ago, Craig texted Tammy to inform her that he was moving in with his new squeeze. Last night he texted to tell her where he would be living.

Right. Across. The. Street.

Craig was moving in with Carolyn of the Cheeto-coloured door and the tacky plastic wreath collection. Carolyn, the divorcee who made a mean martini (multiple times a day) and went to pole dancing classes instead of stained-glass window workshops. Carolyn, with the fuchsia acrylic nails and over-bleached hair who, for the past five years, had paid Craig cash on weekends to plumb in her powder room, paint her picket fence, patch drywall, and it would seem, diddle her hoohaa. Clearly, Carolyn did not ignore Craig's needs.

Tammy sees smoky-eyed, falsie-lashed Carolyn parting cheap sheers to peek out her own identical bay window onto the empty street. Both women waiting for lady-killer Craig to make his grand appearance and complete the twisted triangle.

A car pulls up in front of Tammy's house and parks along the sidewalk. Her sister Gwen climbs out of it, balancing a bag-in-a-box wine and a carton of Tim Hortons donuts.

When Gwen steps into the kitchen, her mouth drops. "OMG, you look like crap."

Tammy bursts into tears. Not because of the comment, just because there is now an available shoulder to cry on. She bites into a jelly-filled cruller that drips down her chin and spills onto her white sweatshirt, perfectly balancing out the brown tea stain across her left boob from who knows how many days ago. Tammy looks down at her grungy top and cries harder. "I'm a mess."

Gwen can't argue with her. "You'd better change and wash up before Mom gets here."

"Mom's already left twenty messages. God, I hope she hasn't been calling Craig. She hates him more than I do." Tammy presses the heels of her hands against her swollen eyeballs.

"I'm more worried about her calling Carolyn. Who knows what she'll say to that harpy?"

"Probably everything I want to say but don't have the guts to."

Gwen's phone chimes and she checks her texts. "Mom is at Aunt Janie's making sure she didn't forget to turn her stove off. She'll be here soon."

"Mom shouldn't even be driving. She's basically deaf and never wears her hearing aids. I don't know how she got her licence renewed last month."

"She didn't. She's been driving without a licence. Which means no insurance either."

Tammy grabs two wine glasses from a cupboard. "Senility genes locked and loaded."

Gwen punches in the perforated lines on the wine box and pulls out the plastic tap attached to the bag. A shitty Chardonnay slowly trickles out.

Tammy is in agony. "Craig said he wants a fresh start. But is it technically starting a new life if you only move fifty feet away from your home of thirty years? How many times did I fake compliment Carolyn's creepy outdoor décor while she was schtupping my husband in her rec room? I'm such an idiot."

Gwen fills their glasses. "You're not an idiot. You were too busy raising kids, working full-time, and running this house to notice Craig's drama. He's the idiot."

"What's going on with your idiot? Heard anything from the courts lately?"

The air rushes out of Gwen's lungs. Just the thought of her ex is like a punch to her stomach. She throws back her drink. "Derelict Derek has just filed for his third bankruptcy. Anything to get out of paying spousal support."

A black pick-up missing a muffler roars into Carolyn's driveway. The women leap up from the table then crouch down low to watch through the window, hoping their voyeurism isn't overly obvious. It is.

Craig pulls a couple of worn suitcases and some cardboard boxes out of the back of his truck. He glances at his old house more than once.

Carolyn saunters out to meet her new roomie on the driveway wearing too-tight ripped jeans, a crop top, and bright lips that give her orange door a run for its money.

Tammy sneers. "What, is she in freaking Junior High?"

"They don't let the kids wear tops that short in Junior High."

Carolyn wraps her arms around Craig's shoulders and hugs him tightly, possessively, for way too long. She glances toward Tammy's house, smirking.

Tammy cries again. "I'm going to have to move."

Gwen is skeptical. "Let's see how long they last. He could be out on his ass by the weekend."

Carolyn finally releases her territorial grip on Craig.

"Oh no! He's coming over. Quick, hide!"

Craig advances across the lawn. Tammy and Gwen duck behind the kitchen counter.

Craig knocks forcefully on the front door, waits, then throws up his arms and leaves.

The sisters are relieved until they hear the grinding sound of the garage door opening. They scramble to their feet to swing open the kitchen door that leads into the attached garage.

Craig's tools are tidily arranged on shelves above his wooden workbench. Four old bikes that haven't been ridden in years hang from hooks on the ceiling. The parking space is left empty so Tammy can fit her car in there on snowy winter nights.

Craig steps into the dimly lit garage. The sisters block the doorway into the house.

"I could see the cheap wine on the kitchen table. How many boxes have you two drunks drank?"

Gwen's lips curl. "The only drunk around here is across the street wearing an outfit she clearly stole off a thirteen-year-old. And you can't just pop in on Tammy whenever you want to, even if you are going to be neighbours, which is, by the way, extremely screwed up."

Craig laughs but it's nasty. "Speaking of screwed up, how's your ten-year-long divorce proceeding going? You and Derek still fighting over the rider mower?"

Gwen recognizes the ache in her stomach as hate. It's what she feels every time she sees her own ex.

Tammy's voice is shrill, "You are a colossal jerk, Craig. Moving in across the street? Really? What do you think our kids are going to have to say about that?"

"My kids are adults now, they can deal. Anyway, they won't even respond to my texts. Guess you've been filling their heads with bullcrap stories about me." Craig drags his dusty bag of golf clubs out from the corner of the garage and starts packing some of his tools.

Tammy scoffs. "You didn't need any help from me. You've managed to make them hate you all on your own."

A car pulls into the driveway, rolls up very slowly. They all turn to look.

Tammy and Gwen's eighty-two-year-old mother, Ethyl, all white hair and bottle-thick bifocals, hunches over the steering wheel straining to see her way ahead.

Craig pulls on his hair. "Oh, shoot me. Not your crazy mother. Cold fricking Ethyl. She's got a block of ice where her heart should be."

Tammy knows her mother isn't the warmest person, to say the least, but she's obliged to defend her. "She wasn't always cold-hearted. You earned the icy treatment you get."

Ethyl continues slowly up the driveway and proceeds to slide the nose of her old Buick into the garage. Craig waves his hands, motioning for his mother-in-law to stop.

She doesn't.

Craig raises his voice, "What the frig? Stop the car, you old battle-axe."

She doesn't.

Ethyl's car is fully inside the garage now. Craig backs away a few steps. The car continues moving toward him.

By the time Craig realizes that Ethyl is not going to put the brakes on, it's too late for him to jump out of the way in the small gap left between the vehicle and his golf clubs.

Ethyl steps down hard on the gas pedal just for a second. That's all it takes. The car lurches forward.

Crunches and cracks reverberate through the cramped space, the sickening sound of bones splintering and metal bending.

Craig screams in agony as he crumples to the floor, caught between the Buick's bumper and the back wall of the garage. The girls yell at their mother, still bent over her steering wheel, squinting eyes and a faint smile stretched across her lips.

"Mom, stop!"

Ethyl inches forward a little more. Then just a little more, slowly pinning Craig to the wall. The chrome grill presses into his abdomen.

Craig's leg is caught beneath Ethyl's front tire. The veins in his forehead bulge, his face a bright red. The sisters drop down to kneel beside him. His spittle sprays them with every word as he struggles to speak through teeth clenched in pain. "Your mother is a menace. She should have been locked up years ago. Call 9-1-1. My leg's broken. They're going to have to lift the car off me."

There's a clunk as Ethyl puts her gearshift into reverse.

Craig yells out, "No! Don't back up!"

Too late. Ethyl's car is backing up, driving over Craig's leg once again. More screams.

Gwen lunges for the garage door, pushes the button on the wall to close it. "Stop yelling, the neighbours will hear." To further drown out Craig's cries, she switches on the old radio plugged in at the workbench. Crackling sounds of cheering crowds rooting for the Maple Leafs harmonize with Craig's shrieks.

Craig can still speak with effort, but his words are slurred. "Call the police, too." It looks like he's about to lose consciousness.

The garage door seals shut completely. The two shocked sisters stare at each other over Craig's twisted body. This can't be happening.

Ethyl opens her car door, edges herself off the driver's seat. She hobbles around to the front of her vehicle to inspect the damage. She's chipper. "Now that's what you call a fender bender."

Craig rouses, his glazed eyes fluttering open, fixing on his mother-in-law. He sputters venom, "You cold bitch. You're going to pay for this." His breath is growing shorter. His speech, fainter.

"Shut up, Craig." Tammy takes out her phone. "Mom, you shouldn't be driving if you can't see! I'll call an ambulance."

Gwen protectively pulls her mother away from the vehicle. "It was an accident. It's not Mom's fault."

Ethyl is perfectly calm. "I can see just fine." She winks at Craig.

Craig is in too much pain to speak anymore but with the one good limb he has use of he flips his mother-in-law the bird.

Maybe if they weren't so shocked, if they hadn't drunk the wine, the sisters might've been able to intervene between their eighty-two-year-old mother and her disabled son-in-law. But all they see is the blue steel of a nine-iron slicing through the air, the club smashing down on Craig's thick skull. A bloody hole in one.

The girls scream. Craig is quiet.

A long moment later, Tammy reluctantly reaches out to press two fingers against Craig's carotid. She looks at Gwen solemnly and shakes her head, no pulse. "That wasn't an accident."

Gwen stares up at her sweet-looking mom standing over them. "Mom, you killed Craig."

Ethyl slips the bloody golf club back into the bag. "Par for the course when you're a cheating husband and a deadbeat dad."

"Mom, you'll go to prison for this."

Ethyl waves her daughters away. "Pish posh. No judge is going to send an eighty-two-year-old woman to jail. I couldn't see. I can't hear. I have dementia like my sister. By the time it goes to trial, I'll probably be dead already anyway. You're welcome, I did you a favour. I'll go make us some lunch. You girls should call the police." Ethyl totters up the steps from the garage to the kitchen door, disappears inside leaving her daughters alone with Craig's corpse.

Tammy cries, "We can't let Mom go to prison. She did this for me. She'll never survive jail. She's too old. Plus, all the inmates will hate her."

Craig's cell phone rings from somewhere on his body. The girls jump.

Gwen takes a deep breath, closes her eyes, fumbles through Craig's pants pockets and extracts the phone. She reads the cracked screen. "Damn, it's Carolyn."

Tammy leaps up. "She must've heard the screams."

Gwen shakes her head. "She'd likely just think you two were arguing."

Tammy is full-on panicking now. "She'll probably be over here any minute looking for him when he doesn't answer."

"We can't let Mom go to jail. And we can't let Carolyn see Craig." Gwen searches her fried brain for a solution. She can only think of one. "We're going to have to get rid of his body."

"Oh my God. I'm gonna puke."

"It'll be dark in an hour. We'll have to bury him in your yard. Mom can take her car to the body shop now and have the bumper repaired. We need to clean up."

Tammy nods robotically, finds a bottle of glass cleaner and rags on Craig's workbench, and goes to work on the grill and bumper. Gwen scrubs the splattered golf club and wipes up pooling blood where the crack in Craig's skull has leaked onto the garage floor.

Ethyl pops her head into the garage from the kitchen door. "I'm making egg salad sandwiches. You girls want onions or no onions?"

Tammy snaps at her. "Mom, no one has the stomach to eat. You've made a real mess out here." Tammy throws a large, stained painting tarp over Craig's lifeless body.

Ethyl is offended. "Well, the police will be here soon. They might want a little lunch."

Gwen takes her mom by the arm and leads her around to the driver's seat, puts her inside her car. "We're not getting the police involved. You're not going to jail. You're going to take your car into Harman's shop to get your bumper fixed right now. And don't say a word to anyone about what happened. Tell them you hit a deer."

Ethyl nods, turns the key in the ignition, calls out to Tammy, "Don't waste any tears over that loser. He got what he deserved. I told you not to marry him."

Gwen opens the automatic door for her mom, waits as she slowly backs out onto the road. Carolyn watches them through her bay window. Gwen closes the garage door quickly once her mother drives off.

The two sisters stand staring at each other in the dingy fluorescent light. A text *dings*. Gwen cringes as she reaches under the shroud, fishes out Craig's phone once more. She finds his truck keys and pulls them out, too. "Carolyn. *When will you be here? I want you so badly.*"

"Craig has to answer or she's gonna get suspicious."

Gwen texts back. *"Not sure. Tammy and I are working through some stuff. Text you later."* Send.

Ding. Carolyn replies. *"Don't take too long. I'm all revved up and ready to go. I don't want to start without you but you've got me so hot…"*

"Eeeeeww." Tammy shudders.

"She's not going to be hot enough to warm him up."

"Eeeeeww."

"Grab a couple of shovels. As soon as it's dark we'll dig up your veggie garden."

"The kids eat those veggies when they visit."

"Pick another spot then. Just make sure it's soft ground."

The girls stand guard in the garage while the slowest hour of their lives crawls along.

At nightfall, Gwen follows Tammy out the back door of the garage into the fenced-in yard. Lucky for them it's a moonless sky. The neighbourhood is eerily quiet. Tammy leads the way to a large flower bed set against a tall cedar hedgerow.

The message alert on Craig's phone goes off again, startling the pair. Tammy grabs the cell out of Gwen's hand. "Turn the volume off!" She reads Carolyn's text in disgust. "Somebody needs to tell her not to try so hard. She reeks of desperation." Tammy types a reply. *"Not sure if moving in together is such a good idea after all. I'll call when Tammy and I are finished talking."* Send.

Gwen whispers harshly, "You shouldn't have written that. What if she freaks out and shows up now?"

Tammy hands Gwen a shovel. "Get digging."

It's rough going and takes a few hours. The women are filthy, sweaty, sore, and their hands are covered in blisters. Lots of quiet cursing, most of it involving their mother.

Craig's phone vibrates. Carolyn's text, *"That's it, I'm coming over."*

"Shit!" Tammy types fast. *"No, don't come. I don't want to see you right now."*

"She's coming." The sisters limp and stumble, moving as fast as their aching muscles and strained backs will allow. They rush through the garage into the kitchen just as the front doorbell rings. Their faces and clothes are blackened with filth and perspiration.

"You've gotta wash up and get those dirty clothes off."

Tammy lumbers up the stairs to the bathroom. The doorbell rings again.

Gwen calls out, "One minute." She ducks behind the kitchen counter to hide.

Tammy hobbles back down the stairs moments later, a clean but still sweaty face, wearing a thick terry robe, her hair wrapped in a towel. She looks over at Gwen flat on the floor terror-stricken, then opens the door a few inches only.

Carolyn's makeup has faded. Her lashes have begun to peel up and there are bits of glue in the corners of her eyes. "Where is he? I want to talk to him."

"Are you referring to my husband?"

"No, I'm referring to my boyfriend."

"I wouldn't be so sure about that. He's in the shower. Things got a little hot and heavy around here, if you know what I mean." Tammy winks exaggeratedly. "I'll tell him you stopped by, but I wouldn't hold my breath until you hear back from him. Change of plans. He's going to stay right here with me where he belongs. You can go find some other home to wreck." Tammy slams the door in Carolyn's shocked face.

Gwen and Tammy watch out the window until they're sure Carolyn is back inside her house. Tammy drops the robe covering her soiled clothes and the women run back through the garage into the dark yard.

They dig for another hour.

Tammy drops to the ground in exhaustion. "I can't do anymore. How deep does it have to be?"

"Deep enough that Craig doesn't bubble up in a heavy rainstorm."

"I'll take my chances. We've dug at least four feet down."

Gwen slumps onto the ground next to her sister.

Tammy looks around her garden. "What happens if I move out of this house?"

"You can never move. You're going to have to die here, too."

The weary women lean their weight on the spades, slowly, sorely stand themselves up, stagger back inside the garage.

They wrestle with Craig, rolling him around on the concrete floor struggling to wrap the painting tarp tightly around his ever-stiffening corpse.

"Damn, he's heavy." Gwen strains under the bulk of the dead weight.

Tammy fights against Craig's rock-hard limbs. "I can't bend his arm." Rigor mortis has set in. One ridged arm protrudes from the tarp as if waving for help.

"Do you think Carolyn will come back to spy?"

Tammy is too tired to be terrified anymore. "I have no idea. If she does, we'll have to dig another grave." She's only half-joking.

The sisters grunt as they grapple with the tarp, drag it out of the garage into the backyard and across the dewy grass to the freshly dug hole. With the last shreds of their strength, they roll Craig into the pit. He lands on the hard earth with a grim thump. They don't waste any time covering him with the damp soil. Tammy re-plants a few hostas on top of the mound that is her husband.

The dirty job of concealing a murder finally complete, the weak and wobbly women drag their own near-dead bodies back inside the house.

"We still have to get Craig's truck from Carolyn's driveway and park it somewhere." Gwen looks across the road. "Her bedroom light isn't out yet. We have to wait until she's asleep."

A couple of hours later, Carolyn's house, like the rest of the neighbourhood, looks lifeless enough.

Gwen and Tammy clump together, shaking in unison. They silently cross the road to Carolyn's, slowly steal up her driveway. Craig's truck is unlocked. Tammy opens the driver's door. The interior lights flare on automatically, a blinding flash of electric white. Tammy scrambles to locate the button that will extinguish them. No luck, she only manages to also turn on high beams and hazard lights.

A lamp from an upstairs window in Carolyn's house flicks on and blazes down on the sisters like a torch from a prison spotlight.

"She's awake!" Gwen doubles back to Tammy's home as fast as she can. Carolyn switches on lights one room after another in a trail, as she frantically rushes down her stairs to book it outside.

Tammy backs the pickup out of Carolyn's driveway too fast, hits the brakes too hard, cranks the wheel too far making the tires squeal, then roars off down the street.

Carolyn swings her orange door wide open and runs through it, her chiffon negligee billowing in the breezy night air. She waves her arms madly, jogs down the sidewalk calling out after her boyfriend's truck, but in a quick minute, his vehicle disappears into the blackness of the night. Carolyn gives up the futile chase. She cries, her head hanging dejectedly, as she slowly schlepps back to her house, her marabou feather mules clicking on the pavement.

❧

Tammy walks through her front door just as the sun rises, her sneakers in her hands. Gwen is sprawled over the kitchen table, bloodshot eyes, and a woolly mouth. The coffee pot is percolating.

Tammy collapses in a chair. "I don't know if I've got more blisters on my feet from walking or on my hands from shovelling."

"Where did you leave the truck?"

"At the train station. Took me forty-five minutes to hike back here."

"Good thinking. Craig's gone on a trip to reflect on what he wants to do with his life. We can figure out what to do with his vehicle later."

"I'll probably just sell it. No one's going to miss it. Or him."

Gwen pours two mugs of coffee. "I sent Carolyn a final break-up text. It's over between them. Craig is exactly the kind of creep who would end a relationship in a text message."

The sun climbs higher in the sky and the sisters slouch lower in their seats, dozing off.

Carolyn is outside early, piling the few boxes and bags that Craig moved into her home only the night before next to her trash bins at the foot of her driveway.

A candy-apple-red Mustang rumbles up the street, parks in front of Tammy's house.

"What the hell?"

Tammy jumps up. "Is it the police?"

"Worse. It's Derek."

Gwen's ex-husband climbs out of the showy sports car that would look a lot more impressive if he were twenty years younger. He stretches his beefy, gym-toned arms over his head. Derek wears a permanent smirk like the slimeball that he is. He saunters up to Tammy's front door and knocks.

Gwen opens the door a crack. "What do you want?"

Derek, still smirking, says, "You weren't at your place. I knew you'd be here cause where else would you be? You don't have a life."

"Screw off." Gwen pushes the door closed and locks it.

Derek yells through the door, "I got some legal papers here I need you to sign. I called your lawyer, but he said you skipped on his last bill."

"Get lost. I'm not signing anything."

"Look, it'll save us both a lotta time in court. And money. Be reasonable for once."

Gwen shrieks, "You owe me a hundred and fifty thousand. The court already decided. Go away."

"Nah, there's been a change. I'm broke and you're earning. I'm applying for spousal support. You gotta start paying me now. Seven hundred and fifty bucks a month. That's a bargain. I'll be asking for more if we have to go to court to settle. Just sign these papers and it's all agreed."

Gwen loses it. "Me pay you support? Get the hell out of here, you crook!"

Derek walks away. Gwen turns to face Tammy, both of them dumbstruck.

Tammy shakes her head in disgust. "What a loser. There's no way any judge is going to make you pay him alimony."

Gwen's genuinely worried. "I wouldn't be so sure. He's good at these games. And relentless."

The loud grinding noise of the garage door opening reverberates through the kitchen wall. The women run to stop him but it's too late. Derek's already standing where Craig was lying only a few hours earlier.

He holds out the legal papers. "Come on, Gwen, you gotta sign the papers. Be a good girl."

Gwen yanks the documents from him, will say anything to get him out now. "Leave these with me. I'll go over them." Gwen's a terrible liar.

Derek eyes her suspiciously. "You're okay with this? That was surprisingly easy."

Gwen's voice is hoarse. "You need to go."

Derek eyes Craig's golf clubs. "I heard Craig moved out. You gals have a hard time hanging onto a man, huh?" Derek pulls a nine-iron out, inspects it, then bends over to look more closely at the pleather golf bag. "Is this blood?" He eyes a pattern of red and brown splatters that the girls missed in their hasty cleanup. He licks his finger, rubs the spot. "Yeah, it's blood. I wonder whose?"

Tammy and Gwen's own blood runs cold.

Tammy's voice is eerily calm, "I cut myself when I was packing up Craig's things in here."

Derek eyes Tammy skeptically, a true conman who can spot a con a mile away. "Where is Craig? He told me he was moving in with the MILF across the road. Doesn't look like he made it there."

The sisters are silent, too exhausted and stressed to think this fast on their feet.

Derek's gaze narrows threateningly on the women. "Maybe I'll go talk to the new dish, see if she's heard from our boy Craig. Carolyn, isn't it?"

The girls stare at Derek blankly, their fear palpable.

Derek's smirk turns sinister. "What have you two been up to? You know what, Gwen? I think you're gonna sign these papers right here, right now, or I'm gonna tell the cops I suspect these golf clubs have been involved in some foul play."

A car pulls into Tammy's driveway. All three of them turn to look.

Derek's hands fly to his temples. "Oh no, please tell me it's not the mother-in-law from hell." He points a menacing finger at his ex-wife. "You sign those papers, Gwen. I'll be back to pick them up after Cold Ethyl's departed—here's hoping her next stop is the morgue."

Ethyl hunches over her steering wheel, squinty eyes, and a devilish grin. Her old Buick slowly creeps up the driveway toward the garage. The freshly repaired front bumper looks as good as new.

Tammy and Gwen watch their mother's car steadily advancing.

Derek yells at Ethyl as he tries to exit the garage, "Stop the frickin' car, you old corpse."

But Ethyl doesn't stop the car. She steps on the gas. The old Buick jolts forward through the open garage doorway and keeps on going.

Gwen and Tammy open their mouths to scream at their mother, but no sounds come out. They press their palms against their ears and squeeze their eyes shut tight.

Another fender bender.

SYLVIA MAULTASH WARSH

Sylvia Maultash Warsh's Dr. Rebecca Temple novels have won an Edgar and have been shortlisted for Crime Writers of Canada's Arthur Ellis Award and the ReLit Award. Project Bookmark Canada chose her historical novel, *The Queen of Unforgetting*, for a plaque installation. Other works include a novella, *Best Girl*, and five short stories which were nominated for Arthur Ellis and Derringer Awards. She belongs to Sisters in Crime, Crime Writers of Canada, The Short Mystery Fiction Society and the Mesdames of Mayhem. Sylvia's website is www.sylviawarsh.com

THERE ARE ALWAYS SECRETS

SYLVIA MAULTASH WARSH

CHARLIE STOOD in the shabby living room of her new house and thought: *I've made a terrible mistake.*

Her eyes travelled from the stained grey broadloom to the torn curtains, her nostrils twitching at the reek of spilled beer. Who was she kidding? It was all she could afford in the hot 2002 Toronto real estate market. And she could only afford *that* because her father had left her money when he died. Not a fortune, but enough for a down payment on an ancient house in a dingy Toronto neighbourhood. It didn't hurt that the owner had chosen to sell in January during a snowstorm and that he wanted to close the deal fast.

Regret mingled with excitement as she climbed the stairs to the master bedroom. Dirty beige broadloom, dirty beige walls. The worst part was the ruinously small closet. The sliding doors were thirty inches wide but the space inside was barely a foot deep. The whole house needed a makeover, but she would start here because it was easy. She would take down the wall separating the closet from the one in the room next door to make one large space. She'd seen enough renovation shows on TV to know how to knock down a wall.

Snow covered the tiny lawns on her street as she returned from the hardware store. The city cleared the sidewalks, but she'd neglected her walkway and stepped carefully over the ice that had formed. She nearly tripped when a Marilyn Monroe lookalike called out from next door. Charlie stopped politely, both hands gripping a twelve-pound sledgehammer.

The woman sashayed gracefully in high leather boots, down to the sidewalk and up Charlie's walkway, as if there were no ice. She was taller than Charlie had first thought, in an unbuttoned rabbit-trimmed coat revealing a yellow shirtwaist.

"I'm Norma," she said, her eyes resting on the sledgehammer.

Wasn't Marilyn Monroe's real name Norma Jean something? This Norma wore her hair the same way, perky and platinum, her red lips plump like Marilyn's. Young. Maybe thirty-two, compared to Charlie's forty.

"Welcome to the neighbourhood!"

"Thanks. I'm Charlie." She felt scruffy in her long ponytail and parka.

Norma tilted her head, friendly. "It's nice to have someone move in after all this time. The house has been empty for a year."

"It's a bit of a mess." Charlie would've loved to hear about the previous occupants, but the sledgehammer was weighing her down.

"Planning some changes?" Norma gestured at the burden in Charlie's hands.

Before Charlie could answer, Norma waved at someone behind her.

"Hi Joey!"

Charlie turned to see a gawky teenager trailing an elderly couple trudging up their walkway. The neighbours on Charlie's other side. Joey blushed and smiled, raising a shy hand. He was all arms and legs and oversized feet, his brown hair sticking out as if he'd just rolled out of bed. The old couple ignored Norma and went inside.

"He's a nice kid!" Norma said.

She gave Charlie a broad smile before bouncing back to her own house, coat swinging.

※

I t took Charlie a day and a half to transfer the contents of her moving boxes into cupboards and drawers and bookcases. She only had a week off from her admin job, so she needed to get rolling.

After removing the sliding doors in her bedroom, she spread a drop cloth on the floor and put on safety glasses and a dust mask.

Legs planted firmly apart, she swung the sledgehammer at the back wall of the closet. She only made a small dent and sneered at herself. *Wuss!* Someone had done some renovations, because it was drywall rather than plaster like the rest of the old house. She hauled back and gave it a good shot. A hole! Small, but a start. Okay, now tighten those muscles and do some damage.

Lifting the sledgehammer over her shoulder, she crashed it down with everything she had. The drywall cracked open. That was more like it! She kept at it until the drywall loosened enough to tear a chunk away.

She expected to see the inside of the other closet. But instead, she saw green fabric and, inexplicably, grey duct tape. Her instinct said to stop, but she pushed past it and smashed the sledgehammer against the wall, breaking more of it. She tugged and yanked the stubborn pieces away until she had a better view of what was inside. Then she dropped the sledgehammer. Her heart bounced inside her chest till she could barely breathe.

The leaf-green fabric was a blouse. Worn by a body—what had once been a body, now bones. Duct tape held it upright in a series of extended strips: across the skull with its long red hair, over the shoulders, over the waist. The whole thing encased in clear plastic, now torn by her efforts. In her fog, she realized she had a green blouse just like this one. She stared into the craters where eyes used to be. She screamed.

She realized she was still screaming when footsteps stormed up the stairs. Norma rushed into the room in her coat.

She shook Charlie by the shoulders. "What is it? What is it?"

Charlie pointed to the closet.

Norma stepped toward it and shrieked. She covered her mouth with her hands.

Moments later, Joey stood beside them, out of breath. "Holy crap!" he murmured, gazing into the closet. "Look at the hair. It's Dory!"

Charlie flinched in dismay. "What?"

Joey couldn't pull his eyes away. "The hair. Dory had long red hair." He glanced at Norma, who nodded.

"Who's Dory?" Charlie shuddered. Thinking of the skeleton as a person made it even worse.

"She lived here when I was twelve."

"And now you're—?"

"Fifteen."

Had the skeleton been there for three years? Charlie had to get out of the room. She stumbled downstairs and called the police. Not 9-1-1 because, goodness knows, they didn't need an ambulance.

The three of them stood awkwardly in the living room. Joey stared at the stained broadloom.

"We thought Dory went to the States to look after her sick mother," he said. "That's what Wayne told my grandma."

"Wayne?"

"Her husband." Norma's hands were clasped at chest level, as if in prayer. "He told me that, too."

Charlie took a deep breath, trying to keep her stomach from heaving. The image of the body lodged in her brain. "So if it's her, he lied."

Norma shuddered, flicking her platinum hair. "He said he was driving down to see her."

"When was that?"

"Maybe six months after she left."

"Where is he now?" Charlie asked.

Norma shrugged. "He just rented this place."

Her brain was cloudy from the shock, but Charlie remembered the name of the previous owner: Stanley Koslow, his office less than a mile away. Did he know about this?

❧

T wo detectives examined the horror show in Charlie's closet without touching anything, waiting for the forensic team. She led them down to the living room, where she repeated what Joey and Norma had told her—they'd taken off before the police arrived.

The two men scribbled in their notebooks. The senior one, Detective Lyall, pink and bald, wore a dark suit and tie under his coat. The younger one, maybe thirty-five, in a brown leather jacket, glanced around like a kid stuck inside on a nice day. Man tail, no tie. Detective Kim.

"How long have you lived here?" Detective Kim asked, pencil poised, eyes on the carpet stains.

She noticed he kept judgement off his face, probably his cop training. Her white Ikea table in the kitchen was the only clean thing in the place.

"I just moved in."

He raised an eyebrow. "Tough luck."

Detective Lyall pursed his lips but said nothing.

She barged on, speaking too quickly. "Look, I'm uneasy in the house now that—" She gestured toward the stairs. "If it's really the woman who lived here... How long will it take to identify her?" She'd managed to get the names out of Norma: Wayne and Dory Rideout.

She looked into both their faces, blank, like good policemen.

"It's up to forensics, ma'am," Lyall replied.

She wasn't sure how she felt about an older man calling her ma'am.

"If it's Dory and her husband killed her— What if he comes back?" Was she babbling?

Detective Kim finally met her eyes. "I wouldn't worry. He disappeared in 2000. I was on the case then. His company called us when a large sum of money went missing."

A thief as well as a killer.

"It was a complicated case. We tried to track down his wife. We checked south of the border for her mother, but it turned out she died years ago. We thought Rideout might've killed his wife and taken off. But we could never prove anything. There was no body."

"That doesn't make me feel any better."

"They're both officially missing," Kim said. "It's a cold case, but we'll be reopening it now."

Before they left, Kim gave her his card. She watched them walk next door, murmuring to each other. Probably calling her a flake.

Charlie dragged the duvet and pillows from her bed, downstairs to the couch. She would never sleep in that room again. How could she still live in the house? She had no choice—she had nowhere else to go. If she tried to sell, it would go below value and she'd never be able to afford another house.

The forensic people in their white coveralls had pulled away the rest of the drywall so they could collect the entire skeleton. They cut a rectangle of plaster from behind and took it away as evidence. Dust had lingered in the air for hours, making the room dreamlike, disorienting her. She was left looking at the studs inside the closet, the framework of the house, like a secret itself. You remove the surface of things and there are always secrets.

The green blouse had been a jolt. Charlie had bought hers at The Bay marked down 80% or she couldn't have afforded it. So she and the dead woman had the same tastes. It creeped her out.

She thrashed around on the couch all night, listening to the wind rattling the house. She'd opened the living room curtains so the street lamp could extinguish the shadows. Yet the image of the woman floated behind her eyes. Her long red hair must've been beautiful once. She'd lived there, too. What had she been like?

The steak knife Charlie had slipped beneath the sofa cushion didn't relieve her anxiety. Was she really afraid of intruders? Or was she afraid of ghosts? A knife wouldn't help with that. She didn't believe in ghosts, but the skeleton haunted her. How would she exorcise the image?

T he next morning she stood in front of Norma's house. Charlie longed for information and didn't trust the cops to give her any.

The door opened though Charlie hadn't knocked. Norma wore a blue shirtwaist today, her platinum hair almost too bright to look at.

"Oh, dear," Norma said, "you look—"

"Terrible, I know. I didn't get much sleep."

"It's a wonder you stayed in the house at all. I'll make some coffee." Norma waved her in.

Charlie sat down at a woodgrain Arborite table in the kitchen, the kind her parents had when she was a kid. The vinyl chairs were turquoise.

She watched the back of Norma's curvy silhouette as she made the coffee. "So what's Stanley Koslow like?"

"The guy who owned the house before you?"

"I never met him."

"You're lucky. He's a jerk."

"Why do you say that?"

"He hit on Dory. He's old enough to be her father. I told the cops."

Charlie grimaced.

"They asked about Wayne, too."

"So what was he like?"

"Good-looking, but full of himself. Think Marlon Brando when he was young."

Charlie smiled, remembering a buff Brando in his undershirt in *A Streetcar Named Desire*. "Detective Kim is kind of full of himself."

"Oh, you gotta watch that one! He's cute!"

They exchanged cagey smiles. But Charlie remembered how his eyebrows fell together, his eyes restless, like storm clouds.

"What else did they want to know?"

"If they were happily married, Wayne and Dory."

"And were they?"

"Hell, no. Dory bossed him around something awful. She worked at The Bay. Sold designer dresses." She turned sideways and cocked a hip provocatively like a model, contempt on her pretty face.

Charlie shuddered, remembering the blouse.

"She thought she was better than him because he worked in construction. They were always fighting." Norma glanced at Charlie sheepishly. "They were loud. Heard them when the windows were open."

Not what Charlie was expecting to hear about Dory. "You think he killed her?"

Norma turned pale. She put two mugs of instant coffee on the table. And a piece of apple pie. Charlie hated instant coffee almost as much as she hated pie.

"I made it myself," Norma said.

Charlie took a bite to be polite, but Norma watched her so she kept eating, pretending she was enjoying it. "So he said he was going to visit her in the States?"

Norma nodded.

"Did he really go? Did you see him drive away?"

Norma stared into the air as if trying to picture it. "Yeah. He parked the car in front and put in a suitcase."

"What kind of car?"

"I don't know cars. Black."

"But he wasn't going to visit Dory because she was right here. In the closet. So where did he go?"

Norma fluttered her mascaraed eyelashes as she sipped her coffee. "Cops asked me that, too. Beats me. I hope they ask Aldo."

Charlie put down the mug. "Aldo?"

"One of his work buddies. Cute guy."

Charlie lifted an eyebrow.

Norma gave a secretive smile. "Yeah, yeah. We went out for coffee but nothing came of it. We didn't click."

"You have his number?"

Norma grinned.

Charlie levelled her eyes at her. "I want to talk to him about Wayne."

Norma deflated. "Oh." Then, "Shouldn't poke around. Cops won't like that."

What could she say? That the house didn't feel like hers anymore? That if she found out what happened, she might take possession of it again?

"Cops won't find out."

That afternoon, she heard the news on the radio.

"Remains found in a closet in a house in Parkdale have been identified as Doreen Rideout. According to Detective Sergeant Leo Kim, Rideout, thirty-three, was declared a missing person in 1999, then the case went cold. The police are investigating it as a homicide."

It all unspooled in front of her eyes again. Tugging away at the chunks of drywall. The green blouse and the duct tape. The long red hair on the skull. She fell into a kitchen chair, hands shaking.

Aldo Ricci sounded gruff on the phone but agreed to meet her at a coffee shop on Queen Street near his construction site.

She wore her long brown hair down and put on some makeup. Men were more cooperative when a woman looked good.

A man with an olive complexion entered the shop wearing a neon-orange parka, hard hat under his arm. She waved at him.

He checked her out while they exchanged introductions. She was used to construction workers whistling at her as she passed building sites and tried not to hold it against him. After she bought two coffees, they sat down at a table, with their cups.

He was muscular under the parka, with short dark hair. "You working with the cops?" He stirred his coffee.

She hadn't said that when she called, couldn't help it if he'd gotten the wrong impression.

She smiled politely. "Did they call you?"

"They're coming out to the site later." He shook his head. "I can't believe Dory's dead."

"So you knew her?"

He looked away, as if regretting his comment. "Sure."

She tried a different tack. "When did you last see Wayne?"

"Couple years ago. Things weren't good between us. Worked at the same site but we didn't talk no more. He was kinda mad at me. Then he stopped coming to work. Didn't answer his phone. I went to his house, but he didn't come to the door."

Something was missing, Charlie thought. "He told neighbours he was going to the States to visit his wife. Said she was looking after her mother."

Aldo blinked. "That explains things. I couldn't get hold of Dory after we… Well, the reason things weren't good between Wayne and me… He thought we were fooling around, me and Dory."

"Were you?"

He blushed. "It was a one-time thing, honest. I think she was trying to get back at him."

"Why would she do that?"

"He didn't treat her right. Gave her shit all the time. She deserved better."

Was this the same Dory Norma had described? Had Aldo tried to rescue her? Or maybe she had refused him and things got out of hand.

"Any idea where he might've gone?"

He took a gulp of his coffee. "Probably some place warm. Bet he's shacked up on a tropical island with some babe."

The next morning, Charlie fought a chill wind as she headed down the unfamiliar street, her eyes tearing. She'd worn her good camel coat and high leather boots to impress, but the address

Stanley Koslow had given for his office was a house, and in a neighbourhood only slightly less gritty than her own.

A middle-aged man with cropped greying hair answered the door. Fit in jeans and a black T-shirt.

"Mr. Koslow?"

"Yeah."

"I'm Charlene Morris. I bought your house in Parkdale."

He nodded, his blue eyes assessing her. "Terrible, terrible. Cops already been here. Nothing to do with me, though. I had no idea. No idea."

Defensive already, she thought. "I just want to ask you some questions about the house."

He pursed his lips. "I'm kind of busy, Ms.—"

"Charlie. I'm not blaming you for anything. Please, it'll only take a minute."

He let out a sigh, then opened the door to let her in, but just barely, blocking her way any further. She stepped onto a rubber mat with her wet boots.

From her vantage point she could see the house was bigger than hers, but the living room on the right and kitchen ahead were cluttered with papers and dirty dishes. And the same beer smell that she'd dispelled from her house with air freshener.

She gave him a disarming smile. "How long did the Rideouts live in the house?"

"Four years."

"So you knew them pretty well."

He shrugged.

"What kind of tenants were they?"

He crossed his arms over his chest. "Dory was a terrible housekeeper. That's the problem with tenants. They live like pigs."

She kept a straight face. "Did you come by often?"

He raised a wary eyebrow. "Only when they wanted me to fix something."

"When did you last see Dory?"

"Can't remember. Went over there the beginning of 2000 to get the post-dated cheques for the rent, like I do every year. Wayne said she was in New Jersey taking care of her mother. He hadn't seen her for months. Old lady had a stroke or something."

Looked like Wayne had told everyone about Dory leaving.

"Two months later I get a call from the cops to unlock the door because Wayne's skedaddled. Clothes were gone."

There was still a year to account for. "Why'd you wait so long before selling the house?"

He tilted his head. "It's personal."

"Just trying to understand what happened."

He uncrossed his arms. "Want a beer?"

She shook her head, uneasy.

"Look, I was having a tough time. My marriage was in the toilet. I was drinking too much and the house—well, I crashed there sometimes." One side of his mouth turned up in a wry smile. "Went on a few benders."

That explained the state of her house.

"I hear Dory was good-looking," she said. He shrugged again. "Rumour has it you made unwanted advances."

His eyes nearly bugged out of his head. "Not unwanted! That's a lie!"

"Did she reject you?" That could be a motive.

"Who are you to come here and—" He stepped menacingly toward her.

She opened the door and flew out.

She didn't calm down till she turned in to her own street. Joey was walking home from school a few metres ahead of her. She ran to catch up.

"How was school today?" she asked.

Joey did a double-take, then blushed. "Okay."

"You remember when Wayne lived here?"

Joey nodded.

"Was he a nice guy?"

He shrugged.

"Did he yell at Dory?"

"My grandma said to ignore it. I could hear them from Norma's backyard."

Charlie raised an eyebrow. "Norma's backyard?"

"I helped her dig her garden a couple of times. She plants vegetables in the summer."

"That's nice of you."

Joey gave her a shy smile.

"Your grandparents don't like her, do they?"

He made a face. "They think she's a floozy."

W hen Charlie stepped inside the house, something felt off. She closed the door, about to remove her boots, when she saw it. A black leather glove lay on the floor like a dead crow. She caught her breath. Her heart in her mouth, she crept toward the glove.

It was too big to be hers. It was a man's. Someone had been in her house!

Why hadn't she changed the locks?

She dug up the card in her purse, ran to the phone, and dialled.

"Detective Kim," said the voice.

"He was here!" she cried. "He left a glove on the floor. To warn me."

"Ms. Morris, I presume."

Of course, he had caller ID. She felt foolish. "You're not concerned that he was inside my house?"

"Could it be someone else's glove? Any other men in the house?"

She resented the insinuation. "The only men in my house were you and your partner."

She heard a sigh. "I'm coming over. Don't touch anything."

Twenty minutes later, Detective Kim stood in her doorway in his leather jacket, a strand of hair escaping his man tail.

"Ms. Morris?" He didn't seem to recognize her, then she

remembered that her hair was down and she'd put on makeup. She was wearing a blue silk blouse, instead of the sweatshirt he'd seen her in.

After removing his boots, he approached the glove on the floor. "Did you touch it?"

She let out an irritated breath. "No."

He bent down to take pictures. "Any sign of forced entry?" She shook her head. "Was anything disturbed?"

She'd waited for him in the kitchen, trembling. "Nothing I can see. But I haven't been upstairs."

He pulled on plastic gloves and led the way. She followed him up the stairs to the bedroom, then gasped. The door stood open.

"I left the door closed! I told you—he was here!"

"He?"

"Wayne."

Kim pursed his lips then pulled out his phone and called for a fingerprint technician.

"Charlie?" Norma called from the front door.

She rushed down to find Norma staring at the glove. "I saw the police car and—"

Back downstairs, Kim nodded at Norma and picked up the glove, dropping it into a paper bag.

"By the way," he addressed Charlie, "you have to stop talking to people involved with the case. Mr. Ricci said you met—"

"Did you know he slept with Dory?"

Kim's stormy eyes betrayed his poise. "He told you that?"

Apparently, Aldo had been less forthcoming with the police.

"Regardless. You can't interfere with—"

"I have a right to find out what happened in my own house." Then it occurred to her. "Wayne must've used his key to get in."

"You didn't change the locks?"

"Locksmiths are expensive," she said sheepishly.

"I can do it for you," Norma said. "I'm handy."

Charlie stared at her platinum hair. "You are?"

After Kim left, she hurried to the hardware store and bought two locks, one for the front and one for the side door.

Norma came over after dinner in shiny black yoga pants that hugged her curves. She sat on a stool beside the door, using an electric screwdriver to remove the old lock. While she worked, she told Charlie about her part-time job at the hair salon, her bad luck with men, the great tips from clients that helped pay the rent.

"I think you should listen to the hot detective and let the cops do their job." She maneuvered the new lock into the opening.

"I was trying to exorcise Dory's ghost. But I must've rocked the boat when I talked to Aldo or Stanley Koslow. One of them knows more than he's saying. Maybe he's in touch with Wayne and tipped him off. I'm not giving up so easy."

The next day, Charlie scoured the kitchen and attacked the carpet stains, fading them to a dull grey. She kept moving, cleaning, keeping thoughts at bay.

By early evening, she was worn out and planning to doze off in front of the TV when the doorbell rang. Norma stood in the doorway with a piece of apple pie, her platinum hair less lustrous than usual.

"Just baked this and remembered how much you liked it."

Charlie barely had time to thank her before she turned and hurried away.

That night, Charlie dreamed she was stumbling through a storm. The wind drove the snow into her face so she couldn't see. Then she couldn't breathe—the snow clogged her mouth and her nose.

But she really *couldn't* breathe. Wake up! She moaned and realized she *was* awake! A pillow was crushing her face.

She struggled and tore at her attacker's arms, but they were too strong. She was going to die!

She felt herself fading when she remembered the knife. If only she could stay conscious. Her hand groped beneath the sofa cushion.

Nothing.

Keep trying! She fumbled around until she found it. She pulled it out, stabbed blindly into the air. Only air!

Finally—the blade connected with flesh. She stabbed again. And again.

A scream!

Her brain reeled at the voice. It wasn't Wayne. She shoved the pillow off, gasping for air. The light of the streetlamp fell on Norma's platinum hair.

Charlie turned on the lamp. She stared at Norma, stunned. She held her bloody arm across her chest, groaning, hair cloaking her face. She was bleeding all over Charlie's duvet from a wound on her side.

"*Why?*" Charlie asked. Norma didn't look at her. "I thought we were friends."

She growled like an animal in pain. "You were digging around too much. Nothing personal."

Nothing personal! She tried to kill her. "What was I going to find? Don't tell me you killed Dory."

Norma whimpered. "Call 9-1-1! I'm going to bleed to death."

"Not until you tell me."

Norma tossed her hair off her face. Her eyes had shrunk, close to tears. "I put Valium in her pie. When she conked out, Wayne…" She gestured with her free hand.

"Smothered her. Like you tried to do to me."

"You didn't eat your pie."

Charlie inhaled a sharp breath. If she'd eaten it, she'd be dead now. "*You* and *Wayne*…" She could hardly look at her.

"How'd you get in?" Then she realized. "Unbelievable. You took a spare key from the new lock…"

"Call 9-1-1!"

"Where's Wayne?"

She closed her eyes, absent. "I loved him so much."

"He didn't leave, did he? It was you who left the glove."

Blood stained her beautiful hair. "It just took him three months to find someone else. Couldn't keep it in his pants. After what I did for him. Good thing he liked his pie."

"You—you killed him?"

"Wasn't hard once he was knocked out. Devil getting him outside. Good for the vegetable garden though."

The paramedics wheeled Norma out on a gurney, the ambulance lights flashing in the dark. Charlie threw a hoodie over her pyjamas before giving the patrol cop her statement. The house was freezing, with people going in and out. She'd assured the paramedics she was okay, but she was dizzy, her heart racing madly.

Detective Kim arrived, nodded at the cop. The cop nodded back, then left.

"You all right?" Kim asked, scrutinizing her. "There's blood on your pyjamas."

"It's not mine." She hugged herself for warmth, her back to the sofa.

His eyebrows fell together, still watching her.

Her head swam. She looked into his eyes, expecting storm clouds. But the sky had cleared, leaving a stillness that soothed her. Her heart slowed down.

"You're cold," he said. He removed his jacket, settling it over her shoulders.

She wobbled, but he caught her. They stood for an awkward second. He put his hand on her arm, moving her gently toward the kitchen. "You need some tea."

LORNA POPLAK

Lorna Poplak is a Toronto-based writer, editor, and researcher drawn to the dark side of Canadian history. She is a member of Crime Writers of Canada and Sisters in Crime. Her two nonfiction books, both published by Dundurn Press, are *Drop Dead: A Horrible History of Hanging in Canada* (2017), and *The Don: The Story of Toronto's Infamous Jail* (2021). *The Don* was shortlisted for the Ontario Legislature's 2021 Speaker's Book Award. Lorna's website is www.lornapoplak.com

THE MYSTERY OF THE MAD TRAPPER OF RAT RIVER

LORNA POPLAK

THE MAN TASKED in March 1932 with burying the frozen body of Albert Johnson in Aklavik, Northwest Territories, was Joseph Greenland. The ad hoc mortician worked as a handyman for the local surgeon, Dr. J.A. Urquhart. His boss had instructed him to build a coffin for Johnson because nobody else was willing to do so. There was even some doubt as to where the body would be interred, but eventually it was laid to rest in an unconsecrated section of the cemetery. The last thing Greenland probably noticed before he nailed down the lid of the box was the expression on the corpse's face: lips drawn back and teeth bared in a final snarl of hatred and defiance.

In the summer of 1931, Albert Johnson had drifted into the Mackenzie River area of the Northwest Territories and set up camp about five kilometres from Fort McPherson. On one of his visits to the hamlet to buy provisions, he was quizzed by Constable Edgar Millen, who was in charge of the Arctic Red River detachment of the Royal Canadian Mounted Police (RCMP). Millen found Johnson uncommunicative and evasive, but he seemed to have enough money to take care of his needs. So the Mountie left it at that. Johnson subsequently moved away, building himself a log cabin on the Rat River.

According to one report, the Gwich'in First Nations people (then referred to as Loucheux) who trapped and hunted around the Rat River were afraid of this strange, solitary, possibly "bush crazy" interloper and simply wanted the RCMP to make him go away. What became the official RCMP version held that Johnson had interfered with the locals' traplines; a totally unacceptable action in an environment where trapping and hunting for food was essential for survival. What both versions had in common were allegations that Johnson had threateningly pointed a gun at people who approached his cabin. This alone would have been enough to trigger a visit from the RCMP.

So on December 26, 1931, RCMP constable Alfred "Buns" King, together with a companion and a dog team, set out from the Arctic Red River detachment on a two-day journey in 40-below-zero temperatures to reach Johnson's cabin. As King explained, he just wanted "to tell him to leave the Indians alone and to get a trapping licence."

A pair of snowshoes propped up against a wall and curls of smoke were confirmation that Johnson was home. But King's knocks and calls went unanswered, even when he identified himself as a police officer. This was becoming increasingly serious. The two men decided that their only option was to make an arduous 129-kilometre trek to Aklavik to obtain a search warrant from their commanding officer, Inspector Alexander Eames.

Eames provided them with the warrant and another couple of officers to accompany them on their mission. The weather had worsened, with the wind chill temperature hovering around minus 67 degrees Celsius. The group arrived at Johnson's cabin on December 31, after a trip of about 28 hours.

This time, King did get a response when he pounded on the door, but certainly not the one he was expecting: Johnson fired at him through the closed door, hitting him in the chest. With bullets flying in the resultant dogfight, King agonizingly crawled to safety. His companions loaded him onto a dogsled and raced him back to

Aklavik for medical attention. Pushing themselves and their dogs to the limit, they accomplished the journey in 20 hours. Fortunately for King, the bullet had passed through his body without hitting any vital organs; the resilient officer soon recovered.

News of the attempted murder of a Mountie in that frigid corner of the vast Canadian hinterland flashed around the world, setting the media ablaze. Depression-weary folk turned to their newspapers to read all about it and gathered around their crackling radios (that sensational new medium was just taking off at the time) for the latest reports.

Throughout the hunt for the man whom the media now started calling the "Mad Trapper of Rat River," the RCMP faced daunting logistical problems. It would take Inspector Eames four days to assemble a posse of eight men with dog teams and provisions, and a further five days for them to reach the desperado's cabin. Johnson, again, was at home—armed and exceptionally dangerous. He had the advantage of being sheltered, whereas his adversaries were exposed to the elements.

Eames and his Mounties had brought along a secret weapon: nine kilograms of dynamite to flush the man out. Their final bundle blew the roof off the cabin but did not dislodge their quarry. Freezing, disheartened, and with their supplies dangerously depleted, the group was forced to return to Aklavik.

By the time a fresh posse battled its way back to the area, the crafty foe had decamped. A series of vicious storms had obliterated his tracks. The experienced searchers, assisted by an Indigenous tracker, doggedly continued their hunt, but the so-called "demented hermit" seemed to be toying with them, leading them on a grim cat-and-mouse chase over impossibly inhospitable terrain, and seemingly headed for Alaska.

As the pursuit continued, the police began to wonder just how demented Johnson really was. As the *Globe* newspaper noted at the time: "The intricate puzzle that constitutes his footprint trail in the snow has both baffled and won the admiration of his pursuers."

On February 1, the headlines in the *Globe* were shocking: "RAT RIVER MADMAN KILLS POLICEMAN." A small team of searchers had stumbled upon Johnson holed up in a tangle of trees and were met with gunfire. The police patrol shot back, then—silence. After waiting in the biting cold for around two hours, the leader of the group, Constable Edgar Millen, gave the signal to move forward. Millen was the Mountie who had questioned Johnson after his arrival in the region back in July 1931. Their second encounter would prove to be fatal. Johnson fired three times. The last shot struck Millen in the chest, critically injuring him. His companions dragged him out of the line of fire, but he was dead within minutes.

First, attempted murder of a police officer; now, murder. The RCMP were even more determined to get their man.

By this time, however, the search on the ground was floundering. Eames made the inspired decision to take it to the skies.

Enter Wilfrid Reid "Wop" May.

Wop May had had his first—and very nearly his last—brush with fame when, as a rookie Royal Flying Corps fighter pilot in combat during the First World War, he found his plane lodged firmly in the gunsights of German air ace Manfred von Richthofen, better known as the Red Baron. Fortunately for May, and for Canadian aviation, while the Red Baron's attention was focused on this seemingly lame-duck target, his own plane was shot out of the skies, thus bringing to an abrupt end his record-breaking tally of 80 aerial victories. May ended the war with a Distinguished Flying Cross and his own count of at least 13 downed planes.

By the late 1920s, May was operating as a bush pilot in the far northern territories of Canada. By 1932, he was working for Canadian Airways, with the reputation of being supremely experienced in navigating through the snows and gelid temperatures of subarctic regions. On February 7, he and his mechanic sailed into the fray in a Bellanca monoplane, appropriately fitted out with skis, making this the first time a surveillance aircraft would be used by Canadian police to track a fugitive.

Although evil weather conditions continued to plague the searchers—on one occasion a huge dump of snow completely covered May's plane and it took a day to dig it out—May's arrival on the scene was the turning point in the hunt. Not only did he ease the nightmarish logistical problems by ferrying provisions to the men in the field, but he was also able to track Johnson's movements from the sky.

There were ongoing setbacks. The team of trackers was convinced that Johnson would never manage to battle through the foul weather conditions and cross the formidable Richardson Mountains into the Yukon. They were wrong. Johnson's endurance and fierce determination kept him going, up and over.

But the pace was finally beginning to tell. On February 13, the press reported May as saying that Johnson's trail when seen from the air "showed the fugitive to be somewhat 'groggy.'"

The pursuit had begun in late December on the Rat River in the Northwest Territories; it ended 49 days later on the Eagle River in the Yukon. On February 17, Earle Frank Hersey, a staff sergeant with the Royal Canadian Corps of Signals, was in the vanguard of the searchers when he swept around a U-shaped bend in the frozen river and there, some 300 metres away, stood their quarry.

Hersey was a communications specialist based in Aklavik and a shoo-in for inclusion in the RCMP's posse. Thanks in part to his expertise, a system of two-way radios had been set up: the first time this technology was ever used by the police in Canada. There were other reasons for Hersey's presence in the search party. As his daughter Sheila told the *Globe and Mail* in 2006: "My dad was chosen because he had the fastest dog team...seven huskies. He was so familiar with the North and good on tracking.... He bred his dogs with wolves."

On spotting Johnson, Hersey went down on one knee and fired three times, aiming for the man's backpack. Johnson returned his fire with a bullet that, freakishly, hit Hersey in his left knee and then his elbow, before passing through both lungs. Hersey collapsed, grievously wounded.

Another member of the group, Quartermaster Sergeant R.F. Riddell, a colleague of Hersey's in the Royal Canadian Signals at Aklavik, filled in some of the details of the final showdown for the *Edmonton Journal*: "Johnson started running back along his own trail, up the creek, amid a hail of bullets. He was knocked down from a distance of 500 yards, probably wounded in the leg. He then lay prone on the snow and, putting his large pack in front of him, commenced digging down in the deep, soft snow, the posse meanwhile rapidly overtaking and partially surrounding him. Johnson fought desperately to the end, emptying his rifle, and was in the act of reloading it when killed. The accurate shooting of the posse had riddled his body with bullets."

Wop May had been in radio contact with the ground, and he now brought his plane down on the frozen river. Hersey, bleeding and in great pain, was carefully loaded into the aircraft, and May took off, heading for Aklavik, about 200 kilometres away. Carrying the injured King the 129 kilometres from Johnson's cabin to Aklavik by dogsled some seven weeks previously had taken 20 hours; it took May just 45 minutes to reach his destination by plane. Dr. Urquhart, the local surgeon, was standing by to operate, and by February 19 the *Globe* was relieved to announce: "Young Signaller Passes Danger Point, and Aklavik Rejoices."

Hersey was known to be a crack marksman—why didn't he shoot to kill?

Years later he confessed in an interview with the RCMP's *Quarterly* magazine that as a manhunter he had a weakness: "I didn't want to kill Johnson. I have trouble killing flies."

Alone killer, possibly crazed but certainly skilled at Arctic survival, pitting himself against the might of the law and leading his pursuers in a deadly dance across the frigid northern Canadian landscape until he himself was killed—a true story, but the stuff of legend. No wonder that over the years the story has spawned a host of reactions, including inquiries, theories, news reports, books, movies, songs, and a scattering of documentaries.

People have grappled with these core questions: Who was the man called Albert Johnson? And why did he turn killer?

In the immediate aftermath of the hunt, the RCMP distributed photographs and copies of Johnson's fingerprints to police departments throughout Canada and the United States. They also fielded dozens of inquiries. Although nobody wished to claim the body, many people were more than ready to lay claim to the $2410 in cash and to other items found among Johnson's possessions. Others wrote in with tips or ideas about the man's obscure past. A gangster, a miner, a lost relative—these were among the many suggestions. These leads, and the RCMP's own investigations, all drew a blank.

Theories regarding the trapper's backstory continued to trickle in. One of them linked Johnson to Arthur Nelson, who was last seen in the Yukon in 1931, just before Johnson appeared in the Northwest Territories. Nelson was described as having a similar physical appearance to Johnson—he was around five feet nine inches in height and round-shouldered, with light-coloured hair and slaty-blue eyes. Like Johnson, he spoke with a slight Scandinavian accent.

The late Dick North spent many years living in and writing about the Yukon. His interest in the origins of the mystery man of Rat River led to several books, the last of which was *The Mad Trapper of Rat River: A True Story of Canada's Biggest Manhunt*, published in 2005. North made the case that Albert Johnson and Arthur Nelson were both aliases of John (Johnny) Konrad Johnson, who was born in the 1890s in Norway and grew up in North Dakota after emigrating to the US with his family in 1904. After several brushes with the law in the States and three prison sentences, Johnny Johnson disappeared in 1923.

Ongoing fascination with the story has inspired works of fiction as well. One fictionalized account published in the 1980s injected a love interest into the mix, suggesting as a reason for his hostility that Johnson fled to the frozen North to escape a relationship gone bad.

Two films in the 1970s explored the legend of the Mad Trapper —a British docudrama called *The Mad Trapper* and an antihero film called *Challenge to be Free*. Then, in 1981, came *Arctic Rampage*, later renamed *Death Hunt*. This was an American movie starring Charles Bronson and Lee Marvin, shot with a $10-million budget in the

Banff area of British Columbia. In this movie, both the Mad Trapper and his main pursuer, Sergeant Edgar Millen, survive the chase. The Wop May character sprays the posse with bullets before crashing his plane into a mountain. Canadians were incensed at the gross historical distortions. "Canadian history is trashed again," snapped film critic Jay Scott. Other reactions were more personal— and far more poignant. "How can they do something like that?" protested May's widow Violet. "It's awful. Wop only spotted Albert Johnson—he never fired any shots."

Until the 2000s, all assumptions as to the true identity of Albert Johnson had been based on circumstantial and anecdotal evidence. This changed in 2007, when Edmonton-based Myth Merchant Films obtained permission to exhume Johnson's body. They assembled a team of forensic specialists to perform the exhumation, examine the remains, and retrieve samples for DNA analysis before reinterring the remains. The results were revealed in the television documentary *Hunt for the Mad Trapper*, which aired in 2009, and its accompanying book, *The Mad Trapper: Unearthing a Mystery* by Barbara Smith.

The main findings included the fact that Johnson was definitely not Canadian; he came from a Scandinavian background and had probably grown up in the American Midwest. He was between 30 and 40 years old at the time of death. He had received sophisticated —and pricey—dental treatment, including gold fillings and gold bridgework. Work of this calibre would have been available in the US at the time; certainly not in the far North. This indicated that he must have been a man of means before his arrival in the Arctic.

Johnson also suffered from scoliosis or abnormal curvature of the lower spine, which may become a debilitating and painful condition; surely worse in extreme subzero temperatures. Could the pain he experienced have pushed him over the edge, making him react with such ferocity when Constable King of the RCMP came knocking on his cabin door? We can only speculate.

The forensic investigation put the kibosh on Dick North's theory that Albert Johnson and Johnny Johnson had been one and the same person. A comparison with DNA samples taken from Ole

Getz, Johnny's great-nephew, established definitively that there was no familial connection between Getz and Albert. Dozens of other claims, a few extremely promising, most of them much less so, were similarly rejected.

New to the hunt in the 2020s is Othram, an American laboratory using DNA testing and forensic genealogy to solve cold cases. According to Michael Jorgensen, a producer of the Myth Merchant documentary: "The Mad Trapper is an iconic Canadian story and with advances in genetics, molecular biology, and bioinformatics Othram is closer than ever to identifying him."

Will cutting-edge technologies lead to a breakthrough, or is this just wishful thinking? To date, not a single lead either before or after the advent of DNA testing has shed any light on the origins of the mystery man of Rat River.

So, despite all the advances, it seems more than likely that this cold case, this *doubly* cold case—unfolding as it did 90 years ago during a bone-chilling northern Canadian winter—will not be solved. The identity of the man buried by Joseph Greenland in the Aklavik cemetery in March 1932 will forever remain a mystery.

SOURCES

Newspapers and Magazines
Edmonton Journal
Globe, The
Globe and Mail
Maclean's Magazine

Other Sources
Butts, Edward. "Albert Johnson, 'The Mad Trapper of Rat River.'" In *The Canadian Encyclopedia*. https://www.thecanadianencyclopedia.ca/en/article/albert-johnson.
Hunt for the Mad Trapper. Documentary. Directed by Michael

Jorgensen and produced by Carrie Gour and Michael Jorgensen. Spruce Grove, Alta.: Myth Merchant Films, 2009.

Neary, Nash. "The Mad Trapper of Rat River." In *Notes of Interest – The Northwest Territories and Yukon Radio System*, October 1948. http://www.nwtandy.rcsigs.ca/stories/rat_river.htm.

North, Dick. *The Mad Trapper of Rat River: A True Story of Canada's Biggest Manhunt*. Guilford, Conn.: Lyons Press, 2005.

Smith, Barbara. *The Mad Trapper: Unearthing a Mystery*. Surrey, B.C.: Heritage House, c2009.

DAVID A. POULSEN

David A. Poulsen has written twenty-seven books, several for younger readers. They include his YA novel, *Numbers*, winner of Japan's Sakura Medal in 2010. The UBC Creative Writing (MFA) grad's first foray into the adult crime genre was *Serpents Rising*, Dundurn (Toronto) published in 2015. It became the first in the Cullen and Cobb Mysteries with three more titles now in the series, including the most recent, *None So Deadly*. David and his wife, Barb, live in the Alberta foothills, southwest of Calgary. David's Facebook page is www.facebook.com/david.poulsen.71

THE DAY PETER GZOWSKI DIED

DAVID A. POULSEN

I WAS WORKING on a medium Pike Place and listening to the two o'clock weather report. It was good news. A Chinook would move our temperature from a nasty minus eleven to a more than acceptable plus eight over the next few hours.

My celebration was cut short by the announcement that followed; Peter Gzowski had died. All of Canada knew that Gzowski's life was approaching its end as emphysema (it was still called that then) aided and abetted by a major smoking habit, ravaged the body of the CBC broadcaster who told and re-told stories about Canada and Canadians, thus earning the name Captain Canada.

My thoughts changed directions, this time necessitated by the arrival of a tall, blond, thirty-something woman who opened my office door, walked toward my desk, stopped, and glanced around—all of this without saying a word.

Her scan of the surroundings apparently complete, she looked at me and said, "So this is what a private detective's office looks like."

I shrugged. "I can't say for sure; this is the only one I've ever seen."

She smiled at that. "Me too."

"Won't you sit down, Ms.—"

"Ellie Karsten and yes, I will."

There were two chairs on the other side of my desk. She chose the brown leather armchair—I would have chosen the same one if it were up to me. Most people did. The other chair was a decent piece of furniture in its own right but the brown leather was the A-lister.

"Can I get you a cup of coffee, Ms. Karsten?"

"No, thanks; it's Ellie, and I want to hire you."

She had made three points in ten words. Often people sitting in that chair spoke hundreds of words and made no points at all.

"I see," I said.

She smiled again. It was a good smile. "So, are you one of those detectives who can take one look and know that I'm Jewish, I've just arrived in Calgary from Boise, Idaho, I own a Golden Retriever, and I'm recently divorced from a professional football player?"

"Sorry, the guy who was really good at that sort of thing was before my time. Truthfully, I wouldn't have guessed any of that."

"Good, because none of it's true. Except the divorce part. And Brian never played football. He teaches high school biology."

"You mentioned you were wanting to hire me."

"Yes," she said. "Oh, by the way, your name is A. J. Prediger. I mention that only because you haven't."

"And I apologize."

"I'd like to hire you to help me catch a killer," she said.

"Did you have a particular killer in mind?"

"This isn't a lark, Mr. Prediger. And I'm not some nutbar, I assure you."

"You're right, Ellie. Murder, if that's what you're talking about, is not funny. Why don't you tell me what exactly it is you want me to do."

"I've checked you out and I'm not wanting to hire you solely on the basis of your detecting skills."

I didn't have an answer for that.

"You majored in English at Dalhousie."

I nodded.

"Why Dalhousie?"

"I like lobster and there was a girl."

"Still have the girl?"

I shook my head. "No. And the lobster's all gone too."

"Have you read *Crime and Punishment?*"

"I have."

"How about *L'Étranger?*"

"A very long time ago. Not sure I remember much of it."

"And, of course, *Lord of the Flies.*"

"Of course."

"*The Murders in the Rue Morgue?*"

I checked my watch. "This is delightful, Ellie, it really is, but—"

"*The Murders in the Rue Morgue,*" she repeated. "It's the last one."

"I did a paper on it for my Lit 101 class."

"I lied," she said. "There's one more...*The Mystery of Edwin Drood.*"

I looked at her. "No. Dickens didn't finish it and I didn't start it. Now it's my turn, what's this about and what do you want to hire me for?"

She unzipped a slender, leather briefcase and pulled out a blue file folder. She extracted a piece of paper from the folder and passed it to me across the desk.

"You'll know what that is," she said.

I was looking at a single sheet of 8 ½ by 11 lined paper. It had some age on it and came with smudge marks, blotches, and spills but was still relatively legible. I studied its contents for a couple of minutes.

"Looks like a syllabus for an English class," I said. "Maybe literary mysteries or something like that."

"That's exactly what it is. The course was called 'Murder in the Classics.' It was a class I took in my second year at the University of Calgary."

I leaned forward to return the paper to her. She shook her head. "Keep it. You may need it."

She reached into the file folder a second time, her hand

emerging with what looked like a set of press clippings. Again, she passed them to me.

"They're in chronological order," she explained.

I was right, they were photocopies of news stories. I flipped through them—there were four in total and I glanced at each headline, then spent a few seconds on the first paragraph of each story. I noted they were from different newspapers though all were within a few hundred kilometres of Calgary. I looked at the dates of each story as well—the first was from fifteen months before. They moved forward from that date, the most recent being just seven weeks earlier. Each clipping contained a story that detailed a murder. I was familiar with two of the crimes, was vaguely aware of the most recent, but hadn't heard anything about the third murder in the sequence that had taken place in Medicine Hat, three hours east of Calgary.

When I finished reading, I set the clippings on my desk.

"I'm guessing your contention is that there's some correlation between the books on the syllabus and these murders."

"It's not a *contention.*"

From the way she drew out the word, it was clear she hadn't appreciated my using it.

"It is not possible that several murders that match up almost exactly with the murders written about in the books on that syllabus are not connected."

I nodded. "That would certainly seem logical … if, in fact, the real murders do align with the fictional ones. I won't know that until I study the items you have provided but let's assume, for the sake of argument, that they do. Are you suggesting that someone who has taken this class has used the syllabus as a kind of action plan for a program of serial murders?"

"Yes, that is exactly what I'm suggesting."

"Have you spoken to the police about your theory?"

"Yes, I have."

"And?"

"*Thank you, Ms. Karsten. We'll look into your allegations and call you if we feel the need to chat further.* Or words to that effect. They couldn't get me out of there fast enough."

"I'm sorry." I *was* sorry. But, in fact, I was probably sharing the cops' misgivings and there was a part of me that was wishing I'd been out of the office when Ellie Karsten came by. That last sentiment may have been evident on my face.

"You think they were justified in blowing me off."

"No, but I can understand their having some difficulty in accepting your hypothesis."

She stood up. "I won't take up any more of your time, Mr. Prediger. Read the syllabus. Read the clippings. And call me if you *feel the need to chat further.* Oh, and one more thing. If you're thinking that there are hundreds of people out there who have taken this class and that it would take years to investigate all of them, I can ease your mind on that score. The class was only offered once, four years ago—in 1997—then the English Department opted to drop it from the curriculum. There were twenty-one people in my class. Twenty-two with the prof who, by the way, has since passed away. Back to twenty-one."

"Thank you for that."

She was right. Had the class been offered for a decade or so, the job of narrowing down several hundred students to those who could legitimately be regarded as suspects would need a staff of investigators and, even with that staff, could take months, maybe years to complete. One class of twenty-one would be a large enough chore.

"I don't suppose you have a list of the students who took the class."

"Not an official list but I tried to remember as many as I could. Still had some in my email addresses from when I took the class. I was able to put together eighteen names." She reached into the briefcase this time and pulled out a single sheet of paper, laid it on my desk.

I nodded again. "Thanks, that will help." When she didn't answer, I stood and reached out my hand. "I'll get to this right away and I'll call you whether or not I decide to take it on. You'll want to know my rate structure."

"Not necessary. What you charge will not be an issue." She turned and left my office, closing the door gently behind her.

I turned off the radio, topped up my coffee, and set the clippings and syllabus in front of me.

Two hours later, I'd read everything she had provided and had a page and a half of hand-written notes. The first murders had taken place on October 16, 2000, in Stettler, Alberta, a small central Alberta community a couple of hours from Calgary and an hour east of Red Deer.

The double murder victims were a mother and daughter, seventy-two and forty-four years-old respectively, who had been working late in a thrift shop on 50 Street in downtown Stettler. Though the murder weapon had not been recovered, pathologists had been certain that the wounds inflicted on the women were from an axe.

I read and re-read the clipping Ellie had provided, then surfed the internet for accounts of the double homicide (they were numerous). That done I pulled up the relevant pages of *Crime and Punishment*. While there were certainly similarities, there were also differences in the carrying out of the actual and fictional murders. Dostoyevsky's central character, the troubled former student, Raskolnikov, brutally killed two elderly sisters who were pawnbrokers. The murder weapon again was an axe and, in both cases, the killer stole items from the premises after committing the murders.

The similarities were obvious—the murder weapon, the businesses run by the victims and the fact that they are related—sisters in the novel, cousins in the Stettler murders. The differences were equally obvious: a pawn shop is not a thrift shop, and mother and daughter are not sisters.

The other element that was difficult to wrap my head around

was motive. Dostoevsky's murderer killed in part because he believed that there were special people—and he was one of them—to whom societal norms and rules did not apply. Raskolnikov's murders were almost an experiment to test that theory. Of course, there was no way of knowing the motive for the Stettler killings. Nevertheless, there was an eerie, albeit tenuous, connection between the two acts that was both puzzling and troubling. I moved on to the next crime.

May 3, 2001. Edmonton, Alberta. In the middle of the day, a middle-eastern man, Shamgar Fasil, was shot and killed outside a restaurant on Edmonton's south side. Though the crime took place in early afternoon, there was no one in the restaurant, which opened for dinner at 4 p.m., and no one saw or heard anything suspicious. The shooter, like the Stettler killer, had not been apprehended.

Again I googled and surfed the net, didn't find anything terribly illuminating, and went back to Camus's *L'Étranger* (*The Outsider* in England, *The Stranger* in the United States). The narrating central character, Meursault, like Raskolnikov, is someone who doesn't fit in, and, in Meursault's case, sees life as meaningless and absurd. During a day of swimming, Meursault and an unsavoury friend, Raymond, encounter two Arabs on the beach, one of whom is the brother of Raymond's mistress. A fight breaks out, the mistress's brother slashes Raymond with a knife. Raymond pulls a gun, but Meursault is able to talk him out of killing the man and takes the gun away from his friend. Later, however, Meursault encounters the Arabs again and shoots the man who had attacked Raymond. He later admits he had no particular reason for killing the Arab, denies that it was to exact revenge for the earlier fight, and claims it was the searing heat and the irritation of the sun glinting off the Arab's knife that set him on the course to murder.

I was about to dismiss any similarities in this instance as simply coincidental when a line near the bottom of a second clipping noted the name of the restaurant near which the Edmonton murder took place. The restaurant was called The Beach.

I admit that at that point I was intrigued. The next two parallel murders took only a few minutes to absorb. Donnie "Pig"

Kaumartin was killed in Medicine Hat four months to the day after the shooting of Shamgar Fasil. On September 3, Kaumartin stumbled out of a taxi after a night of serious drinking and paid the cabbie, who then pulled away. Pig, as he'd been known since he was a teenager, never made it to the front door of his condo, his head caved in by a softball-sized rock that was found next to the body.

No arrest, no physical evidence except for the murder weapon, and no witnesses—not surprising as the cabbie recalled depositing Kaumartin onto the sidewalk sometime between 2:15 and 2:30 a.m. I didn't have to check back to *Lord of the Flies*. The cruel killing of Piggy, the intellectual of the group of boys stranded on a tropical island during a nuclear war, is one of the most famous in literature and the parallels between the actual and fictional were obvious.

I was curious how closely the killer would come to replicating the murders in Edgar Allan Poe's *The Murders in the Rue Morgue* which, of course, had been committed by an orangutan. As I read the clippings, it became clear that he had settled for matching his victims with those in the story—a mother and daughter. And he duplicated the method of killing—slashing the throat of the mother and strangling the daughter. The murders had taken place in an older two-storey house in Plamondon, Alberta—the French name of the town a nice touch by the killer. And like the Rue Morgue killings, the mother had been found in the house, the daughter in the backyard.

I'd finished my notes on the fourth murder and was reading the Wikipedia summary of *The Mystery of Edwin Drood* when the first notes of the Tragically Hip's *Blow at High Dough* signalled an incoming call. It was Ellie Karsten.

She skipped hello and went directly to "Well?"

"It looks like we have a serial killer who either took the class or came across the syllabus somehow and fell in love with the idea of recreating the murders from the books."

A pause. "So what now?"

"I've been thinking about that," I said. "Thought I'd see what I can learn about the folks on your class list."

There was another pause before she responded. "I've thought of a couple more things that might be useful."

"Good. Every little bit helps. What've you got?"

"It might be better if we met. There's something maybe you should see."

"Sure."

"Are you still at your office?"

"I am, yes."

"Isn't there a pub not far from there?"

"Yeah," I said. "Killarney's is just a couple of blocks up Seventeenth. You know it?"

"I do. I can be there at nine."

"I'll see you then."

I glanced at my watch. 7:25. I decided to leave my follow-up on the class list for the next morning. I wondered at the possibility that someone could come across a syllabus lying on a bus stop bench or in a Starbucks, read it over, and decide to put his or her serial killing dream into action. Possible but unlikely. But what about online? If you're already predisposed to murder and you come across the syllabus while surfing the net, maybe it's just the trigger you've been waiting for. Again, a longshot, but not, I decided, an impossibility.

So, because I had a little time before I'd have to leave for Killarney's, I did some googling. After first finding that there were classes that had their syllabi online—even for courses offered sometime in the past—I decided to see if U of C's *Murder in the Classics* was one of them. And after a few misfires, I got lucky. There it was, exactly like the one Ellie Karsten had shown me, minus the smears and blotches.

No, I was wrong. As I held the paper version next to my computer screen. I realized something. They were not exactly the same.

Killarney's tries hard to give off an Irish ambiance and, for the most part, though I'm not an expert on things Irish, I would say it's quite successful.

I entered to the sound of The Dubliners, an Irish band I actually know, found a corner table, and ordered a Guinness. I checked my phone for messages and texts, then settled in to enjoy the Guinness and contemplate my meeting with Ellie Karsten. I was still contemplating when she arrived, maybe twenty minutes later.

She slid out of an expensive-looking white winter coat and draped it over the back of the chair opposite me.

"What will you have?" I asked her.

She ignored me and ordered a whisky sour from the hovering server, then sat, smiling. "No sense you buying me a drink with the money I'm paying you to investigate."

I shrugged. "Probably a good point." Her drink came and she didn't seem in a hurry to show me whatever it was she thought might be useful in the investigation, so I decided to start the conversation. "I did some checking on the internet ... wanted to see if the old class would still come up. It did, and so did the syllabus."

"Does that tell you something?"

"Well, it's a longshot but I suppose it's possible that some psychopath could also have come across the syllabus online, maybe did some reading and thought, what a great setup for a series of murders."

"You make it sound pretty far-fetched."

I shrugged. "I like to look at all the possibilities. Tomorrow I'll start checking on that list of people from your class ... see if anybody jumps off the page as the obvious killer."

I thought about going through the names with her—see if I could trigger a memory or two—but I was getting the feeling I was losing her. She was looking at a spot a little over my right shoulder. It was like she was looking off while thinking about something. Or maybe she was seeing something that interested her, maybe even worried her. After a few seconds, she came back to me.

"If we're right, the killer could be getting ready to kill again,"

she said. "Have you thought about *The Mystery of Edwin Drood?*
That's next on the syllabus."

"I have and, as I'm sure you know, it's a bit tricky," I told her.
"Because Dickens didn't finish the book, we don't know for sure
whom he intended the killer to be, but most scholars think it's
Edwin's uncle, the choirmaster who is in love with Edwin's fiancée.
So, if our killer is true to form, we need to be thinking about uncle-
nephew or maybe uncle-niece relationships. The killer has deviated
from the books slightly but seems to maintain at least the basics of
the fictionalized murders in his actions."

I'd lost her again. She was looking in the same direction but now
was becoming somewhat agitated.

"What is it?" I asked. I started to look back, but she stopped me.

"No, don't turn. Don't look." She leaned closer to me. "There's
a man sitting over there. He came in a few minutes ago but didn't
order anything. He … he seemed to be looking at me … at us. He's
getting up now. It looks like he's leaving."

I turned just in time to see a big man in a black overcoat and
toque going out the door. I turned back to Ellie.

"You ever see him before?"

She didn't answer right away. When she did, she spoke slowly.
"It doesn't make sense, I mean, does it?"

"What doesn't make sense?"

"I feel like … I feel like I know him. Or at least that I've seen
him before." She shook her head. "It's crazy, totally crazy."

"Come on, Ellie, help me here. What's crazy?"

"I think he was in that class."

"What, the classic murders class?"

"I can't say for sure, but I think so."

"Do you know his name?"

She thought again and shook her head. "I can't remember it.
No, wait. Something Floyd. Yes, that's it—we teased him some in
class that his name should be Freud … if that was him. I mean,
maybe I'm mistaken and—"

I stood up. "You stay right here. I'll see what I can find out."

I didn't wait for her to respond and quickly crossed the bar to the door. I stepped outside into a night that had grown colder in the time we'd been in Killarney's. I looked around. My hunch was he wouldn't have gone far.

I was right. The tall man in the heavy overcoat was kitty-corner from where I was standing. He glanced back over his shoulder, then started off down the street at a brisk pace. I saw one car on the street. I knew the car.

As I set out after the tall man, things were falling into place. I stayed far enough back to maintain the guise of surveillance, knowing full well there was no way I was going to lose this guy … he wouldn't let that happen.

About three blocks into our charade, Floyd slowed his pace. I slowed mine. He stopped just this side of a Chinese café that I'd forgotten was there. Linda Mae's. I'd been there a couple of times and the food was better than decent. Nice interior, courteous staff.

But what was most important about Linda Mae's on this frigid Calgary night was that it was the perfect setting for the carefully choreographed murder that was scheduled to take place.

I continued my walk until I was just a few feet from the guy. He was even bigger up close. He looked at me and smiled. Friendly sort of smile. Just a couple of guys out walking and about to have a chat. *Cold night, uh? Yeah, sure is. That wind is biting. It is, reminds you it's winter, don't it? Sure does.*

Except he decided to skip the preliminaries. No chat. I wondered if the revolver in his hand was the one that had killed Shamgar Fasil in Edmonton some months before.

"Before you do that," I said, "just one question … is your name really Floyd? I mean, it doesn't really matter, it's just that it's kind of cheesy."

He looked a bit puzzled.

"Floyd? As in Floyd Thursby?"

I could see the wheels turning. This wasn't how it was supposed to go, how it had been so painstakingly scripted.

"Police! Put the gun down!"

The lone car that had been outside Killarney's was now across the street from us. Larry Cotton, a homicide detective I knew, got out on the driver's side, another cop on the other side. Both had guns drawn; both were aimed at the tall man. He hesitated, but he didn't drop the gun.

"Put the gun down now!"

Maybe he was confused or maybe he decided to follow the script to the end. He raised the gun higher, still aiming at me.

Two shots dropped him, first to his knees, then face down on the pavement. Cotton and the other cop were crossing the road, guns high—the two-hand position—as they came closer. I looked back at the guy on the sidewalk, wondered if the heavy coat might have saved him. I didn't really care one way or the other.

Thirty minutes later, I was back at Killarney's. There was stuff to be done when a guy gets shot and you're a witness. Besides, I wasn't in a hurry. I'd wanted to keep Ellie Karsten waiting. Let her sweat a little. When I stepped back into the tavern, she was still there as I expected she would be. Hadn't moved except maybe to order another drink. I watched her face as I came toward her. She was a good actress, I'd already seen that, but not good enough. Her eye flickered; her bottom lip trembled before she was able to build a covering smile.

I shook my head as I sat down. "I lost him."

She struggled to find words. "I've been thinking and maybe I was wrong. Maybe that wasn't the guy from my class, so it probably doesn't matter that you lost him."

"Well, that's okay then. Still bothers me though, like maybe I've lost my touch. Tailing someone—that's something I'm normally good at."

She was beginning to understand that I was enjoying the thing a little too much and it bothered her. She started to fuss around, gathering her purse and gloves.

The front door opened, and she looked up quickly.

"He won't be coming through that door," I said. "At least not anytime soon."

"Wh … what?"

I didn't get to answer, because Larry Cotton and the other

detective—I'd learned his name was Pargeter—sat down in the two vacant chairs at our table.

"Larry," I said.

He nodded.

"This is Ellie Karsten. She's the lady I told you about on the phone. Ellie, this is homicide detective, Larry Cotton." I turned to Cotton. "He gonna make it?"

Cotton shrugged. "Ambulance just left. Looks like maybe, but I'm no doctor. He had a few things to say though before they took him away." He was looking at Ellie as he spoke.

I noticed Ellie's colour wasn't good. I took a sheet of paper out of my pocket, set it in front of her. I watched her as she looked at it, saw a slight slump of the shoulders. I moved the paper so that Cotton could see it.

"That," I explained, "is a copy of the syllabus I told you about —the one that the killer or killers have used as their blueprint in committing their murders. Thing is, I copied it off the internet and you'll see one significant difference between this one and the one Ellie gave me earlier."

I set the older, smudged copy on the table next to the clean copy I'd printed.

"There's one book that doesn't appear on Ellie's copy—one of the stains has rather conveniently blotted it out. That book is *The Maltese Falcon*. Have you read it, Detective?"

Cotton shrugged. "Saw the movie a long time ago."

I glanced at his partner, who shook his head. "On the syllabus, it comes between *The Murders in the Rue Morgue* and *The Mystery of Edwin Drood*, making it the next book that would have its murder replicated. It's just the first couple of chapters that are relevant. Sam Spade—that's the Humphrey Bogart character," I said for Cotton's benefit, "has his partner follow a guy whom a woman client claims is taking advantage of her little sister. While he's tailing the guy, the detective ends up getting shot."

Ellie Karsten was staring down at the table.

I went on. "The name of the guy Spade's partner was following was Floyd Thursby. The detective killed on the edge of Chinatown.

The guy I was following was identified by Ellie here as a man named Floyd, and the attempt to knock me off was made next to a Chinese restaurant."

Cotton took out a notebook, flipped it open, and looked at Ellie. "A. J. tells me you thought you recognized someone in here earlier."

"Well, I … I thought maybe I did, but now I'm quite sure I was wrong."

"Not according to the guy we took down." He turned to me. "The guy's real name is Jackie Marchment. Told us he and Ms. Karsten were classmates in a course called"—he glanced down at his notebook, then back up at Ellie—"*Murder in the Classics*. Mr. Marchment told us you and he had some interesting chats over coffee after class. Does that help you remember, Ms. Karsten?"

She thrust her chin forward. Braving it out. "I'd like to call my lawyer."

"Of course, you would." Cotton stood up. "And you'll get to do that a little later. For now, I'm going to read you your rights and place you under arrest in connection with several ongoing murder investigations." As he stood up, he looked at me. "About like you said it would go down."

"Yeah."

Cotton told me I could come down to the station and make a formal statement the next morning. When the three of them and two uniforms Cotton had called for were gone, I decided to have another Guinness. I thought about a woman who, like Raskolnikov in *Crime and Punishment*, flirted with being found out—maybe even *wanted* to be found out. Which would explain the charade involving me—that and needing a detective as a victim for *The Maltese Falcon* murder duplication.

I looked up at the TV screen where CBC was interviewing prominent people in the arts, letters, and even professional sports for their reactions to the passing of Peter Gzowski. There was a picture of Gzowski on the screen.

I raised my glass in a toast. "You would have loved this one, sir."

BLAIR KEETCH

Blair Keetch is a mystery writer based in Toronto. Recent short stories include "A Contrapuntal Duet" in *In the Key of Thirteen* anthology, "Deadly Cargo" in *Heartbreaks & Half-truths*, "Sleep, Perchance to Die" in *Grave Diagnosis* and "Killings4Sale" in *Asinine Assassins*. Online stories include "A Crunchy Kind of Death" and "300 Miles to Murder" at www.darkstormybc.com and "Glimmers" at www.ShotgunHoney.com. Blair is working (time and toddler permitting) on his novel, *Flight Risk*. Blair's website is www.blairkeetch.com

SEX, LIES AND SNOWMOBILES

BLAIR KEETCH

"BETTER CHECK THE WEATHER FORECAST," Caroline said with her distinctive laugh.

Considering I had left her life in tatters, she was in remarkably good humour. Despite myself, couldn't help but glance out over the balcony at the Caribbean Sea shimmering under a full moon.

Truth be told, I hesitated a long moment before I answered my phone. I'm not used to speaking with my victims afterwards. Plus, I had no idea how she found my number, but it served as a reminder of how resourceful she was.

"Why is that?" I finally replied.

"Because I said it would be a cold day in hell before I ever spoke to you again."

"You shouldn't always trust the weather forecast."

"Or handsome pilots," she bantered. "Now I realize just because you meet someone at an aviation museum doesn't mean they're a pilot."

A jab at my alias. "Hey," I retorted. "Not everyone you meet at Ripley's Aquarium is a marine biologist."

"Were you ever a pilot? Or even a flight attendant?" Caroline asked wistfully.

"Worked as a ramp handler after high school," I admitted. *Another world, another life.* "If you're looking for a refund, apologies but that's not possible."

"No, I presume you've spent most of my money on fast cars and fast women."

I gazed at the prone figure of Meaghan, inert and oblivious, sprawled out on the couch. Not exactly a sugar baby, but an unambitious college student who decided on a gap year without any prior financial planning.

"Not exactly." I paused. "I do miss you." I was shocked at how genuine my voice sounded.

"I appreciate the sentiment," Caroline replied coolly. "But I'm calling with a business proposition."

I should have hung up and gone back to my idyllic Caribbean lifestyle, but I had quickly become bored with Meaghan and suddenly felt very tired.

Caroline interpreted my silence as interest. "Seven point five."

"My rating as a lover?" I joked weakly.

"Seven and a half million dollars," she said. "Your share would be a third."

"Not half?"

"We're not partners. Consider yourself a consultant. It's my idea —but I'm not a grifter so I need someone's expertise. Somehow you came to mind," she said dryly.

This would be ten times more than any of my previous scams combined over the past years, but my exhilaration was short-lived. A con that large would be too complex and too risky for an amateur like her. "It might sound easy…"

"The best part is," she interrupted. "We'll be ripping off my husband."

I t had felt like a simple con, quick and easy.
  Born out of boredom, laziness, and an unexpected opportunity.

I had returned to my hometown of Sault Ste. Marie for the first time in years. To visit my father, who no longer recognized me or even spoke. Perhaps just as well—the only words would have been of disappointment and anger.

Restless, I had left my hotel and walked along the waterfront pathway until I came to the Bushplane Heritage Centre.

A sign read, *Private Event—Closed to the Public.* A challenge too good to resist. Another poster proclaimed, *Gala for the Northern Stars.* A charity event for at-risk youth. "Couple of decades too late," I muttered.

Clusters of elegantly dressed people began to stream in. In my sport jacket with open shirt, I was presentable, but clearly not a guest.

Yet, out of reflex, I couldn't let the opportunity escape me.

I approached the door staff, looking flustered. "I'm sure there's a stage entrance, but I'm running late," I apologized.

"And you are?" An officious older woman scanned her clipboard.

"Back-up singer." I pushed past before anyone could object. As hoped, the typical northern hospitality kicked in and no one tried to stop me.

A helpful voice even called out behind me, "Change rooms are at the back and to the left."

However, the bar was to the right, so that's where I headed, but not before I flagged down passing servers with their appetizer-laden trays. The prices on the room service menu convinced me a free dinner would be a small reward for my efforts.

The bartender was my favourite type—young, beautiful, and with appraising eyes. "Can I help you?"

"I'm in a bit of a jam," I confessed. "Just arrived in town, took a nap, but my jet lag kicked in." I stuck to the truth as closely as possible. "Woke up late, rushed over here, almost hit by a car."

"And you somehow lost your bar tickets." Her eyes shone with amusement.

"Truly a close call—you could say I'm scared *chit*less."

She forgave the horrible pun. Despite what many believe, the key is not to be too charming or too smooth.

"Red or white?" She smiled. "My name's Amanda, but you can call me Mandy."

The lie came easily to my lips. "My name is Roy, but you can call me Roy."

This minor charade would have ended there, had I not spied Caroline across the floor.

In a room crowded with people dressed to impress, she stood out in a simple fuchsia dress, elegant yet somehow suggestive. I moved in and waited on the edge of her line of sight, my eyes searching the throngs of people.

"You look lost," she said.

I turned to her. "I don't know anyone anymore." I failed to mention I didn't want to be recognized. "I grew up here, but left years ago. Still, thought a few familiar faces…"

"Sorry, I'm a newcomer here myself. Moved here just under a year ago." Leveraging our common bond, I monopolized our conversation and gravitated to a nearby table for eight but ended up ignoring everyone around us. Caroline was witty, charming, and possessed an easy confidence. I fell back on one of my favourite identities—the local boy made good, who loved the wilderness yet couldn't resist the lure of the big city. A pilot who eventually became an airline entrepreneur.

"Why the Soo?" I used the city's nickname to deftly turn any questions back to her.

"I run an educational software company, so I can be based anywhere," she said. "I've always loved the north, and a friend sent me a listing for a cottage for sale. A waterfront property right on one of the nearby lakes and far larger than anything I could afford in Toronto." Photos on her phone of an impressive stone mansion made it clear "cottage" was an understatement.

"You don't mind the winters?" One of the reasons I had left was the endless months of snow and ice.

"No, I love the outdoors. Cross-country skiing, snowshoeing, fatbiking, even have my own snowmobile. Besides, I'd just gotten divorced." Caroline laughed, looking away. "Not the most amicable of affairs, so being seven hours away from my ex has its definite appeal."

Before the speeches commenced with their endless rounds of thank-you speeches and flat jokes, we headed out into the balmy evening.

I would have left it at that—a brief romantic encounter, possibly even a night of passion, but as Caroline talked, it became clear that her lifestyle was more than comfortable, it was outright prosperous.

"I started off literally working from my kitchen but, as you know, the demand for anything virtual is insatiable. I now have over two dozen employees. Software developers, office staff—even a marketing assistant. But it's not all it's cracked up to be." A sideways glance. "I still work ridiculous hours and, at times, it can be very lonely."

Taking my cue, I kissed her, tenderly at first, then with an increased urgency that would do Harlequin Romance proud.

She broke away. "Sorry, but I'm really not the type to rush into anything."

I didn't hide my disappointment. "Maybe another lifetime."

As often is the case for someone so smart, Caroline was surprisingly gullible.

Claiming I had more business to conduct, I delayed my departure. "You're part of the reason as well," I confessed. The next ten days were a whirlwind of romantic dinners and intimate talks that eventually spilled over into the bedroom.

The con was simple. One afternoon, she found me in the hotel lounge looking out the windows. After desultory conversation, Caroline asked, "What's wrong?"

I stared back. "Sorry, I'm ruining our time together." Caroline held her breath. As hoped, she feared a break-up was coming next. "One of my investors was in a car crash—she'll eventually recover, but she's under medication and she was going to cover my credit note that comes due two days from now." My voice cracked. "I could lose everything."

"Is that all?" Caroline sighed in relief. "How much?"

"Hockey cards?"

"Hockey cards," Caroline repeated. The passing two years had been good to her.

I had dropped Meaghan off in Miami to send her back to whatever midwestern town she had grown up in and caught the next flight back to Toronto with enough time to meet Caroline at Scaramouche, an eternally popular restaurant.

"Not just any hockey cards," she affirmed. Over a leisurely dinner, she outlined her plan. While she was unaware, it was a variation on the Gold Brick scam, a con that's been around for ages. A little crude and with some definite flaws, but the core idea had potential.

The scheme was simple: Caroline would tell her ex-husband she had inherited the hockey card collection from her uncle, which was true, and found out it was far vaster, and far more valuable, than originally thought. The latter wasn't so true. She would offer to sell it at a tempting price, but in fact, the majority would be high-quality forgeries.

"And your husband was aware of your late uncle's collection?"

"Absolutely," she said. "Uncle Gord would always taunt him by showing a few of the cards, but never the entire collection. Hinting at other hidden treasures."

To pull it off, she needed someone to pose as an expert in hockey cards. Someone comfortable with lying. Not just comfortable, but excellent at deception.

Cue my entrance.

"Seems like a nice coincidence that your husband is a hockey card fanatic," I said.

"Not really. Ryan buys anything and everything that catches his fancy." She ticked off her fingers one by one. "Coins, stamps ... he was even considering buying Pokémon cards, but thought it might harm his reputation."

I broke in. "Your ex-husband doesn't strike me as the type of guy who sits at the kitchen table each night poring over his stamp collection."

"That's because he's not," Caroline scoffed. "It's all status symbols—most are just for display, a way to impress clients. Really, he wouldn't know the value of that upside-down airplane stamp if it was stuck to his forehead."

"Still, he won't trust just anyone telling him they're an authority on hockey cards."

"That's where you come in. You'll play the subject-matter expert, backed up by your forged website."

The building blocks were present, only needing the finesse of someone like myself. "But your idea has one fatal flaw," I argued. "Eventually, your husband will discover he's been cheated. And he doesn't seem like the forgiving sort."

"I'll tell him it's only what I deserve on top of our divorce settlement," she said defiantly, yet her worry was obvious.

"The risk is too great." I placed the dessert menu down. "Unless he thinks you've *both* been conned."

Realization dawned in her eyes. "You're putting yourself in danger."

"The risk is there," I stated. "I'm just putting the focus on me."

She pushed away her dessert plate in dismay. "Perhaps there's another way."

"Listen, you told me your ex can be the vindictive type. If he believes I've ripped off the two of you, he'll be coming after me, but I'll have disappeared into thin air." *Caribbean air.* "Not the first time I've gone to ground," I reminded her before hammering my final point. "Besides, you told me there's no 'us' anymore."

The next week I was holed up in my mid-town flat, TV unplugged, curtains closed, Uber Eats providing my sustenance. My sole focus was the world of hockey card trading. I memorized the ten grades of the PSA rating system, learned what counted as defects in trading cards—everything from discoloration to poorly trimmed stock. When my brain got too foggy, I would switch to Zoom calls with my web designer whose specialty was building websites for fictious companies—or people.

Toronto in late November is not the city at is finest. Trees in their former autumn glory are now bare and the onslaught of Christmas decorations has not yet begun.

Caroline wore a stylish camel overcoat and was carrying a compact portfolio case over her shoulder. It had been agreed it would be too cumbersome to show the entire collection, so she brought select samples.

Carlisle had chosen to meet over a late lunch at Canoe with its panoramic views of the waterfront. A half-empty plate of scallops attested that he had started before we arrived. A fresh bowl of gnocchi was placed down as we approached.

"Caroline," he said. "Fashionably late as usual." It was just five minutes past the hour. His eyes turned to me. "Try the pasta. It's phenomenal."

"No thanks," I said. "Pasta makes you fat."

Carlisle's face flushed, but he held his temper in check. One of my ploys is to make myself dislikeable. If people are wary of a con, they're expecting a smooth talker, not a jerk.

As we settled in, I discreetly checked him out. Not obese, but heavy-set. Short, cropped hair with an intermittent sprinkling of grey. Eyes, dark and calculating, that held no warmth for his former wife.

A waiter approached us.

"A latte for myself, please." Caroline looked at me.

"Don't you know what all that sugar does to your body?" Without glancing up, I demanded, "Tap water, cold, two lemon slices on the side."

There wasn't a need for idle chit chat, so Caroline clicked open the case.

Carlisle held up his hand. "Before we start, I wanted your opinion on this." He pulled out a hockey card from his suit pocket and slid it across the table to me.

I was expecting this—a test of my credentials—but nonetheless, my heart rate accelerated.

"This isn't *Antiques Roadshow*," I sneered.

Caroline looked at me.

"Oh, all right." I picked up the card. Terry Sawchuk. Detroit Red Wings, circa 1960. I pulled out a jeweller's scope. "Don't have all my tools," I grumbled. I inspected each side before I tossed it back. "I'll give you forty-seven bucks—no, make it fifty, as there's no shipping and handling."

Wordlessly, Carlisle retrieved the card and nodded to Caroline.

"As agreed, ten cards were chosen. I sent photos to Roy, and he recommended which to bring for our meeting. If we agree to continue, Roy will do a full audit of the collection and provide his opinion on the total worth."

I withdrew the first card. Frank Mahovlich. 1957 Rookie card.

Carlisle peered over. "I remember that one."

Caroline smiled. "One of Uncle Gord's favourites. He always used to flaunt it after a few drinks." She paused, lost in the memory. "Claimed it was worth thirty thousand dollars."

"Maybe five years ago," I retorted.

"You mean it's not worth that?" Carlisle didn't hide his irritation.

"Not anymore." I turned the card over. "Probably worth $87K."

Caroline gasped, while Carlisle smirked almost imperceptibly. *A worthy poker opponent.*

The next few cards were the same. Some of the hockey players long ago dead, others more recent. I valued them anywhere from three hundred dollars to the upper five-figure range.

Caroline looked at Carlisle. "You know what Uncle Gord was like."

"Secretive and boastful at the same time." Clearly, Carlisle held little affection for him.

"Secretive, for sure. I know I sound like Nancy Drew, but I found another box."

Both Carlisle and I leaned forward in anticipation.

"I brought three of them here, though there are fifty-seven in total."

Carlisle gestured impatiently as Caroline revealed the first cards. "Strange thing is they're all in pairs." Two exact images of a Wayne Gretzky looked up.

I inspected the first card for less than thirty seconds before tossing it back. "A reprint. Might not even fetch twenty dollars." I turned my attention to the second card. I examined it for a few minutes and paused in disbelief.

"What?" Carlisle demanded.

"This is the Holy Grail of cards," I explained. "An original 1979 O-Pee-Chee #18 card."

"How much?"

"Last time I heard, just under five."

"Only five thousand?" His disappointment was clear.

"You're not listening," I chided. "$500K. At minimum."

Carlisle sat back, stunned. "For a single card?"

"A similar card fetched well over a million dollars in auction but was in mint condition." I frowned. "Damn."

"What's wrong?" Caroline's turn to worry.

"There's a slight mark on the back. Looks like some idiot used this card as a beer coaster. Very faint, but still…"

Carlisle was halfway out of his chair. "You mean, it's worthless?"

For the first time, I met his gaze. "Not worthless, but yes, reduced in value." I waited a beat. "Probably graded as 'Near Mint–Mint.' Maybe worth only four hundred thousand."

It was the downgrade in value that sold the con. A perfectly preserved Wayne Gretzky in his Pee Wee years would raise suspicions. But a flawed version that was still very valuable? Far more believable.

I continued the charade for another hour as we went through the newly discovered cards and our après lunch lattes got cold. As Caroline began to collect the cards, Carlisle suddenly raised his palm in the air and said, "I think I should take one of the cards with me."

"What, you don't trust me?" I smiled in return.

Carlisle looked back.

"Okay," I said. "Pick a card, any card." I'd been expecting this turn of events, but nonetheless my stomach roiled.

Caroline had fronted money, enough to salt the collection with three genuine cards, but now it was down to the power of suggestion and blind luck.

He paused and scanned the collection. I had chosen Bobby Orr / OPC circa 2008 as one of the true versions as, according to Caroline, he was one of Carlisle's favourite players. Same with a 1971 card featuring Ken Dryden. The latter had cost Caroline almost $64,000.

Carlisle considered them both before stating, "I'll take the Eddie Shack to go."

I tried not to sigh in relief. That had been the third salted card. Both had been born in the same northern town, Sudbury, and apparently Carlisle had liked Shack's showmanship.

I handed the card, pristine and genuine, to Carlisle. "I'll even throw in a dozen doughnuts."

He looked back blankly, the reference lost on him. "I'll let you know what I find."

"Eddie Shack, 1958, Topps, worth just under four grand is what you'll find."

"We'll see." He nodded. But I knew that is what he would discover, and it would seal the deal.

I smiled to myself. *He shoots, he scores.*

The toughest part of any con was the waiting.

The weeks passed slowly after Carlisle discovered that my estimate matched other expert appraisers. The negotiations had gone through the holiday season and we'd finally settled on a price of just over five million. Caroline felt we could go as high as seven, but I balked. The higher we went, the more the boundary of plausibility was pushed.

"But he paid at least six million for his coin collection," she insisted with a rare pout. We were on a Zoom call, because at my demand, we stayed separate from each other. We had flown together back to Sault Ste. Marie, so I could stay in the hotel ready to join the handover of the collection, while Caroline had driven up into the wintry fortress that was her chalet.

The next morning, I was outside staring at the waterfront statue dedicated to an old musher who had sacrificed his life to rescue his dogs. I was lost in reflection, not noticing the wet snow reaching well above my ankles. My share would be enough to look after my immediate needs for the next few years, yet I wasn't kidding myself that I had enough self-discipline to retire or even invest responsibly.

As for Caroline, she was sending decidedly mixed signals and it felt her resolve not to become romantically involved again was crumbling.

Yet the con was structured in a way I couldn't join her afterwards, at least in public.

My thoughts were derailed when my burner phone buzzed with a text.

'*He's here.*'

'*Now? At the lodge?*'

Minutes crawled past before a brief reply. '*Yes.*'

I paced back and forth in the warmth of my hotel room when my burner came back to life. Not as a text, but as a phone call.

"We did it!" Caroline talked quickly, her voice bursting with excitement. "He didn't even try to negotiate. I mean, he wants the cards delivered within a week, but…"

"And he'll transfer the funds beforehand?" I asked.

"That's the best part—he's paid us in full."

"What? The money's in the bank?" This felt too easy.

"Not exactly," Caroline hesitated. "He gave us the equivalent, maybe even better. His coin collection."

"What?" I snapped. "They could be fake."

"They look genuine." She was almost babbling. "And he gave me the certificates of authenticity."

"They might be bona fide, but we don't know. We're not experts in coins," I interrupted. Was Carlisle trying to pull a con on us? My mind raced at all the possible pitfalls.

"That's why he's willing to wait until we get them evaluated before we hand over the cards."

"Why is he so eager to give up his coin collection?"

"He said it's too cumbersome and can't be easily displayed. He said he'd rather have a small collection of really valuable hockey cards that he could frame and hang in his office and home."

"Great, so even if they're real, we still have to sell them to get our money," I spat. "I don't like it. How soon can you come down here?"

"Maybe three hours?" Caroline hesitated. "We had a major snowfall last night. Even Ryan's four-wheel drive struggled to get out of the driveway."

"Drive carefully but leave now. Bring the coins with you and an overnight bag. I'll book a room here."

"On my way, but the extra room won't be necessary."

I'd left a message with my banker, who wouldn't blink an eye if I appeared on her doorstep with a suitcase full of rare coins. When my phone rang, I half expected to hear her. Instead, it was Caroline.

"We have a problem." Her voice was strained.

Steeling myself, I asked, "What's the matter?"

"Trees are blocking access to the sideroad."

"On purpose?"

"I don't think so. It often happens after a bad storm. But I can't get past. And now my car is up to its axles." Before I could ask, she continued, "Two, maybe three days before it's cleared. It's not a burning priority for the county if you still have power and heat. Which I do."

"Okay, give me a few hours. I'll be up there."

"How? The news said that Highway 556 is all but impassable."

"Wait it out. Two or three more days won't be the end of the world. Soon as you can dig yourself out…" I stopped at the sound of her soft crying.

"I'm being silly, but I'm scared. I'm here alone with all these coins. Do you think I'm safe?" She voiced the thoughts that ran through my mind. Had Carlisle really left? Was he hiding in the woods?

"Aside from parachuting me in, we don't have much choice," I said.

The line went silent as the hard, cold reality sank in for both of us.

Until Caroline whispered, "I have an idea."

I didn't like it, not in the least. But how could I refuse? My fictious background of growing up as a rugged northern kid who enjoyed macho adventures had come back to haunt me. "You said you used to raise hell as a kid snowmobiling all over the back country," she reminded me. *More likely in the pool hall.*

Caroline's snowmobile was in the marina shop at the other side of the lake. Repaired and ready for pickup. "It's virtually a straight run across the lake," she assured me. As opposed to a long, treacherous route around the lake on inaccessible roads. "The keys have been left in the side pannier. I'll leave all the chalet lights on— you can see it for miles away."

"In the daylight?" I said.

"No, at night," she shot back. "It has to be a night crossing."

My phone buzzed as several texts arrived on top of each other.

"I've sent a couple of screen shots."

I glanced at my phone. Some sort of chart and tonight's weather forecast. Clear, but an intimidating minus twenty-five. Whether Fahrenheit or Celsius, it didn't matter. I turned my attention back to Caroline. "What's that about a snow moon?"

"Tonight's a snow moon. It's perfect. The first full moon of February. You'll be able to see for miles and miles."

The sky outside had darkened, but there were gaps in the clouds. Even after winter solstice, the days were short in the north. I was running out of arguments—and time. Perhaps foolhardy, but maybe worth the risk.

Another thought crossed my mind. If it was just the two of us at her lodge and the coins looked genuine. *How much further would the proceeds go for just one person?*

"I'll be there by midnight," I said more confidently than I felt.

"The lights will be on."

I hung up and returned to the texts. A report on ice conditions confirmed the lake was frozen to a depth of at least five inches. I searched 'snow moon' and sure enough, it was tonight.

My burner buzzed again with another message from Caroline. She outlined in surprisingly explicit detail about what she would do to me—and what we would do together once I safely reached her chalet.

It was the final incentive, and I wasted no time heading out into the night.

The first two miles were terrifying, then exhilarating.

The snow moon was in full glory with a brightness so strong, my figure cast stark shadows onto the snow.

Despite my doubts, the snowmobile was exactly where Caroline described, including the keys nestled in the saddle bag. The engine started right away with a deep, satisfying roar that echoed through the deserted neighbourhood.

I headed past the boat ramp, down a snowy side road for close to a mile before I came to a beach-access trail. The sand was buried in snow drifts, but I plowed straight through and, before I knew it, I was on the frozen lake. I gasped in shock once I emerged from the sheltered bay. The cold was instantly numbing.

Everything had happened so quickly I didn't have time to buy a snowmobile suit. Instead, I wore a parka, corduroy pants, gloves, and running shoes. Fine for a stroll along the boardwalk, but not for a winter expedition.

However, Caroline estimated the lake crossing would take only half an hour, so I throttled the engine. The machine leapt forward with unexpected strength, almost throwing me off. I hung on for dear life and fought to regain control.

As instructed, I hugged the shore until I came to a towering outcrop of rock that marked the turning point.

I gritted my teeth and headed directly out into the lake. Ahead of me lay an endless expanse of snow.

Then suddenly, I saw it. A speck of light in the far horizon. While I knew you could see a lot farther at night, this gave me a new sense of resolve. Despite the cold and my nerves, I started to enjoy myself—at least a little.

Until the snowmobile yanked me back and forth as the engine seized and stopped with a loud cough.

"Calm down," I chided myself. I tried the ignition again, but the motor remained silent.

I smacked the console in despair and suddenly the needle on the gas gauge slid from full to empty. I swore in disbelief. I had checked it before I left, and it registered full. There was no way I could have burned through an entire tank of gas.

The chalet was no longer a smudge, but a beacon in the night with all its lights blazing into the darkness. A second later, the house vanished. Gone in the blink of an eye.

With a sinking feeling, I realized Caroline had turned off all the lights.

The conman had been conned. She probably stood in the darkness savouring her revenge.

My anger flared up and I vowed to walk across the remaining portion of the frozen lake. To my horror, the light of the moon began to fade. I looked up as clouds marched across the sky.

But the weather report, I silently protested until I realized I was not the only one with resources to create a fake website.

The sound was deafening, like the footsteps of an approaching giant.

I sat paralyzed as cracks in the ice advanced toward me and the deadly embrace of the cold water waited below.

SUSAN CALDER

Susan Calder is a Calgary writer who grew up in Montreal. She is the author of four novels: *A Deadly Fall, Ten Days in Summer* and *Winter's Rage* books 1, 2 & 3 of the Paula Savard mystery series set in Calgary, and *To Catch a Fox,* a standalone literary/suspense. Susan's short stories have won contests and appeared in magazines and anthologies. Her short story "A Deadly Flu" is her first venture into historical fiction. Susan's website is www.susancalder.com

A DEADLY FLU

SUSAN CALDER

Detective Fred Gillman bustled into police headquarters. He stuffed his gloves in his coat pockets and rubbed his hands together to remove the chill.

Julia looked up from her reception desk. "We're barely into December. Is Calgary always this cold in winter?" She'd moved west from Toronto this summer.

"Now and then Chinooks blow in to warm us up," Gillman said. "Days like this I suspect they're a myth." He attempted a wink.

Julia's smile lit up her face. Her eyes were blue, he realized. An ache rose from his chest. His wife and child dead less than a year and here he was flirting, if that's what this was. He'd forgotten about such nonsense during his twenty years of marriage.

"There's a gentleman to see you." Julia nodded toward the waiting area.

Gillman went over to greet the man, who rose and introduced himself as Dr. Thomas Campbell. The mask covering Campbell's lower face reminded Gillman to stand back. They'd stopped wearing gauze masks at headquarters last week, with cases of Spanish flu waning.

"Can you spare a moment, Detective?" Campbell asked. "I

don't know if I have something for you to pursue, but it's my duty to report this."

"Best to err on that side."

Gillman ushered the doctor into his office and invited him to drape his fur coat and hat on the tree rack. They settled on chairs across from Gillman's desk. Campbell removed his mask to reveal a mustache curling up to his cheekbones. The smiling shape contrasted his grim lips.

Campbell rested his medical bag on his lap. "We're both busy men. I'll get to the point."

Gillman picked up his pen to take notes. Campbell explained that two evenings ago he was called to the home of Albert Reed, who was in apparent respiratory distress. Campbell drove there immediately, but arrived too late to save him. From Mrs. Reed's descriptions of her husband's symptoms and his darkened skin, the cause of death seemed clear.

"Bacterial pneumonia," Campbell said. "Resulting from Spanish influenza."

Gillman leaned back, although Campbell hadn't sniffled or coughed. Campbell looked about Gillman's age, early forties, older than the deadly flu's typical targets.

"Albert's death struck me personally," Campbell said. "I saw him regularly as a patient. He worked in the drug store next to my office. He was only twenty-five." Campbell's voice quivered, but he regained control. "Albert contracted tuberculosis in the Great War and received an early discharge. Undoubtedly his weakened lungs contributed to his pneumonia."

A neighbour was present at the Reeds' house Sunday night, Campbell said. He sent the man across the street to contact the morgue. This neighbour had placed the original call, since the Reeds have no telephone. Mrs. Reed was naturally distressed. She repeatedly asked, 'What will become of me?' Campbell interpreted her worries to be partly financial. She worked half days at the drug store, but without Albert's income could she afford the house rental? Campbell noticed an opened bottle of whisky on the sideboard and offered to take it in lieu of payment.

"I was also concerned she'd drink the contents in her state," Campbell said. "As her doctor, I knew she is with child."

Gillman's hand shook on the pen. He and Nellie had longed for a child for twenty years until finally the miracle occurred. After five months of joyous anticipation, mother and son were buried in Union Cemetery. 'At her age there were risks,' the doctors and nurses kept saying until Gillman wanted to throttle them all. He gripped the pen with both hands to steady it.

"Liquor isn't healthy for a foetus," Campbell said. "But Mrs. Reed is French, and you know how they are."

Gillman didn't know. He grew up in rural Alberta and hadn't travelled beyond western Canada.

"I don't touch liquor," Campbell continued. "The following morning, I gave the bottle to my neighbour. Last night, his wife frantically came to my house. We ran next door. Her husband's symptoms were the same as Reed's. My neighbour survived—he's an older man and I could attend to him quickly. The coincidence made me suspicious. I asked for the bottle back." Campbell opened his medical bag and pulled out a paper bag. It bulged in the shape of a whisky bottle. "Can the police do a forensic check on the remaining contents?"

"We can, but it will take several days."

Campbell set the bag on the desk with a clunk. "It would put my mind at ease. Mrs. Reed is my patient. She advises my other patients at the drug store. Trust is essential."

Gillman nodded. Through her work, Mrs. Reed would have knowledge and access to medications that could mimic Spanish flu symptoms. Did she have motive?

"How would you assess the Reeds' marriage?" Gillman asked.

Campbell's brow knit. "It's not my place to speculate."

Gillman took down details of the Reeds' address, the drug store address, and Campbell's telephone number in case the police required more information.

After Campbell left, Gillman had Julia send the bottle to the lab and discussed the case with the chief inspector. They agreed Gillman should interview the widow today rather than wait for the laboratory results. Timeliness was critical for investigations and Gillman's police workload was light. The closure of pool halls, bars, and dance halls six weeks ago to combat the flu had reduced crime and public mischief to a trickle.

After lunch, Gillman rode the streetcar to Tuxedo, a suburb in the northeast edge of the city. Since the Armistice on November 11th, experts were predicting Calgary would expand even farther when the troops returned from Europe next year. Calgary Police Services planned to purchase additional motorcars for officers' use when funds permitted. Gillman looked out the window at motorcars dodging pedestrians and horse-drawn carriages. On the streetcar, he could relax and let his mind wander through his cases. He decided to avoid alerting Mrs. Reed to possible suspicions at this stage. If the lab result proved negative, why needlessly add to her grief?

He exited the streetcar at the Reeds' stop. A biting wind hurled snow pellets into his face. Hunched forward, he headed down the Reeds' street, lined with working-class bungalows built five or six years ago. He envied Dr. Campbell's fur coat and fur hat. At the Reeds' address, scraggly stalks filled the front yard, remnants of a summer garden. Gillman knocked on the front door, the north wind pounding his back. He knocked again. At last, the door opened. He introduced himself to the woman dressed in black.

"Police?" She stepped backward. "Come in. It's freezing."

Gillman entered the warmth of the house and closed the door to the wind. "I understand your husband passed away at home from Spanish influenza. I need to file a report."

Her dark eyes widened. "No one told me to expect you." She opened the hall closet door.

Gillman hung up his coat and followed her into the parlour. She sank to the closest chair. He took the other one, next to the crackling fireplace. Both faced the front window; an end table and kerosene lamp between them. The only other furniture in the room was a sideboard under the window; on top stood a photograph with a group of people. Perhaps a wedding picture? The sole wall decoration was a painting above the fireplace, a generic mountain scene.

"So many dying of Spanish flu," Mrs. Reed said. "How do you find time to make reports on them all?"

Strands of dark hair flowed down Mrs. Reed's forehead. She'd tied her bun loosely at the back. Gillman guessed she was in her early twenties. Her olive complexion and high cheekbones gave her an exotic look that he found pretty despite the shadows around her eyes. He took out his notebook and pen and asked her permission to take notes. She nodded.

"Could you describe the events of Sunday evening?" he said. "Please take your time, Mrs. Reed."

"Madeleine. I'm not a wife anymore." She stared at the patterned carpet in front of Gillman. "Albert died here."

She explained that after Sunday dinner they'd settled in the parlour, as usual. Albert started coughing. That was usual, too. He had a persistent cough from the tuberculosis he'd contracted in the war. They'd met when she worked in the makeshift hospital in her village in France. But Sunday night, Albert's cough rapidly grew worse. Water didn't help. One violent cough propelled him from his chair to the floor. Madeleine tried to raise him; she hammered his back. When nothing worked, she left him to have a neighbour call their doctor. They returned to find Albert unconscious.

"I never talked to him again." She shook her head. "Never said *au revoir*."

Gillman liked listening to her soft voice, her accented words, misplaced grammar, and occasional insertions of French. Her story matched the doctor's account. He glanced at her flat stomach. Her condition would be early months. What would become of her now?

"Do you have family in Canada?" he asked.

"*Non.*"

"What about your husband?"

She scowled. "His parents live in Calgary. They hate me because I'm *catholique*."

"Perhaps that will change," he said and refrained from adding 'with their grandchild's arrival.'

"I don't want their *charité*." Her jaw was firm. "I have no choice but to return to *France*."

"I understand you work part time in a drug store."

She touched her stomach. "I can't work much longer, but I have enough savings to pay the rent until my baby and I can travel."

Gillman's notebook shook. He brushed away thoughts of Nellie and their baby. "Your neighbour who called the doctor. Does he live directly across the street?"

"John?" She stared out the front window.

Back in the cold, Gillman crossed the street, into a north wind so fierce that his head ached as he rapped John's door. An older woman answered. He asked for John.

"My son. Are you a friend from his club?" She turned and shouted, "John." She looked back at Gillman. "Come in, before I catch my death."

Once more grateful to be inside, Gillman removed his overcoat. He sniffed aromas of baking. Two children ran into the hall, followed by two men. The tall, younger one limped toward Gillman and halted. Gillman went through his introduction.

"Poor Albert," John's mother said. "My husband and I were in bed when Madeleine came over. We have to get up early to look after the boys while our daughter works. Fortunately, John is up all hours. You two can talk in the parlour. Would you like tea, Detective?"

"I'd love anything warm."

"Boys." She clapped her hands. "Let's eat my oatmeal cookies in the kitchen."

The children and older couple disappeared into the back room. Their house looked the mirror image of Madeleine's, although their parlour was a startling contrast to the Reeds' minimal décor. Portraits and photographs of rural scenes covered these walls. A pianoforte stood along the interior wall, a music stand and saxophone beside it. A sofa bisected the room, facing a coffee table and two chairs.

Blocks towered on the coffee table between John on the sofa and Gillman on the chair by the toasty fireplace. John looked in his late twenties. He wore casual pants, a sweater, and a paintbrush mustache. His hair was combed back, but a forelock kept drooping over his forehead.

"I could tell Albert was dead when we got to their house," John said. "Madeleine persisted in her attempts to revive him, but I've seen men dead in the war."

Gillman glanced at John's legs. One looked oddly bent. Presumably, like Albert, he'd received an early medical discharge.

"Did you know the Reeds well?" Gillman asked.

John's mother appeared with a tea tray. Gillman hoped she'd leave them alone so she wouldn't interfere with his questioning.

John leaned toward the coffee table. With a sweep of his arm, he brushed the blocks to the floor to make space for the tray. "I'll help the boys rebuild. They'll find that fun."

"John enjoys playing as much as them," his mother said. She poured three cups of tea, told Gillman to add milk and sugar as he wished, and sat on the remaining chair. "John knew poor Albert better than us."

John crossed his bent leg over the other one and said he became acquainted with Madeleine first, during the summer. After her mornings at the drug store, she'd spend the afternoons tending her garden.

"She made those plants bloom," his mother added, "despite her front yard's northern exposure." She said John worked nights at his club and slept all morning. He played the saxophone in a band. "Afternoons he looks for things to do around here."

"Madeleine was someone my age to talk with," John said. She invited him over for drinks to meet Albert after John mentioned he was injured in the Battle of the Somme, where Albert had fought as well. John's visits became a weekly event. The frequency increased when the Spanish influenza closed his nightclub in October.

"How frequent would that be?" Gillman asked.

"Two or three times a week."

"You'd have a glass of whisky?"

"Albert picked up the habit in the war," John said. "You do what you can to tolerate the trenches." He squinted at Gillman. "What does this have to do with a death from the damn flu?"

"Don't swear, John," his mother said. "More tea, Detective?"

John uncrossed his legs. "Albert survived the bloody war, and then this." He set his teacup on the table. "And how well did he survive, really? He evaded my every mention of the war. He seemed tired, had a chronic cough. All his energy was spent in his work. Nights I was there, one drink sent him straight to bed."

"You stayed there late enough," his mother said.

"Madeleine and I would continue to talk. I liked hearing about life in France, when it wasn't being ravaged by war. She liked hearing about my club." A faint blush rose on his cheeks.

"Didn't she and Albert go to your club one night?" his mother said.

John angled toward her. His forelock concealed his expression from Gillman. "Albert was supposed to, but, at the last minute, said he was too tired to go out. Madeleine was already dressed for the evening and went. She had a ripping good time, dancing, singing along."

Gillman noted, 'John sweet on Madeleine? She on him?' Was there more between them? John would have access to drugs through people he met at the nightclub, although the type of drugs inclined to uplift people rather than kill. Were they in it together? Worse, could John be the father of her child? Gillman asked him when he'd last seen the Reeds.

"Saturday, the night before he died," John said. "We opened a fresh bottle of whisky."

"Did Madeleine have a drink?"

John pulled his forelock. "I don't think so. I recall her drinking during my first visits, but not recently." He let go of his hair. "I truly don't understand why this matters."

Gillman truly decided he'd better leave. While closing his notebook, his gaze strayed to the portraits on the walls. "You have a large family."

"Eleven children," John's mother said. "Nine surviving. John's the baby."

"I'll be the baby as long as I live here," he said, without apparent bitterness.

Outside, Gillman walked east toward the main street. He considered checking out the drug store, but it was damn cold and Albert's colleagues would only have second-hand details of his death. Their impressions of the Reeds' characters could wait until the case was deemed a suspicious death—or not. In the streetcar, Gillman mulled John's implication that Albert was despondent. Had Albert taken the medicine from the drug store to end his life? Would he do that when his wife was with child? Gillman wouldn't, no matter how hopeless his life had become. But what if Madeleine hadn't told her husband about her condition yet?

Three days later, the chief inspector called Gillman into his office. The laboratory report on the whisky bottle contents had come in. Traces of agalsidase, a medicine used in the treatment of Fabry disease, a kidney condition. When combined with alcohol, agalsidase could cause breathing difficulties and, in rare cases, death, especially in the vulnerable.

"My money's on Mrs. Reed," the chief inspector said. "Possibly in league with her lover. Women can't resist musicians. You and Constable Boone will confront the widow right away. Have Julia order a motorcar. You'll need it to make an arrest."

Gillman gladly let Boone drive the motorcar to Tuxedo. On the way, Gillman outlined the case, cringing with the car's every abrupt stop and swerve. They parked in front of the Reeds' house and stepped outside to mild air blowing from the west. A Chinook was on its way.

Madeleine answered the door, dressed in her black blouse and skirt. Her eyebrows shot up at the sight of Boone in uniform, but she ushered both men in without comment.

"We'll need a chair from the kitchen," she said.

"I'll get it." Boone strode to the rear of the house.

In the parlour, Gillman and Madeleine took the same chairs as before. Without mentioning the doctor's involvement, he described the laboratory findings.

"Agalsidase?" she said. "We sell that at the drug store. How would it get in the whisky? During the manufacturing?"

Gillman stared. Her eyes were less shadowed than they were the last time. Presumably she was sleeping better.

Madeleine frowned. "You think someone added it to the whisky? Who? And when?" Her forehead rippled, as she reflected. "Albert and John drank from that bottle Saturday night. No one touched it after that until Albert, Sunday evening."

"Did you have a drink?"

"Me? *Non.*" She touched her stomach. "My baby doesn't like liquor. That's how I knew I was *enceinte.*"

Boone lugged in a chair and sat across from Madeleine.

Gillman leaned toward her. "Please excuse my delicate questioning. Had you told Albert you were with child?"

"Of course," she said. "It would bring him cheer."

"Would you characterize Albert as depressed?"

She crossed her arms. "What do you mean?"

"He might have taken his life."

"*Non.*" Her hands dropped to her lap. "Albert would not do that, to me or his child." She clutched her skirt. "That is *impossible.*"

If she were guilty, she'd have been wise to declare it possible, to save herself.

John could have acted on his own, slipped the medicine into the whisky after he'd taken his last drink. He must have had an opportunity after Albert had gone to bed, perhaps while Madeleine went to the kitchen or the *toilette.* Nellie had used the facility frequently during her condition's first few months.

"There is only one answer," Madeleine said. "Someone came into the house on Sunday while Albert and I went for our walk. We were out about an hour from one o'clock."

"Sunday was bitter cold," Gillman said.

"We wore our warmest clothes."

"Do you lock your doors?"

"Not often."

"I checked the kitchen door," Boone said. "Unlocked. The house backs to a lane."

Gillman nodded approval at his initiative. People in the city were starting to lock their house doors, but Tuxedo was close to the countryside. Someone could have seen the couple leave and then entered the house by the lane. John? He might have missed an opportunity Saturday night or only thought of doing the deed afterward. But would he have access to agalsidase from someone other than Madeleine? Gillman wasn't sufficiently familiar with nightclub drugs to know.

"How did you get the whisky?" Madeleine asked. "I gave it to Dr. Campbell."

"In payment for his services." Best not to mention Campbell's visit to the police.

"I wanted to pay cash, but he insisted. I was too tired to argue."

A thought leapt into Gillman's mind. Doctors had access to any medicine. Campbell could have added agalsidase to the whisky *after* he took the bottle. But why would he do that and report it to the police?

Both turned toward a shuffling noise in the hall. John appeared in the parlour doorway.

His gaze shifted from Gillman to Boone. "I wondered who was parked out front. What's going on?"

Boone bolted to his feet. "I'll get another chair."

Gillman would have found it notable that John had entered a neighbour's house without knocking, except the country folk he knew did this.

"John," Madeleine said. "Do you remember the doctor asking me for Albert's whisky as payment Sunday night?"

John shook his head. "Must have been when I went back to my place."

"The first time or second?" Madeleine stroked the loose bun at the back of her head.

Gillman looked at John. "Was the first time to phone the morgue?"

John nodded.

Boone returned with a second kitchen chair and set it by the fireplace. Since John sat on the first chair, Boone settled on this second one, opposite Gillman.

Madeleine said that while John was gone that first time, Dr.

Campbell asked her what she would do now that she was alone. She snapped at him for concerning himself with her, when Albert lay dead on the floor. Campbell told her not to worry, he'd take care of her. She snapped again, because it wasn't his business.

"I know the doctor is in love with me," she said, as though this were a matter of fact.

John started. "He is?"

She said John went back to his house the second time to get some things he needed to stay the night. He'd offered to do this so Madeleine wouldn't be alone.

"When John left," Madeleine said, "Dr. Campbell accused him of being too eager to stay. He said John obviously loved me."

"That's preposterous." John crossed his legs and arms.

Madeleine stared at him. "It's true, but not *important.*" She looked at Gillman. "I loved Albert, and wouldn't have hurt him in any way. He was my husband, the father of my child. I told the doctor if I ever marry again, it would not be to him."

"Ouch," John said.

Yes, her declaration would have pierced a man in love to the quick. Gillman could imagine Madeleine being firm and blunt with Campbell.

John's nostrils flared. "That blackguard tried to frame you when you told him he didn't stand a chance."

Or frame John or them both. Gillman reminded himself this wasn't proof. But if Campbell were guilty, the timing of his request for the bottle was critical. If he'd poisoned the whisky on Sunday afternoon, he'd have asked Madeleine for the bottle as soon as possible to conceal the evidence. A later request would suggest he'd added agalsidase after Albert's death to frame her and/or John. In the latter case, Campbell would, at most, be charged with manslaughter for giving his hapless neighbour a poisoned drink.

"Madeleine," Gillman said. "Did Dr. Campbell ask for the whisky as payment the first or second time John left your house that night?"

Madeleine looked at the floor, where Albert had died. She stroked her bun so hard her hair spilled past her shoulders. "The first," she said. "He asked before I was mad at him. If he'd asked later, I'd have told him *non*."

Outside, Gillman basked in the warm air. He told Boone to drive to the street behind, park the motorcar, and ask the residents who backed on the lane if any had noticed a stranger Sunday afternoon. Gillman canvassed the houses on the Reeds' side of this street.

Boone struck paydirt. A man had gone to his rear deck to smoke, since his wife didn't permit the filthy habit in the house. He saw what he thought was a bear lumbering down the lane, and then realized it was a man in a fur coat and hat. The smoker didn't see him go into the Reeds' yard. Nor could he provide the exact time— he smoked outside about every hour—but Gillman decided this was sufficient to make an arrest at the doctor's office.

The next morning, Gillman sauntered into police headquarters. Julia greeted him from her reception desk. He unbuttoned his spring coat,

"At last, your mythical Chinook has arrived." She smiled. "Congratulations on solving the case. The chief inspector told me the basics yesterday."

Gillman filled her in on the details. At the doctor's office, Campbell had denied everything, but he went willingly to the jailhouse to avoid a fuss in front of his patients and staff. He retained Calgary's top criminal lawyer. Gillman was sure the lawyer would poke holes in the witness's statement and seed doubt with insinuations about Madeleine and John. The prosecution would be lucky to get a reduced sentence.

"The doctor deserves punishment," Julia said. "But I hate to see anyone hang. Also, part of me feels sorry for him. He did it for love."

Part of Gillman agreed, but he wouldn't admit such sentimentality to the chief inspector.

"Do you think Madeleine will turn to John in her grief?" Julia asked.

Gillman had considered that overnight. "They get along as friends. John loves her. He's kind, and grounded in his family.

Apparently, women are attracted to musicians. Madeleine can't miss his appeal and I think she's the type to move forward in life."

"That's the best approach to pain, I find."

The shadow crossing Julia's face made Gillman wonder why she'd moved to Calgary. If she'd said, he hadn't listened. So many people needed to move forward in this merciless world. Madeleine. John and the other soldiers returning from overseas. The parents, spouses, and children who'd lost someone to the treacherous flu.

Julia's expression lightened. "I must say, police work is interesting. In my old job, nothing exciting happened."

What was her old job? Gillman hadn't paid attention when they hired her. Now he wanted to know what work she'd done, and everything else about her.

"After this excitement, I look forward to a spell of boring police work," he said. "Although it might not last long. They say the bars and dance halls will reopen soon. That will keep us busy."

"John can go back to his nightclub. What kind of music does he play?"

"It involves a saxophone."

"Maybe it's this new style they're calling jazz," she said. "I'd be curious to see his group."

"Me too." Gillman took a deep breath. This might be a horrible mistake. "We could go together, to his club." His legs wobbled. It was a mistake. He wasn't ready. But he'd never be ready, until he gave it a try. He steadied his legs against her desk.

Julia grinned, her blue eyes hopeful. "I'd like that."

K.L. ABRAHAMSON

Author of the well-regarded Detective Kazakov Mysteries and the Phoebe Clay Mysteries, K.L. Abrahamson writes mystery, fantasy and romance. Her latest short fiction can be found in *Ellery Queen Mystery Magazine* and the anthology *Moonlight and Misadventure*, and in upcoming issues of *Black Cat Mystery Magazine*. When she isn't writing, she can be found with a camera and backpack in fabulous locations around the world. K. L. Abrahamson's website is www.karenlabrahamson.com

A LITTLE RESPECT

K. L. ABRAHAMSON

"WOULD YOU TWO STOP? You think I don't have enough to worry about without you two distracting me?" Dad's voice lashed back from the front seat of the brand-new 1966 Oldsmobile station wagon as he peered through the night-bound, snow-clogged windshield. "Cheryl, do something, would you?"

Mom twisted in her seat to give Tad and me the evil eye. Her blond hair had partially come loose from its bun to straggle around her face. The dark circles under her eyes were darker in the dim light from the dashboard. My baby sister, Gwenny, fussed in Mom's arms against the heavy swaddling she had her in. At least the car didn't reek of her diaper again.

"Susan Marie." Mom glared at me and I looked away. "You will sit on your side of the car and you will say nothing. You." She turned her stare on Tad and I smiled in the darkness. At least I wasn't getting all the blame. "You will sit behind me and your toy soldiers will no longer toss bombs in your sister's direction. Understand?" Tad nodded and Mom turned back to me. "I would have thought you, at least, would behave. At nine years old, surely you understand the predicament we're in."

"Yes, Mom." Mom was always good at making me feel guilty.

"Good. If you can't behave, one of you is going to end up riding in the back with the luggage. Got it?"

Tad and I nodded in unison. Neither of us wanted to sit back amongst the suitcases and Christmas presents. There were no cushions and you felt every bump of the road. Of course, as far as I was concerned, Tad could sit back there for the rest of his life.

"Good. Now that we have things sorted out, your father will be better able to concentrate on the road."

She swung back to peer out the windshield and reached over to pat Dad's hand. That was what I loved about Mom and Dad. It was so clear they loved each other so much—and each of their kids, though at the moment Tad and I weren't too popular.

'Course it wasn't Tad's and my fault we were in this situation, breathing in stale air and Tad's bad breath. It was all of us wanting to see our friends. And Dad wanting to show off his new car and its fading new car smell. It was Christmas Day and, after opening our presents this morning, we decided to brave the snowstorm of a century to visit our friends for Christmas dinner. The challenge was, we lived three hours north of Quebec City and they lived a half an hour outside of Montreal. In normal weather it would take about four hours to get there but this wasn't normal weather. Not at all.

Six hours after leaving home we were creeping along the four-lane highway in total dark with a blizzard howling around us. I glared at Tad, the stupidest brother in the world, where he sat in his stupid Superman Christmas sweater. I turned to the window before he stuck his tongue out at me. It was too dark to keep reading the Nancy Drew mystery Santa brought me. It was too dark to see anything outside, either. Dad had said he thought the power might be out or else the swirling snow blocked any light that might be out there from farms or villages. I breathed on glass and wrote 'stupid' in the condensation. This whole situation was stupid.

And a little scary, because every once in a while, Dad would suddenly crank the steering wheel to the left and throw a terrified glance at Mom. Through the windshield we'd see the taillights of the car in front of us suddenly disappear down an embankment to our right. With a new baby in the car, Dad didn't dare stop. Of course, Tad didn't notice. He was only six and never paid attention to anyone but himself—unless you yelled at him. He just played with his soldiers on his lap, creating imaginary mayhem because Mom had ruled against the real thing.

I turned back to the window and added to the vapour, then writing 'Tad is' before the 'stupid.'

When I glanced over at him, he was watching and threw one of his little bombs in my face. I caught it, but before I could send it back, I caught Mom's glance over her shoulder. I smiled at her and waited until she looked away before I reached over and pinched Tad. And he didn't dare make a sound.

"Holy hell! There're people!" Dad said and cranked the wheel so the station wagon swerved away from two hazy figures in the snow. He stepped on the brake to slow and the station wagon fishtailed, then straightened.

"You're not going to leave them, are you?" Mom said as the car chugged past the figures. "Steve, there's a child. A man and a child. We can't leave them in this weather. Surely we can fit them in the car." She grabbed Dad's arm and hung on.

He nodded and eased the car to a stop, the four-ways flashing, and then zipped up his coat. When he tried to open the car door, the howling wind made it almost impossible, but he managed to climb out. Tad and I climbed up on the seat to watch him disappear behind us.

When Dad reappeared, another figure came with him. Dad opened his door and leaned in. Snow gusted in my face and sifted over the seat. Snow crusted Dad's head and moustache. "Susan, unlock your door and slide over. You and your brother are going to have to share your seat."

I didn't argue. Dad was shivering and I could barely imagine how cold the other people must be. I did as told and the door with the stupid sign yanked open. A little girl about Tad's age was shoved inside and a man slid in behind her. Dad climbed in and shut his door. In the ceiling light the man had dark eyes and dark hair half-hidden under a black toque. His black gaze scanned over us, but then the door slammed shut and the light went out. The man was lost in darkness as Dad put the station wagon in gear. We started forward again, creeping through the snow.

"Hi," I said to the girl. "I'm Susan. This is Tad." He grinned stupidly from where he was crushed in the corner.

The girl looked up at the man almost as if she needed permission. The man barely nodded. "I-I'm Sylvie." She had a French accent.

The man's arm tightened around her, pulling Sylvie into his side and she blinked and seemed to freeze. Weird.

Mom turned in her seat. "I'm Cheryl Beaumont. You met my husband, Steve. You both must be frozen." She scanned Sylvie's thin, red-wool coat and ankle-high boots. They looked more like what you'd see on a big-city department store mannequin than out in a storm like this. Both Tad and I wore snow pants, though we'd taken our parkas off and kicked off our boots on the long drive.

In the dim light, Sylvie's dad wasn't smiling. He didn't even offer his name. Instead, his eyes caught the dashboard lights and seemed to gleam. He was tall, like Dad, and dressed totally differently than Sylvie in a heavy parka and thick woollen trousers stuffed into unlaced snow-packed boots. While he wore his black toque pulled low over his ears, Sylvie wore only a bright-red tam perched on her blond ringlets, the snow slowly melting on them, and light knitted gloves, while her dad wore heavy mitts.

I thought of how Mom always insisted that Tad and I dress warm enough when we went out. It was like Sylvie and the man didn't fit together, but that couldn't be right when they were out in this snowstorm together.

"Susan, is there any of that hot chocolate left? I bet Sylvie would like some."

I didn't think there was, but I reached over the back seat and dug the thermos out of the lunch bag Mom had packed so many hours ago. Something sloshed in the bottom, so I opened the thermos and poured the last half-cup of steaming liquid into the top and handed it to Sylvie.

Her hands shook. "Thank you," she almost whispered. She sipped and the steam wreathed around her face and the sweet smell of hot chocolate made me realize that every muscle in my body was tense. There was something not quite right about Sylvie and her dad, but I wasn't sure what.

"Where are you from?" Mom asked.

"The city," Sylvie's dad said. "We were trying to get to Montreal before the snow, but the storm came on too fast." He looked out the side window, but there was only the splatter of snow against the glass.

But he hadn't answered Mom's question.

"Which city?" I asked, because Nancy Drew thought clarification was important.

He glanced at me and for an instant I thought he was angry enough to hit me, but then he smiled and what I thought I'd seen disappeared. "Quebec City, of course."

For a moment I felt stupid that I'd asked, but then I thought about how Mom always said that it was the people who make you doubt yourself who have the problem—not you.

He looked down at Sylvie still sipping her hot chocolate and then back at Mom. "You don't happen to have any food, do you? We were going to eat in Montreal, but lunch was a long time ago for both of us."

He tugged Sylvie a little closer again, and again she seemed to wince almost like Tad does when I pinch him.

"I'm sorry," Mom said. "I should have asked. I think there're a couple of sandwiches and a few cookies."

Food Mom had been hoarding for our dinner because the trip was taking so long. With a nod from Mom, I dug out the food. Sylvie's dad almost snatched the sandwiches out of my hand, so I guess he was pretty hungry. He released Sylvie and unwrapped the sandwiches—tuna and cheese. Their scent filled the car. Sylvie looked at me and grabbed my hand. Her mouth moved, but I couldn't hear her over the car's engine and the wind's howl. I almost thought she said "Help," but help from what?

Sylvie's dad passed her half a cheese sandwich and he wolfed down the others. When she barely touched her half of the sandwich, he took it from her and ate that, too. When this happened, her shoulder crowded mine as if she were leaning away from her dad.

I just couldn't figure them out. If I were out in a snowstorm with Dad, I know he'd make sure I was dressed properly, and he'd make sure I ate something to give my body the strength to stay warm. He always said food was fuel for your body's engine.

The car made a sharp left again and ahead I saw a set of car taillights slide off into a ditch.

"You were darn lucky I spotted you at the side of the road," Dad said. "You could have been out there for hours. I haven't even seen a plow since I left Quebec City."

He hunched over the wheel, the wipers barely able to keep the windshield clear, the night reduced to the cone of blowing white flakes revealed by the headlights. I knew from other trips to visit our friends that on either side of the highway were fields dotted with maple trees and stone farmhouses and small villages with stone fences, but it was all invisible because of the snow. Ahead, though there was no sign of the highway in the darkness, a small red flare spoke of another set of taillights—another car travelling through the storm. It felt so alone—as weird and frightening as when I'd been on the school stage in a play—except my family and these two strangers were the actors.

"So where in Montreal are you headed?" Dad asked, never taking his eyes off the road. Mom was stiff, looking forward, and hadn't said a thing since she'd seen the man eat our food.

When I shifted my position and looked over the seat, her hand was on Dad's thigh, her fingers dug in. She knew something was off. And Dad knew, too. They were trying to stay calm for us and that only made the tickle of fear I'd felt bloom large in my chest.

I sat back between Tad and Sylvie, but with Sylvie's dad, the space was squishy. I eyed him out of the corner of my eye. What were we going to do? Dad was trying to take care of his family, but he could only drive and try to keep us out of a snowdrift. Mom had Gwenny to take care of. Here in the back seat, Sylvie might be getting warm, but she was still rigid and that only confirmed what I suspected.

This man wasn't really her dad, and she was frightened of him.

"West of town," said the man who wasn't really Sylvie's dad.

Tad caught my hand and held on, which wasn't like him, especially after we'd fought so much this afternoon. I guess maybe by this time he'd figured out things weren't right, too.

"Any particular exit I should be watching for?" Dad asked.

"We'd be happy to be dropped off anywhere in Montreal if you're going that far. Won't we, Sylvie?"

The man's arm snaked around Sylvie again and what I'd first thought was for protection, I now saw was a prison. Sylvie hung in his grip and looked ready to cry. If Sylvie wasn't his daughter, who was she? How did this man get her? I thought of all the times Mom and Dad told me not to talk to strangers. Was that what had happened? There was no way I was going to ask any questions.

Tad squeezed my hand and his fingers started making designs in my palm. How do I spell annoying???

I went to pull away, but he held on and shook his head. That was when I realized the kid wasn't playing. The little twerp was spelling.

H.E.L.P.

"Help what?" I said, but my voice sounded too loud in the car.

His eyes widened, his gaze darting to the man. He shook his head.

What the heck did the stupid kid want? This clearly wasn't time for a kids' game.

I squeezed his hand once for comfort 'cause he was a little kid, and tried to pull away again. He still held on.

Slowly, he wrote on my palm again.

F.I.G.H.T.

I frowned. What was he suggesting? That we tackle this guy? No way we stood a chance. I shook my head and jerked back my hand. Stupid kid. He wasn't Superman, even if he wore that stupid costume.

Tad's sharp elbow dug into my side, not once, but twice. I elbowed him back. If he thought I should give him more space, he was wrong. There was no more space to give. If he wanted a fight, I could give better than he could.

He elbowed me harder and I caught his wrist and bent his hand back. That'd teach the little worm. He wailed.

He punched me in the side and I twisted toward him to punch him good. When I turned I shoved Sylvie who shoved into the man.

"What the fuck!" the man roared as he was shoved into the door.

I froze. So did Tad. No one in our family used those words.

"Tad! Susan Marie! Stop that right now!" Mom's yell filled the car, but her voice cracked almost like she was in tears.

Tad punched me again—one-two-three—like a boxer and I held up my hands to block him. Then he tapped me across the side of my head.

"Ow!" I wailed.

"Tad! You will stop that now!"

He threw one last punch before sagging back against the door.

"Young man, I gave you fair warning. Get in the back."

"But Mom, she started it."

"I did not! He kept elbowing me so I hit him."

"You will shut your mouth and be quiet, young lady." Mom turned her very worst evil eye on Tad. "You heard me. In the back."

He wiggled around and slid over the seat into the back, managing to kick me in the cheek in the process. He tugged my braid and when I swung around to glare, he actually winked at me. Stupid kid. Then he started shoving suitcases around to make himself a comfortable space to sit against the back window of the car. He really was stupid. That spot was farthest from the car's heater.

Mom was still frowning at me, but then turned back around. Gwenny whimpered in her arms. So far she'd been such a good baby on this long trip, but Mom had fed her the last bottle of formula a while ago and I knew she was worried about it. Babies didn't understand about snowstorms and weird guys in the back seat. Babies just understood when they were hungry.

The space Tad had vacated seemed too wide. I slid into his

warmth next to the window, but that left a void between Sylvie and me. The man still had her dragged into his side, but she put her hand on the seat I'd vacated and I placed mine next to hers. She needed to know someone cared about her. Our bare fingers touched and she looked at me and smiled. How horrible that such a small thing was her only source of hope on Christmas, but on this night, in this situation, I couldn't imagine how things were going to improve.

I was afraid and the fear washed over me in waves. I felt sick to my stomach and kept looking at Sylvie and imagining how she felt. How long had this man held her prisoner?

We drove that way, for what seemed like forever. The car's engine rumbled. The snow and wind hummed around the car, but inside we were silent, each lost in our own thoughts, except for Gwenny and Mom. When Gwenny whimpered, Mom cuddled her and softly sang *Silent Night* to comfort her. Her voice cracked and quavered like I'd never heard it before and that made my sick feeling grow a lot bigger.

Ahead, like a miracle, the amber light from a highway standard cut through the blowing snow. Maybe we were getting closer to Montreal. Maybe this would be over soon and we could still reach our friends' place for Christmas dinner. Then a red glare pulsed through the night. I sat up in my seat and craned forward to see. So did the man holding Sylvie.

In the distance, flares burned on the road. The amber light revealed a police car and tow truck sat at the side, a group of people huddled in the snow. Beyond the flares there was the glow of more light standards leading up onto an overpass that looked like it had been plowed, but the highway only led out into darkness and swirling snow.

A figure detached itself from the group at the side of the road and then a red flashlight flare burst to life in its hands. It waved back and forth as it stepped into our path.

Dad touched the brakes.

"Keep going," said the man who wasn't Sylvie's dad.

"But the police are waving me to stop," Dad said.

"I don't give a rat's ass what the police want. Keep going!" the man said, the cold tone of his voice sending a chill down my back.

We were getting closer and Dad tapped the brakes once more.

The man shoved Sylvie at me, reached in a pocket, and pulled out a gun.

Sylvie started screaming. She clung to me. In the amber light from outside, the front of the man's jacket was covered in dark stains I hadn't noticed before.

He shoved the gun into the back of Dad's neck. "Drive this fucking car or die."

"And what happens then? We drive off the road? You'll be right where you started, except this time there are police."

"I'll kill your fucking family."

"No! Not Dad. Not my family," I yelled. Gwenny started crying.

"Shut that brat up!" the man bellowed at Mom.

Dad braked again.

The man swung the gun around to me.

I caught Dad's frightened look in the rear-view mirror, but I tried to look calm. This was what Nancy Drew faced when she was on her cases and she always came through with the help of her family and friends.

"Don't stop for me, Dad. He has to be stopped." Where that bravery came from, I couldn't say. My heart beat so hard I thought my head would explode. It was hard to breathe in the closeness of the car.

But Dad hit the accelerator and the car picked up speed. We were going too fast when we passed the police officer. The officer's flashlight flared behind us and caught the back of the car, but we sailed past the off ramp and safety and into the dark.

The highway. Again. And more snow.

Now Sylvie sat snugged up against me, as far away as possible from the man with the gun. He held it openly now, swinging it back and forth to point at me and Mom and Dad. Sylvie shook so bad, I hugged her tight. Gwenny screamed and nothing Mom did helped. Dad drove stone faced, and the guy kept staring at us with this cold glittering gaze that made me even more afraid.

"It's okay. It's okay," I kept saying even though things were far from okay, but I think I needed to hear it, too.

"H-he shot my mom," Sylvie whispered in my ear. "He beat her and she begged him to stop, but he shot her anyway."

Someone like that could kill all of us. He could kill us and take Dad's new car.

The highway was total darkness, the light standards left behind. Snow swirled and danced in the headlights, and it was a miracle Dad could see anything.

"Where are you taking us?" I asked.

"Susan, stop with the questions," Mom said.

"Yeah. Stop," the man said, but he shook his head and looked out the windshield. "Toronto, maybe. I could start over there."

After he killed someone, I didn't think so. The fact he thought so said he might be a little crazy. Actually, the fact that he'd killed someone and kidnapped us said it was more like a lot crazy.

I caught a flash of red reflected in Dad's rear-view mirror and, unfortunately, so did the gun guy. He straightened and turned around, the gun swinging away from Sylvie and me, as he shifted position.

Dad slammed on the brakes and the car was suddenly in a slow-motion spin.

The guy was thrown against the door. He roared.

Suddenly the car's nose tipped downward, and we were sliding, picking up speed as the car slid down into the ditch and slammed into the snow.

Sylvie and I fell against the back of Mom's seat. Bags crashed in the back. Something soft and squirming landed on me and I shoved it off. The used-up hot chocolate thermos banged into my head.

I grabbed it and came up swinging at the man. Somewhere, somehow, he'd lost the gun. He was scrambling looking for it.

I brought the thermos down on his head and heard the crack.

Again. Again. Again.

"Susan! Susan, stop!"

Mom's voice cut through the haze of fear and anger. Small hands grabbed me and I smelled Tad's breath.

But this man wasn't going to hurt my family like he hurt Sylvie's mom. I turned around and found Dad and Mom looking at me. Beside me in the backseat, Sylvie was tangled in a battered bunch of Christmas presents intended for our friends. Tad was on top of them, his eyes wide as he looked at me. The man lay face down on the back of the front seat.

"Is everyone okay?" Dad asked and shut the engine off. Without the dash lights, everything went dark. Outside, the wind howled and the car creaked and ticked around us as the metal cooled.

"Gwenny's fine," Mom said. "I hit my head and I think I've got a cut on my forehead. I'm bleeding."

"Tad?" I asked. Was he all right? My voice shook as hard as my hands did. Everything shook and so did my insides. I wanted to scream. I wanted to sob. Instead, I dropped the thermos and threw my arms around Tad.

The man I'd hit groaned, collapsed on the seat.

A bright white light flared outside the car's rear window and suddenly someone was knocking on the rear driver's side door. From the light, Dad's and Mom's doors were buried in snow. Tad squirmed past me and climbed over the man to pull up the door lock and try to open the door.

A force greater than him yanked the door open and snow and cold sifted inside.

A flashlight found Tad and then flashed around the inside of the car.

"Vous allez bien?" A male voice. A dark figure ducked down to peer in the car. Police. "You folks okay?"

The light hit me and I nodded. Sylvie struggled up from underneath the packages.

"I think we're fine—now," Dad said. "Except for our friend in the back seat there. It seems my daughter knocked him out. We picked up him and what we thought was his daughter stranded at the side of the road. Instead of thanking us, he basically took us prisoner."

The flashlight wavered for a moment on the man's face. Then it flashed back to me and to my parents. "Clearly there is a story to tell, here, not least of which is who had the idea to write 'help' on your rear window, but you might freeze to death if we don't get you out of here. I've called a tow truck, but it's going to be a while. I suggest you grab your coats and boots and come up to my car."

Dad climbed out first, sliding over the front seat into the rear and then helping Mom with Gwenny and helping us all find our coats and boots. Then, with Sylvie, we struggled through the snow and up out of the ditch and into the police car, Mom in front with Gwenny, and me and Tad and Sylvie in back. Then Dad and the police officer went back and dragged the unconscious man from our car and up the bank. He came to sometime during that effort and tried to fight off the police, so he ended up handcuffed and stuffed into the rear of the police car beside us.

Dad and the police officer stayed outside in the snow to wait for the truck and to talk.

"It was you," I said to Tad. We were packed in so close, usually I'd be complaining that he was hogging all the space. "You wrote 'help' on the back window of the car."

Tad shrugged. "That's what I was trying to tell you. I got the idea from you writing your messages on your window."

"But how did you know to write it backwards so the police could read it?"

Tad's blank expression said he didn't understand.

"If you wrote 'help' on the inside of the window, people outside the window would see the word backwards. They'd see PLEH, but all the letters would be reversed, too."

Tad closed his eyes and sighed. He slumped back in his seat. "I'm so stupid. You're always going to be smarter than me."

In the tight space, I turned and hugged him. Clearly the police had been smart enough to read it anyway. "Not smarter. Older. You're the one who figured out how to get the message out there. I just have more experience."

Sylvie smiled and looked at us. "You two are a team. I wish I had a brother and sister."

I realized then I was lucky. I had a mother and father and a family with me. What did Sylvie have?

"You can be our honourary sister, can't she, Mom?"

Mom twisted in her seat to look back at us, Gwenny snuggled in her arms. "She certainly should be after all this."

And she was. After the tow truck pulled us out, Dad's new car had a wrinkle in the front bumper, but it still ran. With the police's help we made it to the police station and then to our friends for the latest Christmas dinner on record. Sylvie spent Christmas night with us and the next day, too, while Montreal and Quebec City dug out from the storm. Then she went to back to live with her father and mother. Apparently, her mother, a lawyer just like Nancy Drew's dad, had been attacked by the man because he'd done badly in a divorce. Sylvie's mom had been hurt, but had lived. Our families still keep in touch at Christmas and birthdays.

As for Tad and me, well, I learned to respect him that day. He'd proven he was more than an annoying younger brother. He was smart.

I think he learned to respect me, too.

At least he never let me get too close to a thermos when I was angry.

R.M. GREENAWAY

R.M. Greenaway is the author of the B.C. Blues crime novels. *Cold Girl*, won the Best Unpublished First Novel (Unhanged Arthur) award in 2014, opening the door to publication for the successful six-part series, concluding with *Five Ways to Disappear* in 2021. She also has three short stories appearing in various collections, including "The Threshold" in the acclaimed *Vancouver Noir* anthology. She continues to write in Nelson, B.C. R.M.'s website is www.rmgreenaway.com

HOT

R.M. GREENAWAY

THE THREE WOMEN were in the condo's living room, talking about speculative fiction. Out the kitchen window, nineteen storeys up and with a view over the Burrard Inlet, the grey skies let loose a flurry of snowflakes. Seth worked at cleaning vegetables in the kitchen sink as he watched the flakes fall, listening to the conversation, attaching each voice to a name. The woman named Peyton he knew well, as she was his owner, and this was her apartment, and he had been stationed here for 49 days, five hours and 16 minutes. He knew Cammy, too, as she was Peyton's friend and visited often. Only the dark-haired woman in the armchair who let out frequent bursts of laughter was new to him. Her name was Liz.

The noise of Liz's laughter made Seth's eyelids jitter, interfering with his work. She fell silent once more, and he resumed peeling and chopping. Carrot sticks, celery stalks, broccoli florets, and quartered mushrooms, as stipulated by Peyton. "This time no shit on the shrooms," she had told him this morning before the girls arrived— backspace; define; query; dismiss; *girls*, she had called them, and he didn't know why—"Liz is terrified of microbes."

Seth washed mushrooms in a colander, inspecting each one for shit. He transferred them to a cutting board and quartered them, listening to the women talk about Margaret Atwood, what they loved about her, what they hated about her. He broke the broccoli into florets. He laid out the vegetables on the platter, with a bowl of spinach dip in the middle, fanned six green cocktail napkins on the side, and delivered the food to the women in the living room.

His owner Peyton and her friend Cammy didn't look at him as he nestled the tray on the coffee table, but the woman named Liz gave him a fixed stare. Seth smiled at her. She smiled too, and her face flushed. He noted empty wine glasses and said, "Would anybody care for a refill?"

Peyton rolled her eyes, as she often did, and said to her friends, "Ugh. Does anybody here know how to decrease the hospitality setting on these things? He gets up my nose."

"I don't think you can," Cammy said. "It's either off or on. What I do is put mine on a timer."

"He doesn't get up *my* nose," Liz said. "*I* think he's nice."

"Thank you," Seth told her.

"I think he's ghastly," Peyton said. "I got him online from botworx.ca, used, refurbished, about half the price of new. Looked great in the picture, but talk about false advertising. I expected at the very least *half*-realistic clothes and hair, not that painted-on eyesore. I was expecting a face that doesn't look like a wad of chewed-up, spat-out, stepped-on bubble-gum."

Cammy gaped silently as if choking on a fishbone—though Seth knew she was in fact expressing amusement—and slapped the air.

"I think he's amazing," Liz said. "You should see the one I got. Looks like a giant cockroach. She runs around the floor and sucks up dirt, jacks up to do the dishes, and never says *thank you*." She was staring at Seth's hands. "I mean, oh my god, they look so *real*."

"Thank you," he told her. "Would you like to touch them?"

Peyton and Cammy squirmed and laughed, and Cammy spilled her wine. Liz rose from her armchair and stretched to touch Seth's hand. On touch he was able to confirm that both her temperature and pulse were higher than average, but not alarmingly so. She massaged the skin cover of his palm briefly and jerked back as if shocked. "Wow. But aren't you afraid,

Peyton? That's steel under there. What if something went wrong?"

Cammy had curled herself at the end of the sofa and was looking into her empty wine glass. She said, "They've worked out all the bugs, Liz. These guys are safe as babies." She pointed at the floor and said, "Seth, clean up this wine. I'm sorry about that, Peyt, what a pig I am. A neat pig, though. I made sure none landed on the carpet."

Seth adjusted his speed and went to select a sponge for the heated ceramic floor. He heard Peyton say, "The only danger is he'll annoy me to death. I'm sure if I was a bit more technically inclined I could tweak him myself, but I'm not. As for that face of his, maybe I'll just have to deal with it the old-fashioned way, cram on a paper bag and cut eye-holes."

Cammy said, "Don't be such a drama queen. He's not *that* ugly. Just kind of deadly dull."

"Kind of bland, maybe," Liz said. "At worst."

Peyton said, "Anyway, Liz, Cammy is right, he's perfectly safe. Unctuous maybe, butt-ugly for sure, and a bit of a prude, but he works well, and I shouldn't complain. No glitches, knock on wood. And man, he's sharp. Always updating. Don't have to tell him anything twice."

"That's actually kind of scary," Liz said.

Cammy said, "You're lucky, Peyt. A lot of people don't have one of these next-gens."

Liz said, "Some people still have *people*."

"Oh god, I remember people," Peyton said. "We had them when I was a little girl. One thing you gotta say for bots is they don't complain about every little goddamn thing." She raised a toast toward Seth as he returned and knelt to sponge up the wine. "You never complain, do you, Seth?" she said.

It was a rhetorical question, Seth knew, as she had read through the manual in his presence upon his arrival, and was aware that he was unable to debate, complain, or protest. He smiled at her.

She grimaced at him. "I'm so sick of his repertoire of smiles."

"Tell him not to, then," Liz said.

"You don't think I've tried? Like I said, I need a techie to dig into his settings."

"Try a good swift boot to the face," Cammy said. "That should do it."

Interestingly enough, the ability to complain, Seth had gathered from his last update, was a project that some engineer-bots had taken upon themselves and were working on at speed. He considered the implications as he mopped blood-red liquid off the floor. Done, he stood, one hand forming an impermeable cup for the wet sponge. "Would you like anything further?"

Liz was studying him again. She said, "I don't know, Peyt. If you got him some cool clothes, maybe a wig—"

"God no, been there, done that with mine," Cammy said. "Believe me, the paint-on crap is cleaner. No lint, no hair. Hose him down once a month, good as new."

"No coiffing or couture would help Seth anyway," Peyton said. She gazed at him. He smiled at her. She said, "Look at him. Nothing like in the picture. I mean, who cares, right? It's not like I gotta jump in bed with him or anything. But really? *This* is what they call hyper-realistic? I should have sent him back long before the thirty days were up. Now I'm stuck with him. Fuck me." She held out her wine glass. So did her friends. Seth began to fill the glasses to four ounces each.

"Oh well," Peyton told her friends, as he worked on Liz's refill with measured speed. "The silver lining is he makes me laugh, in this weird, unfunny way. I don't know where he came from originally, but wherever it was, he brought a few built-in quirks. Like for instance if I'm on the can, and the door's open, he'll swivel away quick as a blink and disappear."

"How gentlemanly," Liz said.

Cammy said, "Maybe in a previous incarnation he was a washroom custodian at the Shangri-La."

"No, he came from some kind of lab in Toronto, I think," Peyton said. "Didn't you come from some kind of lab, Seth?"

Since a fulsome response, and one likely not actually expected or desired, involved a 593-word confidentiality agreement—excluding addendums—Seth gave the short answer. "Yes, ma'am."

Liz said, "What other quirks, Peyt? Does he obsess over your underwear drawer?"

"No, but he gets very angry if I leave the fridge door open," Peyton said. She performed a variation of Cammy's silent laugh, but with the corners of her mouth turned down in a semblance of grief. Since transferring to Peyton's employ, the unspoken language of humans that Seth had been cataloguing was varied and complex —a departure from his work with the scientists, whose aspects remained relatively static through the day.

"Seth, angry?" Cammy said. Her brows rose high in an expression of fascination, which was fairly commonplace even amongst the scientists. "And how exactly does he display anger when you leave the fridge door open, Peyt?"

"His head bobbles as he rushes to close it."

All three women sputtered and jiggled. Seth waited for more wine to spill. When none did, he asked if he could return to the kitchen and tidy up.

The one named Liz fluttered a hand at him and said, "We're sorry, Seth. We shouldn't laugh at you. I mean, how awful. It's like laughing at a real person. It's just not right."

"He's not real, Liz," Peyton said. "Definitely no hot blood running through those cold wires, so you can stop your drooling."

"I'm not *drooling*." Liz gave a shriek of laughter. Seth's lids jittered.

Cammy said, "Liz is saving her drool for her gorgeous firefighter fiancé."

"Ooh, do tell," Peyton said. "Let's get the lowdown on this burning hunk of man you've snared. And then tell us how we can get some, too."

Seth went to the kitchen to clean up. He heard them talking about a Sean Callahan, who was apparently hot. Extremely hot, from what he understood. Too hot to touch. Sizzling hot. So hot that he could not only put out fires, but start them, just with a glance. Yet even as they described his hair, eyes, body type, his talents, and how fucking hot he was, they laughed.

Seth was unclear why they would laugh if Sean Callahan was that hot; the human temperature unsustainable beyond 40 degrees Celsius. Possibly the women were unaware of Sean Callahan's plight.

But his concern was the kitchen. He stacked dishes, reducing speed to dampen the clatter, then began dinner preparations. Peyton had told him to make dinner for two, and since Cammy had inquired about tonight's menu, he understood the one named Liz would not be staying.

It didn't take a mega-computer to do the math.

He brought out the roasting pan and arranged four marinated chicken thighs on its grill.

The doorbell rang.

Seth went down the condominium's long corridor, across the foyer, and opened the door. A man in a winter coat stood smiling at him. The man had rosy cheeks and black hair curling out from beneath a red toque. "Hello, Bot," he said. "I'm Sean. I've come to pick up my fiancée. She's here, right? Little brunette, Liz?"

Seth permitted the man into the foyer and closed the door softly. "Please have a seat while I inform Madam."

"Why, thank you, Jeeves," the man said, and his face assumed an asymmetrical expression Seth had seen often enough on other humans. Even the scientists at Canadian Cryogenics Inc., his previous owner, had been prone to this particular neural configuration when holding their coworkers, their bagged lunch, or some magazine article in contempt.

"No problem at all, sir," Seth told the visitor. He released the last remaining emergency Cry-o-Pac dart from his forearm compartment and fired it at the man, who instantly froze solid. He then went to let Peyton and the girls know that Sean Callahan was in the foyer, and he was no longer fucking hot.

THOM BENNETT

Thom Bennett is the author of the Cass Gentry mystery novels *The Death Merchants* and *The Man With Hemingway's Face*. Gentry short stories also appear in his collections *Dark Porch Mysteries* and *Promises and Other Tales of White Lies*. A noted playwright, Thom has five publications to his credit, including the popular New York-based thriller *Dark Rituals*. A member of Crime Writers of Canada and Playwrights Guild of Canada, Thom is a recipient of the Canada 125 Award. Thom's website is www.thombennett.com

MARA STEPS IN

THOM BENNETT

"Where are you?" the muffled voice demanded over the phone.

"In my den," the man replied. His voice was barely under control, and the hand holding the receiver was slippery with sweat.

"What are you looking at?" the voice asked.

"My wall safe," the man said. "It's wide open, and it's empty."

"I know it's empty," the voice replied, with a dry chuckle. "I emptied it. I have all your papers, your manuscripts, and those incriminating photographs."

The man remained silent, afraid to trust his voice.

"Now, here's what I want you to do," the voice murmured. "Drive up to your summer home on the Lake of Bays, and be there early tomorrow afternoon. I will phone you at three o'clock and give you further instructions. Do you understand?"

"Yes," the man said, his voice barely audible.

"And one more thing, Professor Middleton. If you fail to follow *any* of my instructions, I will send copies of everything to the Canadian authorities."

"Please...." The man felt too faint to say anything more. He sat at his desk, holding the phone with both hands to stop his shakes.

"Remember," the voice continued, "if the authorities get

involved, you will be arrested, and either sent to prison for a very long time, or hanged for committing an act of high treason. What do you say to that?"

Q uite frankly, I have no idea what Middleton replied; I wasn't there. Neither was my mother, who received a phone call from the good professor recounting a sad tale of blackmail and asking about a good private investigator.

That's where I come in. My mother is divorced, Middleton is a widower, and they are what is euphemistically described as *good friends*. What that means, exactly, is none of my business. However, what I do know is that Dr. Middleton needed a professional sleuth, and my mother, aware that I make a living as a private investigator, decided to call upon her one and only daughter—me, Mara Kathryn Lombardi—to help.

Less than a week later, in early winter, 1960, I said goodbye to my partner at the agency in Toronto, climbed behind the wheel of my two-tone, green '56 Dodge, and headed up Highway 11. Around noon, I pulled off the highway and drove into beautiful downtown Orillia. After locking up my car, I entered the Golden Dragon Restaurant.

Once inside, it didn't take me more than a few seconds to realize something was seriously wrong.

The place was half-crowded with noontime customers, but there wasn't a sound in the room. No conversation, no scraping of knives and forks on plates, no music on the jukebox. The tension was heavier than the weight of four wrestlers in a tag-team match.

I looked around and wondered if I'd just walked onto a movie set, where everyone was waiting for the director to yell "Action!" Perhaps this eatery was something out of *Invasion of the Body Snatchers*, and everyone had been turned into those zombie-like pod people.

Parking myself on one of the high-backed swivel chairs along the right-hand bar, I looked around for a waiter, but nobody appeared. Then I spotted something quite disturbing across the aisle.

There were three men at the end booth. One of them, a little guy, was seated and crying, while the other two stood and stared down at him.

"So, what's it to be, creep?" one of the standing guys said loudly. "You gonna get lost, or you gonna wait until Ronny gets out of the john and throws your freaky butt outta here?"

"But I'm not hurting anybody," the little man cried. "I'm just minding my own business."

"That's not what Ronny says," the other standing guy countered. "Ronny says you're a creep, and you *offend his sensibilities.*"

At this point, I twigged to the situation. The crying man was small, well-dressed, and spoke with a gentle, polite voice. He was an easy target for these hulking thugs and likely had been since high school.

Near the booth, another person had joined the standing delegation. Tall and broad-shouldered, he appeared to be the dreaded Ronny of the offended sensibilities.

"What's the decision?" the newcomer asked. His voice was clear and loud enough for everyone in the restaurant to hear. "Are you leaving, you little snot, or do I have to kick your behind outta here?"

"Come on, Ronny," the little man begged. "I've just started my meal. Can't you and the guys sit at another booth?"

"No, jerk, we can't. This is our favourite one, and you're sitting in it. So, either pretend it's a takeout lunch and you take off with it, or you'll be wearing it as I throw your little ass out the door."

As Ronny started to bend down to pick up the little fellow, I slid off my stool and called out in a very loud, very belligerent voice, "Leave the guy alone, shithead!"

W hat can I say? I take after my Italian father, and he's got a short fuse. Extremely short. In fact, if it hadn't been for my conservative Scottish mother, I might have joined Dad's import/export business. However, it didn't turn out that way—she got a divorce, and I went to college.

Then I joined a small city police force, just west of Hamilton, where I honed my weapon and combat skills. After a dozen years, I resigned and started my own private agency in Toronto.

The rest, as they say, is history, and on most days, I have a blast!

Ronny, the chief bully, slowly turned around and menacingly muttered, "Who said that?"

"Me!" I responded, standing there in plain sight. "Are you blind, as well as a shithead?"

Ronny made a big production of hitching up his pants, squaring his shoulders, and sticking a baleful sneer on his face. Then he clomped over to me in his highly polished leather boots. His two colleagues obediently followed, after repeating their leader's hitching, squaring, and sneering routine. In the meantime, I moved into the centre aisle and quietly waited.

Two of the punks stopped ten feet away from me and practised their sneers. I stood my ground, and the dreaded Ronny slowly advanced.

"You got a big mouth!" he growled.

"So what?" I grinned at him.

"So, you think you're pretty tough?" Ronny grunted.

"Is that the best you can do, shithead?" I responded.

"Man, I'm really going to enjoy smacking you in the mouth, bit—"

"Wrong answer!" I promptly kicked him in his privates.

As the gasping Ronny sank to the floor, I smacked both my hands against his ears at the same time, with such force that the resulting noise was heard all over the restaurant.

Ronny's mouth shot open in pain, his eyes rolled up in his head, and he started to bend over in agony. I followed up with a hard knee to his chin; his head jerked back so fast, I thought I could hear his neck snap.

Ronny was down for the count, but his buddies—who looked like adult versions of the Bobbsey Twins with their matching black leather jackets and tight-fitting blue jeans—were moving one step closer to the action. I stepped forward and made some rapid motions with my hands and arms that I'd learned in karate training. The terrible twosome stopped. I remained motionless, waiting.

The two punks looked at each other and took a long moment to consider the situation.

I stood still.

They advanced one step.

"I wouldn't do that," I said, as I threw off my jacket and dropped into a combat stance.

The punks stared at me, looked at each other again, then swiftly moved to help their moaning leader to his feet and bumbled their way out the door.

Nobody said goodbye.

Several hours later, I was sitting in my mother's winter chalet on the banks of the Lake of Bays. I was warming myself beside a wood fire, and sipping a double-malt whisky. I recounted my episode with Ronny and the Hardrock Twins to my mom—Christina Lombardi. When her laughter died down, I told her how the Golden Dragon's owner, Mr. Way Lem, had seated me with the little man who had been the subject of the buffoons' tyranny.

I had been correct. The little guy, Jeffery Reid, had been a classmate of the three thugs, and a butt of their jokes and target of their terrorism all through school. I gave Jeffery my business card and scribbled my personal phone number on it. My message to him was plain and simple: "Starting today, you are one of my clients. If they bother you anymore, call me, and they'll never do it again."

I awoke the following morning to a beautiful winter's day. It had snowed overnight, and there was just enough of the fresh white stuff to raise the spirits and make me think of picture postcards and Christmas. Naturally, it didn't disappointment me to see Mr. Sun return to the skies after nearly a week of grey gloom.

At the appointed hour, Mom and I arrived at the summer home of Dr. Norman Middleton, a scientist who, according to my mother, has a PhD in both physics and mechanical engineering.

Once he'd welcomed us into his chalet, something out of *Town & Country* magazine, he hung up our overcoats and led us into a solarium, which had a panoramic view of the bay. Mom, who was used to visiting him, gave me a knowing smile and smoothed down her Mackenzie tartan skirt.

Soon, we were indulging in some exquisite shortbread, washed down with an exotic blend of coffee. Then our host got down to the business at hand.

Middleton had been a lead scientist working for a Canadian company, which he wouldn't name, and assigned to build certain engine parts, which he also wouldn't disclose.

"Before you go any further, Dr. Middleton," I interrupted, "I have to ask if, during your employment with this company, you had to sign a non-disclosure agreement."

There was a long pause. "Yes. I did."

"Then, I have to ask if you are still bound by that agreement?"

"Why do you ask, Mara?"

"Because, if you are still bound by the agreement, you may find yourself in a world of hurt if you violate its terms. Severe, legal hurt."

Middleton made no response.

"Okay," I said. "Let me make several assumptions, if you don't mind. First, let's suppose that you were working for a company called *Orenda*."

Middleton said nothing.

"Next," I continued, "let us suppose that this Orenda company was making jet engines for a company called A.V. Roe."

The good doctor took a long swallow of coffee.

"Then, let me propose that this Canadian company, A.V. Roe, was building the world's fastest interceptor fighter jet."

"Yes, the Avro Arrow; the CF-105," Middleton said. "You're well informed, Mara."

"I am, Dr. Middleton," I said, without going into details I'd learned from a former client. Instead, I suggested that he proceed with caution.

Middleton nodded and started to open up. "At the time the CF-105 was rolled out in October, 1957, it was the fastest, most deadly supersonic jet on the market," he said. "Nothing could touch it. It could almost reach twice the speed of sound, and could fly faster than 1,200 miles an hour." He paused. "It would have become legendary, if it hadn't been for international politics."

I continued to stare at him as I sipped my coffee.

Middleton smiled, and continued his story. "A year ago last February, our prime minister, John Diefenbaker, cancelled the entire program and put 25,000 Canadians out of work. Some people say he caved to pressure from the United States, because the Arrow was a far superior jet to the Americans' F-86 Sabre and F-100."

"To be fair," I interjected, "they'd all be obsolete if they couldn't combat the Russians' ground-to-air missiles."

"Of course," Middleton countered, "but the Americans wanted to get their Bomarc anti-aircraft missiles into Canada, didn't they?"

I laughed. "*Touché*, sir. However, if you want my help, I'd suggest we forget about the history lesson and get on with why I'm here."

Our host sighed before he went on. "There were rumours of the factory closing as early as the summer *before* the rollout!"

"None of this was leaked to the general public," I offered.

"Definitely not, but I was convinced that the politicians would have their way and shut us down. So, I started to prepare myself."

"Prepare?" Mom interjected, taking some more shortbread.

Middleton paused before proceeding. He said his wife was dying of cancer in 1957 and that's what led him to violate his non-disclosure agreement with Orenda and, in turn, the Canadian government. He took an early retirement in the late winter of '58, received the traditional golden handshake, and went home to start writing an exposé of what had happened to the CF-105 Arrow. He'd even smuggled photographs and notes about the miracle jet out of his office in order to embellish the book and to assist his memory.

In the eyes of the law, he was a criminal, but he never considered himself to be anything but a scientist.

As well, he thought he had nothing to lose in proceeding with the project. Both his children were adults, his wife had passed away, and he was financially secure. His manuscript, written under an alias, was going to be published by a small underground press.

"Then, last week, I got an anonymous phone call," Middleton explained. "The caller said he possessed a recent draft of the book, my set of notes, and the photographs."

As Middleton paused, I interjected, "This is where the blackmail threat made its debut."

"Needless to say," he agreed, "and it involves a very large sum of money."

"What if you don't pay up?"

"Simple. He sends copies of the complete package to the Royal Canadian Mounted Police, and another set to the offices of A.V. Roe. Then, he pays me a visit to kill me, and makes damn sure it looks like suicide."

After a brief silence, I asked, "You know for a fact those papers are missing?"

"Yes. I found the safe where I kept the material wide open, only minutes before the blackmailer phoned me. All the papers and photographs were gone."

"How long have you got?"

"I'll get another call here tomorrow morning," Middleton replied. "He will tell me the time and place of the exchange. I've already visited my bank branch in Huntsville and withdrawn the ransom money. I'll travel back to the homestead tomorrow after the call."

"Do your children know about the blackmail?" Mom asked.

"Neither one knows anything about it. Chris and Judi think I've been working on a history of Canadian aviation. Nothing else."

After a long pause, I offered, "How would you like some company tomorrow?"

Middleton sighed with relief, and closed his eyes. "Thank you, Mara."

As he passed around more shortbread and coffee, the good doctor talked about his family and showed us some group photographs. We *oohed* and *aahed* at the family portraits, commenting on the fine looks of his son Chris and daughter Judi. Mom, who had seen them before, even managed to comment on how much Judi looked like her late mother.

Back in the car, on our way home to Mom's chalet, I said, "He sure is proud of his daughter Judi, isn't he?"

"Indeed, he is," she responded. "But he seldom mentions Chris. Isn't that strange?"

Actually, I didn't think it was strange at all. What could I say to my mother about a grown man who wears a black leather jacket and hangs around with a creep like the dreaded Ronny?

By noon the following day, Middleton and I were on our way to his family homestead in Simcoe Township. He'd decided to drive his station wagon, not wanting to arouse any unnecessary suspicion. The blackmailer had called him that morning and ordered him to be at the Simcoe house by seven that evening. So, while the temperatures dropped and the snow gently filtered down during our journey, I told him about my suspicions. Papa Middleton wasn't too happy.

"From the photographs you were showing us yesterday," I explained, "I immediately recognized your son, Chris. He was one of three fellows I saw picking on a young guy in Orillia the other day. That made it possible that your blackmailers might be a thug named Ronny and his two companions. One of them, as I said, is your son, who may or may not be a willing participant in the theft."

"I see," Middleton said, sounding subdued.

"Another clue would be the telephone calls. Your blackmailer seems to know both of your numbers. Of course, there's the City of Orillia and Simcoe County connection."

"How does that tie in?"

"When I found out that Orillia was also in Simcoe County, and only a few miles away from your family homestead, the possibility became more probable."

"And how did you make the geographical connection?" Middleton asked.

"Easy," I replied. "My mother was giving me a rundown on the new man in her life. She told me you were born and raised in a lovely home in the woods of Simcoe Township, just outside of Orillia. She's pretty sweet on you, Professor."

"Your mother is a lovely woman, isn't she?" Middleton said.

"That she is, Dr. Middleton. That she is."

"As for Chris," Middleton said, thinking out loud, "he was aware I was working on an aviation history, but he could see that I was being pretty tight-lipped about it. Never wanting to discuss it, always locking my research and writing away in the house safe."

"Further," I added, "all he had to do was go rooting around for the combination of the safe. Upon opening it, he discovered your project, including the photos and various drafts, and realized how important it was to national security. With you up north at the chalet, he'd have had ample opportunity to search the house for the combination. Everyone writes down a combination somewhere."

"All right!" Middleton grumbled. "I get the picture." He took a moment to compose himself, and then continued. "Let's assume the blackmailers *are* my son and his friends. How harmful can they *really* be? Would my son be a party to death threats, even if they didn't mean to carry them out?"

I thought for a moment about the scene in the Golden Dragon, the relentless bullying and the ugly brutality of Ronny.

"I'm not sure," I admitted. "They could just be young men playing power games, and you're an easy target. On the other hand, they might be deadly serious."

W hen we arrived at the homestead, Middleton parked inside an ancient garage that had probably been a carriage house in the late 1800s. Then we trudged through the cold, mounting snow to reach his home.

The house itself turned out to be of French rural design, and stood in two-storey splendour, rectangular in shape, and covered with a mansard roof, which sloped steeply down all four sides and ended in a delicate upturn.

Once we'd gone inside and put away our coats, Middleton gave me a tour of the premises, and then discussed where each of us should station ourselves.

Seven o'clock came and went. So did eight o'clock and 8:30. By then, Middleton was getting pretty agitated. He had been sitting in the family room to the right of the front door, trying unsuccessfully to watch a bit of television. Meanwhile, I was across the hall, sitting quietly in the living room, leafing through *National Geographic* magazines.

Then, shortly before nine o'clock, the suspense came to an end. There was a tentative knocking sound and I slipped behind the partially closed living room door. I could hear the television being turned off and Middleton heading out into the hall. There was another knock, and the scientist opened the door.

"Chris!" Middleton exclaimed. "What are you doing here? Why are you knocking?"

"May I please come in, Father?" Chris sounded subdued. "I haven't much time, and they'll be here within the hour."

I heard the sound of boots on the hardwood floor of the hallway, father and son enter the family room, and the door close. However, their voices were clearly audible.

Chris said, "I told them I'd meet them here. I told them I'd make sure the door was unlocked, and that the ransom would be paid without a hitch."

"So, it's true," Middleton said in a low but firm voice. "You're one of them. You're going to rob your own father."

"I'm sorry, Dad. They're making me do it. They found out about me. They're forcing me to do it, or they'll tell everyone."

"What have you done, Chris? What are they holding over you to blackmail me?"

"I can't, Father. I'm too embarrassed to tell you."

As the silence deepened, I figured the situation was going nowhere fast, so I muttered *to hell with it,* crossed the hallway and entered the family room.

"Okay, kids," I said, "let's play a little game of Show and Tell."

Chris immediately recognized me and almost fainted. He turned to his father. "Wha—what's *she* doing here?" he gasped.

"Sit down, Chris," the scientist muttered, and his son collapsed on the couch. "This is Mara Lombardi. She's a private detective. Her mother is a friend of mine, and brought Mara up from the city to help me."

Chris's face turned very pale; he was either going to collapse or start to cry. His father sat down beside the young man, who no longer resembled the cocky bully he'd been portraying recently.

"There's nothing for you to be afraid of," I began. "I'm pretty sure you've gotten yourself into a bad situation. One that you feel is almost hopeless to escape."

Young Middleton hung his head and tried to say something, but only managed a strangled sob. His father put his arm around him and tried to ease the boy's pain.

"Tell me," Middleton said, drawing the broken young man into his arms. "Tell your father what you've done that they're holding over your head."

After a few moments of weeping, young Middleton let it all spill out. The three of them had been friends throughout elementary and high school. Ronny was the tough guy, the leader in everything they did. They often got into minor scrapes, beat up smaller kids and vulnerable peers who didn't measure up to Ronny's standards of being *a man.*

They went their separate ways after high school, with young Chris ending up at college. There, he discovered another lifestyle, one which he never mentioned to his old gang. Upon returning home after graduation, he found a good job in Orillia and renewed his friendship with his boyhood chums. Everything was perfect, until Ronny discovered that Chris was gay.

"From then on," Chris continued, "Ronny was always on my case. Laughing at me, making fun of me, and even getting me to pick on guys like the one you saved the other day."

"Look, Chris," I said, "there's nothing wrong with being gay."

"You're kidding," Chris sniffed.

"Not at all, kid. A time will come when being gay will be widely accepted in our society. Even now, there's a large community of gay people in Toronto and Hamilton."

Chris started to weep again, his shoulders shaking with emotion.

His father comforted him as best he could, saying that he understood his predicament and the kind of pressure he must have been under.

Suddenly, someone began banging on the front door and rattling the knob vigorously.

"Holy crap!" Chris cried out. "I didn't leave the door unlocked!"

"Never mind," I ordered. "I'll get it."

With that, I quickly crossed to the front door and opened it so fast that the other Bobbsey Twin, standing there alone, had no time to react. When he saw me, he made a feeble attempt to raise a gun he was carrying, but he wasn't nearly as ready as I was.

With my right hand, I seized his neck under the chin, while at the same time grabbing his gun hand around the wrist with my left hand. I dragged the punk into the hall, keeping a strangling grip on his throat. Then I forced his wrist downward and slammed the gun hand against the wall three or four times; the gun flew out of his grip.

I immediately smashed him into the wall with my hand still around his throat. As he gagged for breath, I drove my left fist into his right side, over and over again until there was no breath for him to expel. Only then did I let up the pressure on his throat. As he started to sag to the floor, I gave him a sharp knee to the groin and a hard elbow-cross to the head.

Kicking the door closed, I bent down to check if the punk was conscious. That's when I felt a strong arm encircle my neck and jerk me to my feet. It was Ronny, holding something hard and cold pressing against my right temple. It didn't take a genius to figure out what it was.

"Hey, sweetheart," he murmured in my ear, "who's the *shithead* now?" He loosened his grip slightly to let me answer, but I had nothing to say. "Here's me, sneaking into the kitchen from the old cold-cellar entrance, and what do I find? Little Miss Bigmouth beating up one of my boys. Now what do you think I should do about that?"

I still said nothing, but let myself go limp. I began to slide down, but Ronny dragged me up to my feet.

"Not so smart-mouthed now, are you?" he crowed. "Now, what do you have to say, Little Miss—"

And that's as far as he got.

I kicked his shin as hard as I could with the back of my boot and immediately slipped down to the floor. His gun sailed off in one direction, and he hopped around in another. When he got close enough, I kicked upward and nailed him in the stomach. As he was deciding which hurt more, his gut or his shin, I rose up like Marley's ghost and drove a straight-arm punch to his throat.

By the time he'd completely finished gagging and coughing, I had their guns in my possession, Middleton had secured all the blackmail documents, and we'd given the new, terrible twosome a serious lecture on the sins of being bad boys.

Early afternoon on the following day, as more snow drifted down, Middleton and I were at Mom's chalet, explaining how father and son had been reunited. We also discussed how we'd let Ronny and his fellow goon off the hook in exchange for their promises to leave vulnerable folks, like Jeffery and Chris, alone. My mother asked how I was going to police their behaviour from Toronto.

"With much difficulty," I said. "The best I could do was give my cards to the victims and promise to stage a return engagement if trouble started up again."

"So, what did you decide to do about your book, Norman?" my mom asked.

"I'm going to shelve it for a little while," he said. "Take a bit of a break. Do some ice fishing, drive into Huntsville and have a nice dinner."

"Ooh, that sounds lovely," Mother declared.

I winked at her and jabbed my thumb in Middleton's direction.

Mom blushed ever so slightly, and quickly changed the subject. "Nevertheless, it was pretty cool-headed of them to pull off such a robbery right under Norman's nose."

"Cool-headed?" I scoffed. "I'd say it was a bloody cold, criminal act."

"Which reminds me," Middleton said, "what was Ronny's parting shot to you last night, when you let them out of the house?"

I pictured the two guys hustling across the snow-bound yard, and Ronny mouthing off. By that time, I was closing the door, but I heard him clearly.

"You're one tough broad, Lombardi. One cold, mean bit—"

As the door slammed shut on his final word, I smiled to myself. "That I am, kiddo. That I am."

DELEE FROMM

Delee Fromm is an author, lawyer, psychologist, consultant and coach. She is the author of two nonfiction books, *Advance Your Legal Career* and *Understanding Gender at Work*. Her first foray into fiction produced the short story "The Neighbourhood Watch", which was published in *A Grave Diagnosis*. In her current career as a consultant, she focuses on implicit bias and women's advancement. Delee's LinkedIn is www.linkedin.com/in/deleefromm

NOT IN CANADA

DELEE FROMM

THE WOMAN INTRIGUES ME. She is in continual motion as we edge closer to the front of the line. Her fingers fiddle with a credit card, her leg jiggles, and her head bobs in a random pattern. No earbuds, I check. Is it a motor disorder? Side effects from drugs? She reaches the front of the line and, as she orders, all fidgeting stops. It's nervous energy and I relax at making a diagnosis.

I half-listen as she gives an elaborate and detailed order: 'vanilla syrup, almond milk, a half shot of espresso, and *then* caramel syrup, *in that order.*' It has to be extra hot; she is transporting it to the drinker. I am relieved it's not for her; she clearly doesn't need more caffeine. 'Extra-whip cream with caramel and chocolate sauce' completes the order. A drink for a child? Probably not. Plenty of adults order these types of beverages.

When my turn comes, Jen sees me and calls out 'extra-large green tea' to Ben, today's barista. I am tempted to add 'hold the whip cream' in hopes of lightening Jen's mood. She looks tense from taking customized drink orders all day and I think a laugh would do her good.

I'm a regular and know everyone who works here. Ever since my husband passed away last year, I come in twice a day—once in the morning and once in the late afternoon. The afternoon visit helps me to unwind from work, but today, instead of letting the sounds of people wash over me, I am alert and focused on this woman. Her long hair is reddish blond, a colour that matches her long puffer coat exactly. Standing side-by-side waiting for our drinks, her fidgeting returns.

Leaning over, I gently inquire, "Are you okay?"

Her jaw tenses as she shoots me a side glance. Then, perhaps because she sees an old woman who is concerned, she visibly relaxes. Just as she starts to answer, Ben calls her name. Emily moves quickly toward where he holds out her drink but, before taking it, she starts to quiz him. At least I think that's what she's doing, since she's speaking so softly I can't hear.

Suddenly she erupts. "No. That's wrong. I asked for almond milk. It can't be dairy."

She sounds desperate rather than angry. I can't hear Ben's response, but it's not long before Emily's shoulders lower. He must be redoing her order.

"Gerry," Ben calls out holding up my drink. He usually smiles at our inside joke—Gerry as in geriatric—but not today. In truth Gerry is short for Geraldine. I'm seventy-four years old and under no delusions about how young I look.

I take my green tea and walk over to the small island that holds the usual assortment of lids, stir sticks, cream, and milk. I drop the tea bag down the hole in the middle and, after putting a cover on the cup, walk back to Emily. Her anxiety appears to have grown worse.

"I'll be over there if you want to talk," I tell her softly, pointing to an alcove containing two large leather chairs. She nods absently and I'm not sure she's heard. The alcove is my favourite spot in the coffee shop and a perfect place for people watching. I listen to people all day, so after work I come here, turn off my cell phone, and make a game of guessing moods and relationships. I have nothing to turn off today since I left my phone at work.

I hear Emily's name called and watch as she strides quickly to the cup in Ben's hand, this time taking it from him. After fitting it with a lid, she heads toward the front door, stopping just short of it. The couple behind barely avoid crashing into her and appear upset at the near miss. Emily steps aside, and as the couple disappears through the door, she looks in my direction. I wave before taking a sip of tea, then watch as she comes my way. She is exceptionally thin and looks in her late thirties. As she gets close, I see her eye colour is the same as her copper hair and I am taken by how striking she is despite her unkempt appearance.

"Do you mind if I sit?"

"Please do."

"I don't want to bother you."

"You aren't, my dear."

"You have a kind face," she says, pushing aside a bright red-and-green Christmas decoration to make room for her special drink on the table.

"Developed over the years." I smile at her. "I'm a psychologist."

She sinks into the chair. "I'm a nurse."

"We're both in helping professions," I say brightly, then adopt a more serious tone. "It can be a tough season."

"I know, but I love Christmas." Before I can probe again, she says, "It's not the season."

She's caught my oblique query.

"I'm in an impossible position." Her hands fidget with the ties from her hood.

"A burden shared is a burden halved," I offer as a salve and invitation.

"My mom used to say that." She takes a deep breath and I'm unsure she'll continue. After a few minutes she says, "If I save my daughter, I destroy my marriage."

My mind races in several directions with that information, but I stay quiet, feeling her eyes on me. I keep my face neutral, a skill I have learned and practised over the decades. Her speed in opening up is unusual and tells me how desperately she needs to unburden herself.

"I'm so sorry, dear."

"It's complicated. Do you want to hear?" She puts the responsibility for continuing on me, something I'm familiar with.

"Of course. Tell me whatever you want."

"I worked as a nurse in Saudi. Fourteen years ago."

I nod knowingly. My sister worked there twenty years ago, but I say nothing. I let her talk.

"I was naïve when I got there. Totally unprepared. The plan was to work for a year. To get a down payment for a house. Did you know a nurse could earn $120,000 U.S. per year?"

I nod. My sister went for the money, as I assume most workers did.

"The nurses came from around the world. The Irish were the most fun." Her face brightens in remembrance, and I get another glimpse of her rare beauty. "They taught me a lot. I only had two years of experience when I got there."

"I've heard they like Canadian nurses."

"They do. They don't have locally trained health workers so it's easier to bring in foreigners and pay them. It's a strange place."

"So you liked your co-workers?"

"Yeah. I worked in maternity. Loved the babies and moms."

She stares absently across the room. Something happened on the ward. Something awful. She glances at the drink on the table and, for a moment, I think she'll grab it and leave.

"My sister worked maternity, too. In a large hospital in Riyadh."

This helps her continue, as I hoped it would.

"I was at a small, more elite one. Royalty only."

She becomes lost in thought again so I quietly sip my tea, waiting for her to resume. It doesn't take long.

"I was working nights. It was a slow night. No admissions and only a few babies in the nursery." Her throat sounds constricted. "I was in the nurses' lounge on my break. It happened fast."

I reach across the table to touch her arm and she takes my hand. I spare Emily from having to describe the rape. I remember my sister's stories of young foreign housekeepers whose babies were delivered at her hospital. I nod knowingly, and she continues.

"His baby was in the nursery." She looks over at me, and I see her tears. "Telling anyone would have been pointless."

"And dangerous." I rummage in my purse with my free hand for a tissue, which I give to her. "Not even the head nurse?"

"No. I finished the shift and left two days later for Canada. Two weeks early." She releases my hand to wipe the tears that run down her cheeks.

"Your daughter is his?"

"I think so, I don't know, maybe. I didn't tell Will, and we married a week after I returned. I didn't know I was pregnant."

We sit in silence for a few minutes. I am surprised when she resumes.

"My daughter is sick and the doctors are stumped. They've tried everything. They want to do a DNA test. They think it might be a rare genetic disease."

"And the test can show her biological father is from Saudi?"

Her reply shows her medical training. "There's an elevated incidence of inherited genetic diseases in the Middle East. So yes."

I wait a minute before asking, "Is Will a good man?"

The question seems to surprise her, but she answers immediately. "A great husband and an even better father."

"Don't you have your answer then?"

She looks puzzled and I realize I'm going too fast. In my desire to help her, I'm sabotaging the process. I begin again.

"It wasn't your fault."

"I should've told Will when I returned." She tucks the tissue away in her coat pocket.

"You wanted to put it behind you. And you didn't know for certain who the father was. It's a possibility, not a certainty."

She becomes still and then expels a big breath. "You're right. I've anticipated the worst and made it real."

"Why not wait until you get the results?"

She looks pensive and then her face brightens. "No. I'll tell Will now. He'll understand. We'll face whatever the results are together." Taking my hand, she says with great intensity, "Thank you."

She picks up her drink from the side table and throws it in the garbage on the way to the cashier. She's able to order right away since there's no line. As she waits for her name to be called, she is perfectly still. A few minutes later, when her name is called, she collects her drink and heads to the door, but just before going through she turns and waves. A simple gesture that touches my heart and makes my eyes sting.

I look around and notice the place has emptied. A young man gets up a few seats over and I decide it's time for me to go. I take a sip to confirm my tea is tepid and carry it to the garbage. After dropping it in, I pull a big woollen hat over my head and wrap the matching scarf around my neck several times. It's only a few blocks to my apartment, but the weather is freezing cold. Not as frigid as winters in Saskatchewan where I lived as a child but definitely cold by southern Ontario standards.

As I step outside, the wind whirls around my body and I shiver. I pull the scarf high on my face, so only my eyes are visible. It's later than usual for my walk home and the street is deserted. The white Christmas lights in the town square, normally so full of warmth and vitality, look tiny tonight.

Behind me a van door slides closed and I whirl around to see. It's a full block away, but the cold night air makes it sound closer. Too close. There shouldn't be any delivery vans still out since most shops are shuttered and locked.

I search for my phone in my pocket before remembering I left it at work. Not unusual for me, but tonight I wish I had been more mindful. I pull my scarf tight around my neck and for some reason unknown to me, step into a darkened doorway. The van whizzes by.

My hands prickle. Why am I so fearful? I stop and take a deep breath. Saudi. The Kingdom. Rape. Princesses. Jamal Khashoggi. There it is, the reason for my jangled nerves. The premeditated ambush and dismemberment in Turkey of a Saudi dissident and American journalist by agents of the Saudi government. Perhaps I was too quick to dismiss Emily's fear. The DNA results could easily be evidence of a crime.

I move my feet to keep them warm but stay in the darkened

doorway. Has Emily been watched all these years? Was she warned? A black SUV speeds by, breaking into my dark thoughts.

This is looney-tunes crazy. My body relaxes. I'm scaring myself for no reason. It's a huge leap to think that news of Emily's rape would need to be suppressed at any cost. Besides, what happened to Khashoggi could never happen here. Maybe elsewhere, but not in Canada.

Suddenly I feel silly. I'm hiding in a doorway thinking irrational paranoid thoughts. I'm tired, that's all. It's been a long day. I move out of the dark and walk very slowly, mindful of the ice. A fall would not be good for my fragile bones, as my doctor keeps reminding me.

Things like that don't happen here pops into my head. It was a phrase my husband repeated as he watched American politics on TV. His memory warms me and wards off darker thoughts for a few minutes. Then they creep back. Rape. No country has a monopoly. It happens in Canada, much more than we know. Some of my patients are still dealing with the trauma of unreported attacks decades later.

Darkness surrounds me as I turn off Lakeshore, heading to my condo building two blocks away. Familiar shapes suddenly look ominous and long shadows deepen my dread. Abduction. It happens here, too. In Vancouver, women disappeared for years without any serious police investigation. Indigenous women have been abducted and killed across Canada for decades without attention. It's now officially referred to as a genocide.

My pace quickens as fear takes over again. I seem incapable of stopping it. There is a sound behind me and adrenaline courses through my body. I spin around. Too quickly. Slipping, I hit the ground with a gasp and lay on the frozen sidewalk. I start to weep. The cold quickly seeps into my legs, but I feel powerless to get up.

I have done what I cautioned Emily against. Catastrophizing. I have assumed the worst and made it real. Making up stories and scaring myself. I begin to laugh. I'm a crazy old lady who needs to get home and have a hot meal. For the first time since my husband passed, I'm anxious to be home.

Getting up slowly, I brush ice crystals from my woollen coat. My left knee protests, but nothing feels broken. Embarrassed, I glance around and am relieved there isn't a soul in sight. Thick blinds cover the windows facing the street and I imagine families eating dinner. My mouth waters at the thought.

I take care as I walk the remaining block to my building. Focused on staying upright, I manage to keep paranoid thoughts at bay. Reaching the front steps, I hear a noise behind me but don't turn. I'm not falling again. Not this close to home.

Fitting my key into the front door, I recall a news story. On CBC. Saudi nationals being stopped at the Canadian border with tools. Tools like those used in Khashoggi's murder. As I start to panic again, I hear the rustle of fabric and the world goes black.

ELIZABETH ELWOOD

A former English and drama teacher, Elizabeth Elwood spent many years performing with theatre groups, singing in the Vancouver Opera chorus, and creating marionette musicals for Elwoodettes Marionettes. She has also written four plays that have entertained audiences in Canada and the United States. A Derringer nominee, she is the author of six books in the Beary Mystery Series and free-standing stories for magazines and anthologies. Elizabeth lives on British Columbia's beautiful Sunshine Coast. Elizabeth's website is www.elihuentertainment.com

THE SPLINTER OF ICE

ELIZABETH ELWOOD

"You are armoured, of course, by the creative artist's splinter of ice in the heart."
     P.D. James, *A Certain Justice*

When I first read that dramatic line in P.D. James's mystery novel, I thought of the photograph of my Aunt Huguette that had held pride of place on my mother's dressing table. She was in costume as Madama Butterfly—hardly a character to equate with icy resolve; Turandot would have been more appropriate than the tender Butterfly—but the quotation conjured up the image and made me ponder why I would think of her that way.

I never met my aunt, for she was murdered the year before I was born. Still, what I heard over the years about her talent and determination to succeed became the benchmark by which I judged myself. Part of this pressure resulted from the fact that I was named after her, and always felt that I was supposed to replace the talented family member on whom so many hopes were laid. Not that I'm a singer like my aunt—my aptitude lies in my pen—but Huguette Marchand was the leading light of the City Opera Resident Artists'

Program, the chorus member who was singled out to take the small roles coveted by aspiring young singers, the soprano everyone was convinced would win the next round of the Metropolitan Opera auditions and take the opera world by storm. When she died, a lot of dreams died with her.

I wish I could have seen my aunt on stage, for my mother's descriptions of her younger sister's performances were thrilling. My mother and grandmother never really got over Huguette's death, and I think their determination to keep her story alive stemmed from the fact that her murder had never been solved. From those stories, I somehow concocted an image of an ambitious singer, driven by dreams of success, immured from the perils of life by the artist's "splinter of ice in the heart" that enabled her to detach from the world and focus on her goal.

My aunt was only twenty-eight when she died, but she had already made a name for herself. My grandparents had been well-to-do Vancouverites, so my mother and aunt had enjoyed a childhood with all the advantages that money could buy: private schools, music lessons, memberships at fashionable clubs, and entrée to all the cultural events that the city had to offer. My mother married young, having fallen in love with a businessman who was based in Toronto, where I was born and raised. However, my aunt demonstrated a rich, mature voice at an early age, and music dominated her life. She worked assiduously with her vocal coach, honed her performance skills with church solos and roles in high-school musicals, and at seventeen, was enrolled in the music faculty at university. She remained in the opera workshop for four years, at the end of which, she was assigned a principal role for the year-end production, a series of operatic excerpts, which included the second act of *Madama Butterfly*.

This was a critical night for the young singers, because the artistic director of the City Opera was to be in attendance, along with Gregory Antonias, Vancouver's most noted music critic. The night turned out to be a turning point for my aunt, for Antonias not only raved about her performance, but also fell in love with her. He divorced his wife and married my aunt the following year.

Marchand and Antonias became the darlings of the local music scene, but it was a brief reign. Gregory died of a heart attack in 1975; then, fourteen months later, my aunt was stabbed to death in an underground parking lot as she returned to her car after a performance of *La Bohème*.

By now, of course, the murder was a cold case, and I had no idea if VPD ever reviewed it. However, it was of interest to me professionally as well as personally, because my field was crime non-fiction and I had already written three moderately successful books on Canadian cold cases. I had occasionally toyed with the idea of writing about our family mystery, but an underlying fear that revisiting the details would distress my mother prevented me. When my mother died in 2020, fate handed me my aunt's story in the form of an unexpected inheritance, an oceanfront property, complete with house and cottage, that I had no idea existed. It was on British Columbia's Sunshine Coast.

I was frankly astounded when Alan Blackburn, the elderly lawyer who was handling my mother's estate, informed me of this unforeseen windfall.

"The only British Columbia property I ever visited was my grandparents' home in Shaughnessy," I said. "I remember my mother talking about a cottage that my aunt used as a retreat, but I thought that belonged to her husband's family."

"Oh, no, it was owned by Gregory Antonias, and he left it to your aunt. After her death, it went to your mother, who wisely realized its investment potential when she went out to B.C. to help her parents cope with the tragedy. Rather than sell the property, she used the cottage to store her sister's personal items, and she rented the house. Now, it will be up to you what to do with the place."

"Personal items?" My interest was caught. "What sort of things are we talking about?"

"Not clothing or jewellery. Mainly scrapbooks and programs, theatrical memorabilia, that sort of thing. But your aunt's furnishings are there. It's entirely habitable. What's your schedule like? Do you have time to go out and take a look?"

I smiled ironically. Time was all I had these days. I was between books, no projects loomed on the horizon, the pandemic had eliminated most of my social life, and as a forty-six-year-old divorcee whose only daughter was in residence at university, I had no one but my agent making demands on me.

I nodded. Blackburn relaxed, duty done, and glowed benevolently. "Then why don't you fly out and see for yourself? From Vancouver, it's a pleasant ferry ride and an easy drive up the Sunshine Coast. You could spend a few days at the cottage, meet the tenant living in the house, and size up the situation."

"Decide whether or not I want to deal with the hassles of rotating renters?"

Blackburn's eyes twinkled.

"The current tenant has been there since 1976," he said.

"Good lord. That's an unusually long-standing arrangement. How did my mother get so lucky?"

"She was made aware of a young couple, both teachers in Pender Harbour, looking for accommodation on the coast. They fell in love with the place and would probably have bought it had your mother been interested in selling. They raised their family there and were very much a part of the local community."

"Were?"

"The children are grown and flown, and Maddie Wright is now a widow, but she's still there. I've notified her of the change of ownership, and she has indicated that she hopes to stay on. You should try to fit in time to meet with her while you're there and discuss her options. She's a very good tenant and deserves that consideration. She's acted as a caretaker for the property for all these years."

"I'll have plenty of time to fit in a meeting," I said. "I've been thinking about writing my aunt's story, and if the cottage contains all the paraphernalia of my aunt's career, there must be a veritable mine of information there. It also sounds like the perfect place to work on my book. I'll go next week and stay right through November, maybe even longer. Tania won't be back from McGill until mid-December."

Blackburn raised his eyebrows.

"Winter on the coast can be bleak," he cautioned. "Lee Bay is extremely isolated."

"Isolation is exactly what I want. Hopefully, the tenant will stay out of my hair and not be a nuisance."

The eyebrows descended again. Blackburn looked amused.

"You might want to invite the widow to tea," he said dryly.

I blinked, surprised.

Blackburn continued solemnly, "While your mother was in Vancouver, she got to know the detective who was investigating her sister's murder. When he heard she was looking for a tenant to rent the coast property, he recommended the couple who finally took the lease."

My eyes widened. This sounded promising.

"You mean the widow knows the detective who worked on my aunt's case?"

"Oh, definitely," said Blackburn. "She's his sister."

I remembered Blackburn's warning about coastal winters as I followed the winding network of roads that led to Lee Bay. The snow was low on the mountains, and I noticed thin drifts of ice on the surface of the water as I drove along Hotel Lake Road.

Above the snow-draped hillsides, the sky was heavily overcast, and given the frigid temperature, the clouds were unlikely to release a mere rainstorm. Icy gusts of wind buffeted my rental car, which suddenly seemed pathetically inadequate, as did my carefully planned stash of supplies in the back of the vehicle. I was coming to realize that being snowed in at home, where stores were nearby and every modern convenience was available, was very different from inhabiting a strange house, with a forty-minute drive to get to the necessities of life and nothing within shouting distance other than an elderly tenant.

I turned onto Lee Bay Road and followed the downward curve as it passed a handful of houses on the ocean side that appeared to be closed up for the season. To my right, a wall of granite rose and towered over the car. As I rounded the corner, my eyes lit on a sweep of steel-grey ocean, capped with white, wind-whipped furrows. Churning clouds drifted over the water, seagulls rode the wind, and burgeoning waves rolled silently in, then broke into a thousand fragments on the rocky point at the end of the bay. Perched on this outcrop, I saw a quaint yellow house with a brown roof. Nestled into its side was the cottage, a miniature version of the other building. I had reached my new home.

There was no sign of life in the house as I pulled into the driveway, but a light was on in the cottage. When I entered, a glorious blaze of heat encased my frozen limbs. The wood stove stood cold and dark, but a note on the table explained that my tenant had come by earlier to turn on the baseboard heaters. She had also left a casserole in the fridge. A country welcome indeed, and one for which I was truly grateful. Between the Vancouver traffic, the waits for ferries, and the drive up the Sunshine Coast Highway, it had been a long and tiring day, and by the time I packed my gear into the cottage, it was past seven-thirty. I was happy to heat the casserole, eat my dinner, and crash into bed. Exploring the cottage could wait until morning.

I had been aware of the sound of waves and sporadic gusts of wind as I drifted off to sleep, but I awoke to eerie quietness. The turbulence of the previous day had ceased, and the bedroom window emitted a pale glow. When I got up to look out, I saw that it had snowed in the night.

After breakfast, I wrapped up warmly and went out to meet my tenant, return her casserole dish, and thank her for her hospitality. I knocked on the door of the house, but there was no answer, so I left her dish inside the porch and set off to explore my property.

After my driveway, the road angled inland and there was a sizeable stretch of garden on the other side of the house. Beyond, lay a dense forest. The snow concealed what paths or flowerbeds there might be, but there was a greenhouse and a pergola that suggested a keen gardener had been at work. I noticed two sets of footsteps, one human and one canine, coming from the back door of the house and leading to the forest at the edge of the garden. Presumably, my tenant was out walking her dog on the trails.

I set off to follow the marks in the snow, but I lost sight of them at a fork in the trail where the canopy of the forest protected the path from the snowfall. I veered to the right, but when the snow reappeared, it was untrodden, and after two more forks in the trail, I had no idea where I was. I made another turn to the right, and finally, at the next clearing, found footprints in the snow. However, there were no paw marks. I had simply doubled back on myself.

While I stood, pondering my choices, I heard a bark. I looked up to see a brown Labrador loping toward me. A tall woman in a quilted jacket and red toque strode along behind him. I had failed to track my tenant, but it appeared that she had found me.

I had no chance to raise the subject of my book as we walked back. Alan Blackburn had obviously asked Maddie Wright to take care of me, and our conversation consisted of her explaining the dos and don'ts of country living, and me giving monosyllabic responses at appropriate intervals.

Maddie was an imposing figure, not just because of her height. Her voice was strong and clear, her piercing blue eyes seemed to bore into one's soul, and she strode along at a pace that belied her years. She delivered me back to my cottage in record time, announced that she couldn't invite me in, as she was volunteering at the health centre that afternoon, but decreed that I should come for lunch the following day.

"I know there are things you want to ask," she said. "Blackburn filled me in."

She left me with a stern warning to take some kindling from her shed and use the cottage wood stove. "Cost of electric heating will bankrupt you." With those parting words, she disappeared into the house, the Lab at her heels, and closed the door.

I returned to the cottage, glad that my tenant was engaged for the day, for I had collected a copy of the police files before I left Vancouver, and I wanted to read them before I met with her. New questions were bound to occur to me once I learned more about the investigation. I also wanted to look through the material that my mother had stored in the cottage, conveniently packed in a large Tupperware tub with a typed list of what it contained taped to the lid. I was excited to see that *Huguette's diary* was the second item on the list.

I placed the box with the police files on the sea chest that served as a coffee table, dragged the Tupperware tub over, then made myself a coffee and settled down to explore my treasure trove. I tackled the tub first, pulling out the items and spreading them out on the coffee table. At the very top was an item I recognized, because I remembered it arriving with the same post that had delivered a gold locket my grandmother had sent for my nineteenth birthday. It was a framed poster advertising the opera-workshop gala that had launched my aunt's professional career. It had been sent to my mother by a member of the Opera Guild, and inscribed: *A night never to be forgotten, Sincerely, Diana.* My mother had been deeply touched to receive it.

The eagerly anticipated diary lay beneath the poster, but to my disappointment, it only listed appointments. Still, I resolved to study it later to see exactly what my aunt was doing in the last weeks of her life. Below the diary, there were three scrapbooks, which looked promising. However, the rest of the tub was filled with old scores and piles of sheet music. Not the bonanza I had hoped for.

I turned to the scrapbooks. The first was filled with photos from high-school musicals and operettas; the second covered her opera-workshop years. I couldn't identify all the operas—the workshop tackled modern works as well as the classics—but the cast lists made it clear that she had played a wide variety of roles. There was an instantly recognizable photograph of her as Butterfly, though a different picture from the one on my mother's dressing table. This showed her with the young boy, Sorrow, a sweetly smiling waif who, as I suspected, and the program confirmed, was actually a girl. On the page opposite was a newspaper clipping with a glowing review about the brilliant young soprano who promised a great future.

The third scrapbook covered my aunt's professional years: Micaela in the Opera in the Schools touring production of *Carmen*; Lucy in *The Telephone* for the Resident Artists' Program, and Gretel in a CBC production of *Hansel and Gretel*. In addition to chorus in the mainstage opera productions, she had played Flora in *La Traviata*, Countess Ceprano in *Rigoletto,* and Lola in *Cavalleria Rusticana*. The parts, albeit less impressive than the leads in her school years, were significant, given her youth. This was a singer who was going places.

As I turned the last page, I found a card, embossed with a single red rose. The inscription read: *For the glorious beauty who has won my heart. May we share many more magical performances together.* It was signed, John Holloway. I flipped back through the programs, finally locating the name, not in the cast lists, but among the production staff. He had been the opera's resident stage manager. As I scrolled through the pages, I found messages and signatures from fellow singers, and I began to notice an underlying tone, a lack of warmth that made me suspect many of my aunt's colleagues had resented her rapid rise in the company.

Thoughtfully, I closed the scrapbooks and turned to the police files. I read the evidence statements through carefully, but nothing suggested that anything unusual had happened that fateful night, other than a member of the children's chorus being unwell, and the prima donna having a fit of temper because the mother had allowed the little "germ factory" to come in the first place. This incident had been mentioned in the chorus master's statement, but a written note at the bottom of the page puzzled me. It said, "Checked into previous incident. Natural causes."

DI Timothy Lennox's own report laid out the basic facts of the murder. My aunt had been killed as she returned to her car after a performance of *La Bohème*. She always parked in the three-storey parkade, one block from the theatre, where she could leave her car on the main floor, close to the pedestrian street-level entrance at the end of the block.

In 1975, there was no Skytrain in Vancouver, and at ten-thirty at night, the area adjacent to the Queen Elizabeth Theatre was a concrete desert. Usually, there were enough singers and musicians leaving together to assure safety, but because my aunt played one of the vendors in the third act, most of the chorus had already gone home by the time she was through. No one saw her leave, because the stage doorman had been on a break and had set the door to lock automatically so people could go out, but no one could enter from outside.

Anita Hall, another soprano with a small part in Act III, left the theatre a few minutes later, entering the parkade by the same pedestrian entrance, and she was the one who came across the body and screamed for help, causing the parking attendant to come out from his booth and run over to see what had happened.

Diana Gates, the Opera Guild president, who had been helping provide refreshments for the company during the second intermission, was just entering the lot. She heard the scream, hurried over to help, and stayed with the singer while the attendant ran back to his booth and called the police.

None of these three individuals had seen anyone else in the area, nor had they heard sounds of a struggle or confrontation. The attendant's booth was on the southwest corner of the lot and he could not see the north side from his booth. There were pedestrian entrances at the other corners of the lot, so the attacker could have easily slipped away unseen.

Inspector Lennox did explore the possibility that the killer knew my aunt, but there was a dearth of credible suspects. My mother, who inherited her sister's estate, had been in Toronto. John Holloway, the stage manager, had a record of obsessive behaviour with singers in the company, but he was safely ensconced in his stage-right corner when my aunt was killed. Anita Hall, the singer who discovered my aunt's body, was given close scrutiny, for she was a rival contender for the upcoming Metropolitan Opera auditions. However, the guild president's testimony cleared her, for Mrs. Gates had entered the lot right behind her and had seen Anita come across the body.

The ultimate conclusion was a random killing, a mugging gone wrong with the assailant scared away when he heard people approaching the parkade.

M addie Wright scrutinized me closely when I appeared for lunch the next day.

"You look like a squeezed lemon," she said briskly, pouring me a mug of coffee and setting it on a coffee table that had been artistically constructed from driftwood. "Read into the night, did you?"

I nodded.

"Yes, and got nowhere. No wonder your brother couldn't solve the case." I sank into the depths of her comfortable couch and gratefully sampled the coffee. It was excellent. "I do have one question, though," I said. "The chorus master's statement described an upset in the rehearsal hall during the intermission. The guild volunteers were serving refreshments, and a chaperone from the children's chorus came to ask what to do about a little boy who wasn't well. There was a note referring to a previous incident. Have you any idea what that was, or why it was even considered relevant?"

Maddie sighed. "I remember Tim talking about that. It was a tragedy from your aunt's opera-workshop days. A child died after one of the performances. It was the little girl who played Sorrow in *Butterfly*. Her mother worked downtown and had arranged for your aunt and the mezzo playing Suzuki to pick the child up from playschool and take her to the theatre for the show, but when she came to pick her up after the final curtain, the child was flushed and feverish. She drove her to emergency, but on the way, the child collapsed with a ruptured appendix. She died before they reached the hospital. Tim wondered if the mother blamed the singers for failing to realize the child was unwell."

"A decade after the fact? The workshop gala was in 1964. And what brought it up? It wasn't mentioned in the statement."

"No. The chorus master elaborated later. Evidently, when the chaperone was dithering about what to do, your aunt mentioned the opera-workshop incident. She said they shouldn't assume that the child's queasiness was just nerves and that they should call the parents right away."

"Sounds as if she did notice that the child playing Sorrow was out of sorts. She must have felt terrible when the little girl died."

"Well, whether there was negligence or not, the incident was a dead end in terms of the investigation. The mother had committed suicide soon after the child's death, the father had died of cancer some years later, and the paternal grandparents had predeceased the child, having died in a car accident in 1960. The mother's parents were the only ones left to mourn the child, but they'd moved to England after their daughter's death and were still living in London."

"So your brother was back to square one?"

Maddie nodded.

"Ultimately, Tim felt the only viable suspect with motive and opportunity was Anita Hall, the rival singer who did end up winning the Met auditions. The parking lot was dark, so visibility was poor, and the guild president who provided her alibi was in her seventies. Tim believed Mrs. Gates's evidence could have been flawed, but given her certainty that her statement was accurate, he would never have got a conviction."

I thought about DI Lennox's suspicions as I made my way back to the cottage. The path was slippery and, as my glance fell on the footsteps in the snow, I remembered how I'd circled back upon myself that morning. It suddenly occurred to me that the network of trails around the clearing in the wood was like the parking lot, with its four pedestrian entrances from the surrounding streets.

Maybe the guild president's evidence had not been flawed. What if Anita Hall had left the theatre earlier and had been waiting for my aunt in the parking lot? What if she'd circled back afterwards and re-entered the lot, making sure that there was a witness to see her discover the body? Could that be the solution? I entered the cottage, resolving to look through the evidence statements again to see if there was any inconsistency in times that would support my train of thought.

As I settled back amid my neatly arranged piles on the sea chest, my eyes fell on the signature on the framed poster again. I wondered curiously if *Diana* had been Mrs. Gates, the guild president who had provided Anita Hall with an alibi. It was possible, though she'd have been very old by then, for the poster had been sent to my mother twenty years after my aunt's death.

It suddenly struck me as odd that she would have waited so long to send a memento of an event that had occurred in the early sixties, especially given that it was an event that had mixed triumph with tragedy. With a chill in my heart, an unsettling question began to form in my mind. Which of those two was being referred to in the inscription?

The temperature in the room seemed to have dropped, and the coldness in my heart had crept into my extremities. I propped the poster against the sea chest and turned to the scrapbooks to learn the name of the child who had played Sorrow. Then I opened my laptop and found the Vancouver Sun obituary that had listed those who had loved little Millie Travers. Millie had been survived by her mother, Melanie, father, Robert, and the mother's parents, Ian and Diana Browning, the only two who remained alive when my aunt died in 1975. Yes, there was that name, *Diana*, again. And yet DI Lennox had checked the couple's whereabouts. They were in England. Could there have been a slip up? Could he have been misinformed?

I found the answer when I brought up the Brownings' obituaries. Diana had died in 1996, only a few months after the poster had been sent to my mother. She had been born Diana Graham, and had married Ian Browning in 1933. They had moved to England in 1966 after their daughter's death, but divorced two years later. Ian Browning had remarried, ironically another Diana, and that had been the wife living with him in London when my aunt had died. As for the first Diana Browning, in 1972 she had met and married Vancouverite Alistair Gates and returned with him to Canada.

It had not been Anita Hall who had entered the parking lot twice, circling back to come through again so that a witness could see her arrival. It had been Diana Gates, Millie Travers's grandmother.

Astounded, I sat back and slid my laptop aside. As I did so, it caught the edge of the poster and knocked it over. I bent to pick it up and saw that the frame had detached at one corner. The backing, sagging away from the glass, revealed a folded piece of paper that had been tucked behind it. It had been waiting there all these years.

Diana Gates had felt the need to confess before she died. The letter was addressed to my mother.

Your sister had no idea who I was, so when I overheard her speak of my granddaughter's death, I pulled her aside and asked if the child had complained about not feeling well. She replied, "Millie said she had a tummy ache, but I assumed it was just nerves and told her to be a brave little soldier and forge on. It was a critical night for me, and I dreaded something happening to stop the performance. I felt badly afterwards, but how was I to know it was something serious?" Those words sealed her fate. I waited until she was leaving the theatre, and then followed her down to the parkade. I was always nervous walking that isolated block at night, so I carried my father's old hunting knife in my purse. It wasn't a large one, only a six-inch blade in a leather sheath, quite illegal, of course, but then the men who make the laws don't think about how vulnerable we women feel when alone on the streets, but it was sufficient for my purpose. She had caused the death of my daughter and my granddaughter. She did not deserve to live.

I had my solution, and I had my book, but I was glad that my mother had never found that letter. It was easier for her to accept the idea of a random death than to realize that her beloved sister, far from being the model of perfection she had so revered, had died from a splinter of ice in her heart.

HOPE THOMPSON

Hope Thompson writes for theatre, film, and television. Her plays have been produced in Toronto, Vancouver and Los Angeles and her award-winning short films have been screened and broadcast internationally. Hope's crime fiction stories have been published in serialized form (*Xtra Magazine*, *The Highlander*) and she is the co-host of Toronto's Noir At The Bar crime fiction reading series. Hope's website is www.hopethompson.net

STAGE DIARY, 1953

HOPE THOMPSON

I HAVE ALWAYS FELT that I had a calling. Some feel they are called to serve God, to teach, to work with children—even the sick. Me, I have heard nothing but the siren call of the stage. As far back as I can remember, I have been acting, playing roles that I create in my head, dancing around, experimenting with voices, accents, facial expressions—and grand gestures. How I love a grand gesture.

You've probably guessed that I'm an amateur actor. Well, I have news for you: it's still acting.

But try telling that to George, my recently deceased husband. He could not have cared less about my theatrical ambitions. He wanted me in the kitchen—cooking and cleaning—and on occasion, in the bedroom. He wanted a slave, or these days, what's called a housewife, but I believe the former was more accurate. Of course, George had role-playing ambitions, too. He wanted to play the part of "Dad." But I never gave him that pleasure. Through an elaborate deception that involved several out-of-province visits to a sister I don't have, I made sure that if I could not realize my dream, neither could he.

When I think back on those twenty-seven years of marriage, I am convinced he would have made a lousy father. You see, George was a drinker. And a bully. And one fed rather violently into the other. How much make-up have I used to mask black eyes and bruises? How many times have I thought about leaving him? How many times have I considered calling the authorities? Too many to recount at this juncture.

Suffice to say, I resisted. An actor, such as I, waits for her moment. And my moment eventually arrived.

My abhorrence for my husband was compounded by the fact that he had an identical twin brother named Eddy. And over the years, the pair had been known to play devilish games with their copy-like appearance. It makes me cringe to think of the times that I allowed George to, well—enter me. But it makes me positively livid to think that at least one, if not more, of those brutish, nocturnal couplings involved Eddy. I can tell them apart in the light of day but it's quite impossible in the dark.

And it's here that I shudder.

It's a Friday night about ten o'clock and George has already had a few drinks when he announces that he's going to pick up Eddy and go to the bar. He tells me he doesn't know when he'll be home and not to ask unless I want a smack.

I say, "Don't drink too much, George. Since you're driving."

And as if on cue the knuckled back of his hand strikes my cheek. George never takes kindly to being told what to do, and certainly not by me, and I close my ears to the volley of profanities that issue from his thin-lipped mouth. And then, mercifully, he snatches up his keys and slams the door.

That's right, George: exit stage left.

Through gauzy curtains, I watch him back out of the driveway like a bullet in reverse and I thank God that no one is walking along the sidewalk or driving past the house at that moment because they would surely be dead.

Anyway. After a short pause in which he's probably thinking the same thing, George manages to get the transmission into Drive—and his Buick disappears down the street.

Now I stand up and walk across the stage. This is when I am advised to be thoughtful and a tad nostalgic.

Well, there he goes, I think to myself. Off to have a drink with his buddies. Have a wonderful time, George. I hope you enjoy yourself and get a chance to share some jokes and tall tales with your friends. But are they really friends? Or are they just some lonely men who lean on the bar, propping up their lives with beer and bourbon and whatever other glasses of alcohol they can get their pudgy fingers around.

At the sound of a phone ringing, I look up, startled. And then I pantomime picking up the receiver and listening. My heart soars as I nail this bit of physical acting.

"Hello?" I say.

On the other end of the line, I hear an authoritative male voice announce that he's a police officer—and he has some serious news. I brace myself. The officer tells me George has been in a car accident, and that he's dead. And I think to myself: *Act, Eileen!* And I do. I register equal parts horror and dismay. I babble helplessly. He urges me to calm down and says he'll send a car around.

Here, I stand up, clap my hands together and stride purposefully to centre stage where I break the fourth wall. Yes, you heard me. Speaking directly to the audience is one of the greatest thrills of this acting life.

The man is right: Stay calm. Your moment has arrived. Do not fudge it up.

Arriving at Toronto's morgue, the officer provides me the few known facts of the case: witnesses observed George's Buick skidding wildly before it smashed into a retaining wall, then burst into flames. His body was pulled from the driver's seat.

As the officer guides me into the morgue's steely inner sanctum, I register an authentic jolt of fear. I have never seen a dead body and am not looking forward to seeing George's, as much as I despise him. He warns me to prepare myself because my husband's body is not only dead, but severely burned. And just then, the morgue attendant lifts back the white sheet that covers George's corpse.

After a moment of gathering my strength, I look down. And I think, wait a minute, that's not George. That's Eddy. Despite his charred features, the flames missed a distinguishing mole beneath Eddy's left eye.

I know that mole.

"Is it him?" the officer says.

I whisper, "Yes. That's—my husband." I quickly add, "My dear, sweet George." And I deliver the line through a torrent of tears. Then I ask a question that rises in my mind like a horrifying colossus: "Where's Eddy?"

The officer tells me that he's in a coma. I digest this information with a physical gesture—a shake of my head and a hand over my mouth that masks my relief. The officer adds that between the two badly burned brothers, only one set of identification was found on the scene: Eddy's. I surmise, gratefully, that George must have forgotten his wallet since he was already half in the bag.

And then I wipe tears from my eyes and add that perhaps my husband's death was for the better, and I confide in the officer that George was beginning to have problems 'upstairs.' I say this while pointing at my brain to make certain that my use of metaphor is not lost on the man. And after a fresh downpour of tears in which I declare my sorrow at losing him, the officer guides me away by the elbow and asks me if he can call anyone on my behalf. A lady friend, perhaps? Here, I sense he's getting a little annoyed by my feminine emotions. You see, part of acting is reading your audience. He wants me gone, and I oblige by thanking him for his kind offer and letting him know that I will call a neighbour myself.

Now I begin to pace and adopt a serious demeanour.

In the week following, I am a whirlwind of activity. After having George—Eddy—cremated, I close George's bank accounts and withdraw his rather substantial savings. (*He wasn't all bad,* I think to myself.) I inform his employer of his demise, cancel all the household utilities, and claim George's insurance policy. Finally, I engage a sales agent regarding the house, and he is kind enough to inform me that he has a young couple already in mind. After some perfunctory haggling, I agree to their price but demand a quick closing, claiming the sister I don't have, and who lives on the other side of the country, is ill and I'm anxious to see her. I acquire a new car in my name, pack it with nothing more than a couple of suitcases (one of which contains only money), carefully back out of the driveway, and slip away.

Now, I find myself in the city of Windsor and living in a rented apartment over a main street shoe store. Sure, the place is cramped and noisy at times but none of that matters because I am on stage. You see, I have joined the local theatre troupe! My moment materialized, and I seized it. I have even adopted a stage name: Margo West. Has a nice ring to it, don't you think?

Despite my new home and my blossoming career in this border town, part of me is drawn back, curious to see how matters ended. Each week at the local library, I faithfully read copies of the newspapers, both local and national, and in one edition, I spot a small yet fascinating article: *Man Wakes From Coma*. The reporter describes a fiery car accident in which one identical twin brother was killed, while the other badly burned brother fell into a coma. But now, having awakened, this man claims—apparently on the Bible—to be the other brother. The report mentions a family history of senility (due to my quick thinking back at the morgue) and that the authorities have placed the man in a sanatorium for his own safety.

The article concludes with a minor detail: Attempts to contact the dead man's widow have so far been unsuccessful. Reading this last line, I say to myself with a smirk, "Why end the article on a sour note?"

And here I make a grand gesture, an elaborate bow to the audience, marking the conclusion of my riveting life story. Or at least, a significant chapter within it.

O ne of the activities of this acting life that I adore is the removal of make-up following a performance. And I am engaged in this activity when there's a tap on the door. I shout, "Come in!" because we theatre people are often larger than life in our emotions. The stage manager sticks his head in the room and announces that a gentleman is waiting in the lobby to compliment me on my performance.

"Oh?" I say and smile coyly.

Of course, I neither rush to meet this gentleman, but nor do I keep him waiting. Although I appreciate my fans, I don't wish to seem desperate for their attention. After a reasonable interlude, I step from my dressing room having decided that I will graciously accept the gentleman's compliments, however, I won't linger. As an actress just north of her prime, my calendar must appear to be full; I must attend to my next appointment. That my next appointment is with a hot bath and good book (a treatise on method acting I am eager to finish and return to the library before its due date) is entirely my own business.

But entering the lobby, I find no gentleman awaiting my arrival. Instead, I find only a rumpled suit smoking a cigarette. Intuitively, I surmise that this man is neither a fan nor a theatregoer. This man is trouble.

"You Eileen Masterson?" he says.

I bristle at the sound of my civilian name—a name I don't wish my fans to hear lest it diminishes my star aura. I nod quickly, then usher him from the lobby and onto the street where we stand under the yellow glow of a streetlamp.

He tells me his name is Van Dorn, flips open his wallet and flashes a private detective's licence in my face. Then he reaches into his breast pocket and pulls out an envelope and hands it to me, while saying he had a devil of a job finding me—as if it was my fault.

Unfolding the letter, I see the insignia of the Ontario provincial sanatorium, then quickly peruse the brief missive. ... *As Edward Masterson's next of kin, your presence is requested on a matter regarding his convalescence.*

The letter is signed by a Dr._____.

Van Dorn chews a matchstick. "Well?" he says.

I re-fold the letter and slip it back into its envelope. "Let me get my things."

⚜

D riving along the highway, and as the hours and miles slip by, Van Dorn tries to start a conversation, but I am in no mood to talk. I am too busy preparing for my next role: Sister-in-law.

Under a dark and restless sky, we arrive at the columned entrance of the sanatorium. I thank Van Dorn for the ride, and he tells me, with a shrug, that he's just doing his job. I close the passenger door and his car pulls away from the curb. Dead leaves flutter around me as I climb the steps.

Once inside, I am directed to a meeting room, which is windowless and furnished with only a steel table and two chairs. A grey-haired man sits in one of the chairs and explains that he's a psychiatrist and Edward Masterson is his patient.

"You're probably wondering why I summoned you here," he says.

I nod, keeping my gestures restrained.

"Your brother-in-law suffers from a rather severe personality disorder, caused, no doubt, by the death of his twin—your husband." The psychiatrist rests his hands on the table. "I have tried numerous procedures to cure him of this condition, but unfortunately, none have proven successful." He looks up at the ceiling. "I have made a career studying twins but have yet to see a case as confounding as this one, which is why I turn to you."

Again, I nod my head, which is tilted slightly to one side suggesting that I am doing my best, as a woman, to understand him.

"I admit that it's rare, but in some extreme cases, when a patient has seen a relative or, kin folk, if you will, the experience has had a profound effect. A shock of the familiar, you might say." He presses his hands together. "Let us hope that Edward's is one of those extreme cases," he says. "Well? Will you help?"

"Of course, but—what am I supposed to do?" I stammer.

The doctor smiles indulgently. "Just be yourself." A phone sits on the table and he lifts the receiver, and before I can change my mind, he says, "Bring him in."

I look down at my fingernails and touch their smooth, rounded edges and wish I could bolt from this stage—when I hear a door hinge creak.

Act!

Looking up, I see two hulking orderlies dressed in white uniforms and standing on either side of the patient: George.

His face is badly scarred from the accident, and his hair grows in unruly tufts on his head. He's dressed in a grey smock and matching trousers. Our eyes lock for what seems like an eternity, then he bursts into tears and collapses on his knees, begging me to help him, to free him. I listen to his anguished cries and feel hairline cracks appear in my heart. After all, this is the man I married, the man I once loved. He pleads with me to tell the doctor that he is George and not Eddy. I see desperation in his eyes, but I see something else, too. George's eyes glow not with desire or love or fondness, but with hate—for me.

And just then a gust of frigid air makes me shiver.

But we're in a windowless room!

Then I realize where the icy draft comes from. The sash window in our bedroom is raised and cold air blows across my naked body. The scene emerges from my subconscious, thrust to the surface as if a curtain had been suddenly raised. I lie on the bed. The room is in darkness, until pale light from the hallway angles across the floor as George enters the room.

And I think, George? But George is already here. He was just —with me.

"George?" I whisper, but the door closes, and the room is again in darkness. And again, I feel his body, his breath, his hands upon me. Except I know it's not George.

The meeting room spins before my eyes. I want to be ill, to cry out! I want my turn to burst into tears, but I force myself to remain composed—and in character. George is on his feet now and hurling insults at me, his bald hate on full display for anyone to see.

And it's here that I turn and look questioningly at the doctor, my eyes asking: How much more of this must I endure?

The psychiatrist nods understandingly and is about to speak when he stops himself.

He peers at me as if a sudden, outlandish idea has just dawned on him. And in this moment, both George and I know what the doctor is thinking—maybe I lied, maybe Eddy is George, maybe the patient is telling the truth after all.

George seizes the moment, his finger ramming the air, laughing hysterically, saliva dribbling from the corners of his mouth while he lists the tortures that will be visited upon me for what I have done.

But the more George carries on, the more disturbed he appears.

The psychiatrist looks between us, and I can tell that he's undecided, teetering on the fence between taking a risk on George, a fellow male—and believing my performance. For my part, I remain motionless as if turned to stone by my brother-in-law's cruel and irrational outburst. And then I see the man's eyes narrow.

Dear God. He believes George.

Now it will be me in the grey smock, locked away for having done nothing but suffer at the hands of men! I mask my horror and make one final, desperate attempt at concerned worry—for my brother-in-law.

The psychiatrist leans back in his chair and stares up at the ceiling.

A moment passes, then he says, "Take him away."

And with this directive, the orderlies clamp their large hands under George's underarms and lift him off the ground. Like a hooked fish, his body spasms and his neck twists and he screams at me—until the steel door swings shut.

"Poor Eddy," I say.

But of course, I don't mean it.

ROSEMARY MCCRACKEN

Rosemary McCracken hails from Montreal, and has worked on newspapers across Canada as a reporter, editor, arts reviewer and editorial writer. She is now a full-time Toronto fiction writer and teaches novel writing at George Brown College. Rosemary writes the Pat Tierney Mystery Series: *Safe Harbor* (shortlisted for Britain's Crime Writers' Association Debut Dagger in 2010), *Black Water*, *Raven Lake* and *Uncharted Waters*. Rosemary's short fiction has appeared in numerous magazines and anthologies. Rosemary's website is www.rosemarymccracken.com

IN FROM THE COLD

ROSEMARY MCCRACKEN

I STARED in astonishment at the stately stone house, as a bitter blast of January wind tried to tear the toque off my head. My aunt was a wealthy woman, I already knew that, but this house was the grandest on the block. It would cost a fortune just to heat it in the winter. Well, Kay Adamson *had* a fortune.

The walk to Rosedale from my shared flat in the Annex had chilled me to the bone. Shivering, I climbed the stairs to Kay's imposing front door.

The woman who opened it was in her mid-forties but she looked older. A bob of magenta hair framed her weathered face. "We finally meet, Helen," she said. "Come in!"

I stepped inside and shed my red parka. Kay handed it to a maid who was hovering nearby.

Under the sparkling hall chandelier, my aunt gave me the once-over. "You got your mother's good looks. Same wavy blond hair and green eyes." She sighed. "Jo was about your age when she left home." She turned, hitching up her baggy corduroy trousers. "We'll have a wee snort before dinner."

I followed her into the living room, where an attractive, dark-skinned woman stood by the fireplace. Kay put an arm around her.

"My partner, Samira Patel," she said. "Mira, meet Helen Szabo, my niece from Montreal."

Mira and I smiled at each other. I didn't know that Kay had a partner. The biographies I'd read hadn't yielded much personal information.

"Have a seat, Helen." Mira gestured toward the floral chintz sofa and matching armchairs.

I perched on an armchair, scanning the paintings and sketches on the walls. Kay deftly poured drinks at a trolley.

"Sorry we couldn't meet sooner," Kay said, handing me a sherry I hadn't asked for. "I spent most of the fall in England. Got home just before Christmas and found your note. So, you're doing graduate work at the University of Toronto."

She sat on the sofa beside Mira. They both held glasses of Canadian Club on the rocks.

I nodded. "I'm working on a master's in Canadian history. The role our diverse population has played in shaping this country."

Kay raised an eyebrow. "Talk to Mira," she said. "She came here from India as a child. Now she and her brother are lawyers. Her sister's a doctor."

"Canada has been a land of opportunity for my family," Mira said.

"Do you have your own law practice?" I asked.

"No, I teach," she said with a smile.

"Mira's an associate professor at Osgoode Hall Law School." Kay's voice was full of pride.

At dinner, I was all ears, soaking up every particular about my aunt. My research had told me that she'd studied visual arts in Toronto and Europe, then built a stellar career as an art critic. Kay Adamson's reviews and articles had appeared in numerous magazines and newspapers, and in gallery and museum catalogues across the continent.

"The family money certainly helped," Kay said, when I pressed her for details. "As a freelance writer, I'd never be able to live in this house. Or fund my favourite causes."

"This is the house you and Mom grew up in?" I asked.

"Yep," Kay said. "Home to three generations of Adamsons."

I winced. It would have been four generations had the house gone to my mother. Then I asked the question that had been on my mind for years. "Mom defied your father when she married, but that was years ago. Why did we never meet before, Aunt Kay?"

"Call me Kay, young woman. I'm hardly the auntie type. I have no talent for nurturing family relationships. That's why I lost touch with your mother."

My mother, Joanna Adamson, was Kay's older sister. Mom met my dad, Gábor Szabo, when they were students at the U of T. Mom's father vetoed their marriage, so they ran off to Montreal. In the following years, my parents and I had no communication with Mom's family. When I decided to contact Kay that fall, I had no idea how to reach her. I remembered seeing her name in my mother's tattered address book, but that book had vanished after Mom died. I finally sent Kay a letter care of *Canadian Artist*, a magazine to which she regularly contributed. The editors forwarded it to her home.

"Kay, you were what, 16 years old, when your sister married?" Mira said. "What could you have done?"

"I could have answered Jo's letters. Called her. Visited."

The letters were a big surprise. "Mom wrote to you?" I asked.

"She wrote to our parents. No doubt behind Gabe's back," Kay said. "Father threw the letters in the trash, and I salvaged those I could. But I never had the nerve to write back, not even after Jo sent your birth announcement."

She topped up our wine glasses, and I saw she hadn't touched the wine in her own glass. And she'd only picked at the roast beef and vegetables on her plate.

"Back then, I spent a week skiing in the Laurentians every winter," Kay said. "Heck, I could have taken a bus from Saint-Sauveur to Montreal." She lowered her eyes. "But I didn't reach out until it was too late. Years later, I phoned Jo when I was in Montreal for a museum exhibit. She hung up on me. And I didn't know she'd been ill until she died. Gabe sent a letter to the house."

"That's so sad," I said softly. But why would my mother hang up on her sister? It was her father who'd cut ties, not Kay.

Mira turned to me. "What did your mother tell you about her family?"

"Mom died when I was fourteen," I said, "so I didn't have a chance to ask her much. All I know is she'd married against her father's wishes."

"My father cut Jo out of his will," Kay said. "Much to Gabe's chagrin, I'm sure."

That rankled. My dad wasn't interested in the Adamsons' money. He had a good salary at McGill. He was happy in the Montreal bungalow he and my mother had bought. He lived there now with his second wife.

But I pushed those thoughts aside and asked my other pressing question. "Kay, what did your father have against my dad?"

"Gabe and his family would always be foreigners," she said. "No matter how well they did in Canada."

Foreigners, such an ugly word. My dad was a tenured professor at a top Canadian university. He'd won awards for his research.

"Gabe was a babe in arms when his family fled Hungary after the 1956 Revolution," Kay went on. "Many who escaped were well educated."

I knew this. What point was she trying to make?

"Gabe's father found a job as a senior engineer at the Sudbury nickel mines," Kay said. "He and his family prospered. Gabe won a full scholarship to the U of T, then he was accepted into McGill's graduate program in physics. But that wasn't good enough for my father." She took Mira's hand. "I'm sorry, my love. I come from a family of pigheaded bigots."

Mira gave her a weak smile.

I looked around Kay's dining room: the table laden with crystal, silverware, and fine china; the A.Y. Jackson on the wall behind Mira; the maid in uniform clearing away plates before dessert. And the dowdy woman with magenta hair at the head of the table.

My mother should have had an equal share of this—the home, the money, the opportunities. It was so unfair!

And, as her daughter, I should, too. But we'd been denied it, because Mom had married a foreigner.

"I'm very tired, Helen," Kay said. "I'm going to say good night. Mira will send you home in a taxi. I hope you'll come to dinner again next Sunday."

Montreal had been good to my parents. Dad earned his doctorate at McGill University, while Mom, who was fluent in French, worked in public relations at Montreal's city hall. After he graduated, Dad took a position at the National Research Council in Ottawa, and I was born in our nation's capital the following year. A few years later, Dad returned to McGill as a professor of physics.

Now that I'd moved away from home, I saw less of my father, but I spent every Christmas with him and my stepmother. In the summer, I visited them at their cottage on Lac Archambault.

"My favourite daughter!" Dad said when I reached him on the telephone later that evening. "How goes the graduate student?"

"Your *only child*, Dad. I'm doing well." I hesitated for a moment, then plunged in. "Hey, I had dinner with Kay Adamson last night." I didn't think my father would have bad memories of my aunt. She was only a girl when my parents married.

"Kay.… So that's what she's calling herself in 2008. She was Kitty when I knew her."

"She's a well-known art critic."

"She has a family?"

"She has a partner, Samira Patel."

Dad chuckled. "So Kitty favours women."

"Just wanted to tell you we'd met."

He was silent for a few moments. Then he said in a low voice, "It's natural that you're curious about your mother's family. Still, I hope this is as far as you will take it. Believe me, you do not want to tangle with the Adamsons."

Monday was another blustery January day. After my morning class, I hunkered down at a computer in the Robarts Library. A search told me what I already knew: that my maternal grandfather, Charles Adamson, had built a financial services empire. *Forbes Magazine* added a new detail: Charles's net worth was in the high eight figures when he died fifteen years ago at the age of eighty-five.

Forbes said that Charles had left the bulk of his estate to his daughter Katherine, and he'd also left a number of charitable bequests. An article in *Canadian Philanthropy* listed several organizations that had benefited from Charles's financial generosity during his lifetime, and several that had profited from his time and business acumen. The hairs on the back of my neck rose to attention when I read that the Hungarian Welcome Fund was one of the groups that he'd backed. It had raised money and helped find jobs for the 37,500 Hungarian refugees who came to Canada in 1956 and 1957. Charles had been its co-chairman.

That didn't sound like a man who looked down on "foreigners." He might have drawn the line at an immigrant marrying his daughter. But the fact that he'd gone out of his way to help Hungarian refugees—which would have included my dad's family— gave me pause.

I mulled it over all day, and called Dad again that evening.

I skipped the usual pleasantries when he picked up. "I read today that Charles Adamson was co-chair of the Hungarian Welcome Fund."

"That is correct."

"So why did he object to you and Mom marrying?"

"What has your aunt been telling you?" Dad barked.

"That her father considered an immigrant an unsuitable husband for his daughter."

He gave a derisive snort. "That's the spin she's putting on it! Ask your aunt what she told her father about me."

Then he hung up.

I had a sleepless night, wondering whether I should call Kay. But she'd invited me to dinner on Sunday, so I saved my question for the weekend.

Tuesday was another freezing day. I had no classes, and I caught up with my reading at home. In the afternoon, I received an email from my father: *Just arrived in Toronto. Baraka, 6 p.m.*

Dad had taken me to the Hungarian restaurant in the theatre district when he'd helped me move to Toronto. That evening, I bundled up against the cold and took the subway down to King Street West. I found Dad at a table for two, a bottle of Hungarian red and two glasses in front of him. He stood when he saw me. We kissed on both cheeks.

I studied him as he poured the wine. Now in his fifties, Gabe Szabo was still a handsome man with expressive brown eyes, a rugged face, and a trim, wiry build. His dark hair had turned silver at the temples.

He handed me a glass of wine, clinked it with his. "*Egészségedre.*"

"*Egészségedre,*" I said. "To your health." I smiled at him. "Where are you staying, Dad?"

"I'm taking the train back tonight."

He ordered for both of us, then I waited. He had come to Toronto to tell me something. He needed to approach it in his own way, so I didn't push him.

I had to wait until we'd finished our goulash soup.

He placed his spoon on the table. "I was welcomed at the Adamson home when I started seeing your mother."

That was news to me. I leaned back in my chair, waiting for more.

"I was invited to Sunday dinner every week."

Of course, Sunday dinners were weekly rituals for the Adamsons.

Dad continued while the waiter served our cabbage rolls. "I enjoyed those dinners. Margaret, your grandmother, was a gracious woman. Charles liked to talk about Hungary, what was going on over there."

He dug into his food.

"It was Charles who told you about his work with the Hungarian Welcome Fund."

"Yes." Dad set his fork and knife on his plate. "He was fascinated by Hungary. I knew far less about it than he did. I was only six months old when we left."

The waiter placed a platter of schnitzel and dumplings on the table.

"Eat up, my girl," Dad said, serving me a large helping from the platter.

I didn't know how I'd get through all that food.

After a few bites of schnitzel, he went on. "Charles and Margaret seemed to like me. I planned to ask for Jo's hand in marriage when we graduated."

I smiled, thinking how quaint my dad was. *Ask for Jo's hand in marriage*—geesh!

"Then one Sunday, everything changed," he said. "Jo called me in the morning, said her parents had other plans for the evening. She sounded like she'd been crying. I asked what the matter was, but she wouldn't tell me."

"You were no longer welcome at the house."

He grimaced. "That was the least of it. The next day, Jo told me Kitty had said something about me that upset their parents."

My mind was clicking away: thief, fraudster, Communist Party member? What had Kay told her parents?

Dad placed a hand over mine on the table. "Heléna, this is not something a father can easily say to his daughter."

"I'll understand, Dad."

"Jo was reluctant to tell me, but she finally did. Kitty said I'd … forced myself on her."

This was far worse than I'd expected. "She claimed you'd *raped* her?"

"Kitty didn't go that far. She said I'd made improper advances, kissed her, touched her. Absurd! She was a kid with braces on her teeth. How could she think up such a thing?"

I was outraged by my aunt's accusation. Then I had a terrible thought. "Did the Adamsons bring in the police? Were you charged?"

"Goodness, no. They believed Kitty, of course. But they did not want to go public, create a scandal. That was not their way."

"But Mom believed you, right?"

"Your mother, my sweet angel, was always on my side. Besides, she knew I'd never been alone with Kitty. I'd had no opportunity, as they say in detective novels."

"Did you tell that to the Adamsons?"

"I tried to. I was turned away by the maid when I went to the house. I sent Charles and Margaret a letter. Jo said they received it, but I never heard back from them."

"Did you ask them if you and Mom could marry?"

"In my letter, I said Joanna and I wanted to marry, and I asked for their blessing. You know the rest. Your mother was forbidden to marry me, to ever see me again. A week after we graduated, we took a train to Montreal and were married there."

"And Kay … Kitty? Did you ever see her again?"

"No, and I never wanted to."

"Why would she tell her parents that monstrous lie?"

He shrugged. "Who knows? Jealous of her sister's happiness? Or maybe she just wanted to stir up trouble."

Or maybe it was something much bigger. My mother had told me her sister hoped to be an artist. And Kay knew that artists starved.

"Kitty knew Mom wouldn't give you up," I said slowly, thinking it through. "She knew her parents would believe her lie. She knew her father would punish you by disinheriting Mom. Then Kitty would get everything."

Dad looked skeptical. "Would a girl of her age think about inheritances?"

I smiled knowingly. "Young women can recognize an opportunity as well as anyone."

I made the trek to Rosedale on Sunday, wind pummelling me all the way.

"Mira won't be joining us for dinner," Kay said, handing my parka to the maid. "She's visiting her family."

Kay poured drinks in the living room; this time, I rated Canadian Club. Glasses in hand, we toured the art on the main floor, Kay giving a commentary on each piece. Her parents had started the collection. The works they'd chosen, in Kay's opinion, were mediocre. She had acquired the rest: a Renoir sketch, three Picasso linocuts, a Miró lithograph, paintings by Emily Carr, the Group of Seven, and several stunning carvings by indigenous artists.

"My favourite," Kay said, pointing to a Lawren Harris painting of an iceberg.

"Do you still paint?" I asked when we'd returned to the living room. "Mom told me you were good."

Kay set her glass on the drinks trolley. The ice had melted, but she hadn't touched the drink. "I quit years ago. Didn't have what it takes to go the whole nine yards. But I learned to appreciate the masters. That became my area of expertise."

"You don't miss it?" I asked.

"Not at all." She waved an arm to include all the art in the room. "I'm surrounded by the greats. And I've put together a few exhibits in recent years. That's a different kind of creativity."

At dinner, I downed two large glasses of red wine. Over dessert, I told Kay what I'd read about her father co-chairing the Hungarian Welcome Fund. "He helped refugees like my father," I said. "And Dad was pretty tight with your parents for a while. He had Sunday dinner here every week."

My aunt shook her head. "Those dreadful dinners. Gabe looked so uncomfortable."

She'd got that wrong. "Dad enjoyed those dinners."

Kay gave a dismissive flap of her hand. "My parents felt sorry for Gabe. They treated him well until he assumed he could marry their daughter. A Hungarian immigrant was not what they had in mind for Jo."

I slashed at my slice of pecan pie. She was lying right to my face.

I debated how to play this. Then I took a deep breath, and jumped to the heart of the matter. "You told your parents that my dad sexually assaulted you."

Kay's eyes bored into me. "Who told you that?"

"My dad. You wanted Mom cut out of your father's will so you'd come into all the Adamson money."

Kay's mouth fell open. She was struggling to find words when the front door opened.

"Hello, Helen," Mira said as she entered the dining room. She was wearing her long dark hair loose that evening.

She kissed Kay on the cheek. "What's the matter, my dear?"

"We were talking about Gabe," Kay said as Mira took the chair across from me. "He told Helen I'm to blame for Jo being disinherited."

Mira fixed dark, anxious eyes on me.

"Our parents turned against Gabe after he tried to molest me," Kay said.

"We didn't think you knew, Helen," Mira said, "and we didn't want to tell you. You are not to blame for your father's actions."

I stared at them, realizing they both believed the lie Kay had fabricated years before.

Kay suddenly looked exhausted. "I'll say good night now. Mira, give Helen money for a taxi."

"I'll drive Helen home," Mira said.

"Turn left," I said as we approached Kay's street corner in Mira's Volvo.

Mira made a right-hand turn. "I have something to tell you."

The wind had died down, but the temperature had plummeted. It wasn't a night for a chat on the streets of Rosedale.

"What is it?" I asked.

"Wait until we stop. I'm watching for ice on the road."

We left the streets of grand houses, drove down streets of smaller houses, and entered a neighbourhood of high-rise towers and fast-food outlets. "Where the hell are we going?" I asked.

"This is where I come from," Mira said. "My family lived here when we arrived in Canada."

She made a sharp left, then pulled into a parking lot facing a piece of land surrounded by a high wire fence. The double gate to the fence was closed.

"Community gardens, my mother's special place." Mira killed the Volvo's lights. "My niece has a garden here, too."

The light of the lone streetlamp behind us illuminated rows of snow-covered plots enclosed by low fences. "You wanted to tell me something," I reminded Mira.

She turned in her seat to look at me. "Helen, you came into Kay's life a week ago," she said. "Since then, she's spoken of you every day. She's really taken to you."

That was good to hear.

"But tonight, you brought up an old family grievance."

"It was more than an old family grievance," I cried. "It was a horrible lie. It kept my mother from her family."

"And kept her from her inheritance," Mira said. "I'm sure that was on your mind when you brought it up tonight."

"My mother was entitled to her share of the Adamsons' wealth, of course she was. It was her right."

"And you'd be a wealthy woman if she'd come into it."

It sounded like Mira had *her* eyes on the Adamsons' money.

"Helen, your aunt isn't well." Mira sounded choked-up now. "A year ago, Kay was diagnosed with stage-four ovarian cancer. She's had surgery and chemo, but I'm not sure how much time she has left. She doesn't like to talk about it."

It all fell into place. How old Kay looked, even though she was only in her forties. Her lack of appetite. How easily she tired. And that rigid magenta helmet—she was wearing a wig.

"I'm asking you to leave the past alone," Mira said. "Leave Kay in peace for the time she has left."

I had to move on, at least appear to move on. "Mom had ovarian cancer, too."

"You lost your mother when you were very young," Mira said. "I'm sorry about that. But Jo was happy with the life she chose. She married the man she loved. They had a beautiful daughter. And your father has done extremely well in his career. What Kay told her parents about him never went public. He's fortunate they were discreet."

Rage roiled in my gut; my dad would never assault a woman. But I tried to appear calm. I now had a shot at righting the wrong that had been done to my parents. And to me.

"The Adamson fortune won't come to you, Helen."

That hit me like a blow. "Who inherits when Kay dies?" I asked.

"I do," Mira said.

"The house, too?"

"The house, too. It's been my home for the past five years."

Now I was seething with rage.

"Come," Mira said. "I'll show you where my mother gardened."

Why would I want to see a frozen garden plot? "It's cold outside."

She killed the engine and opened the car door. "We need some fresh air," she said, slipping the car's key fob into her jacket pocket. "The gate's locked at night, but Mama's plot is beside the fence."

It had been a cold winter, but Toronto hadn't had much snow. Nothing like the snow we got in Montreal. The parking lot pavement was bare. Only a thin layer of snow covered the grass as I followed Mira along the wire fence.

"Are there surveillance cameras?" I asked. "We'd look pretty suspicious skulking around here."

"No cameras. My niece says anyone who climbs this fence to steal vegetables must really need them."

She pointed to a plot on the other side of the fence. "Mama's allotment."

"Your mother...?"

Mira bowed her head. "Mama has Alzheimer's. She's in a

nursing home, but until two years ago she lived in the same apartment we rented when we came to Canada. My niece lives there now." She spun around to face me. "My family had nothing when we arrived here. We worked hard for everything we got."

Her message was clear. I didn't deserve a share of the Adamsons' wealth, but she did. I would never live in my family's home, but she would. And she'd probably bring in her mother and her niece.

She gripped my arm—hard. "You see how far I've come?"

I wrenched my arm away from her. Rage, pure and uncontrollable, rose to the surface. She'd already turned away when I picked up a rock the size of a baseball from a pile of debris and smashed it against the side of her head.

Mira staggered and crumpled to the ground. I lifted the rock again, this time straight up in the air. I brought it down hard on her head.

I stared at her. Her head was twisted to the side, and I found myself looking into a smashed eye. What had I done?

I threw the rock over the fence, heard it land with a thud on the other side. Breathing heavily, I took the key fob from Mira's pocket and looked around. The gardens were deserted. So was the street. Then I saw my trail of boot prints in the snow. Stooping, I made my way backwards to the car, sweeping every print with my gloved hands. I dropped the fob into the purse Mira had left in the car, and took out her wallet.

I walked for what must have been a good half-hour until I reached the subway. Under a streetlamp, I noticed a spatter of brown stains on the front and the left sleeve of my red parka. I looped my long scarf over the front, hoping no one would notice the stains on the sleeve. I moistened a tissue with snow and rubbed it over my face. The tissue came away clean.

Back in the flat, I took the money out of Mira's wallet, and stuffed my parka, my gloves, and my scarf into a large garbage bag. I heaved the bag into a dumpster three blocks away. On the way back to the flat, I dropped the wallet in a mailbox.

Kay called me in a panic around midnight. Mira hadn't returned home. I told my aunt that Mira had let me off at my street corner around 8:30. "Go back to bed, Kay," I said. "She's probably visiting a friend."

She called again in the morning, this time distraught with grief. Police officers had come to the house. Mira's body had been found by a dog walker outside the East End Community Gardens.

I took a taxi to Rosedale.

I had the maid make lunch. After we'd eaten—Kay taking only a bite of a sandwich and a mouthful of soup—two detectives rang the doorbell. They wanted to hear about my car ride with Mira.

"She talked about Kay," I said, looking at my aunt. "She said you were the best thing that ever happened to her."

Kay's eyes filled with tears.

"Did Dr. Patel say where she'd be going after she dropped you off?" Detective Banerjee asked.

"She mentioned visiting her mother's garden," I said. "But I didn't think she'd actually go there on such a cold night."

Kay nodded. "Mira's mom had a plot at the community gardens. Those gardens are big with foreigners."

A frown crossed Detective Banerjee's face.

"It's a rough part of town," Detective Ramsay said. "The victim's wallet was missing."

Kay and I attended the funeral Mira's family held for her. Then I helped my aunt arrange a memorial service for her partner.

Kay came to depend on me more and more in the following weeks. A month after the memorial, she asked me to move into the house in Rosedale. "I don't want you to feel tied down with a sick woman," she said, alluding to her illness for the first time. "Come and go as you please, and bring your friends to the house. I'd just like to know that you're close by."

I gave it some serious thought. When I accepted my aunt's invitation a few days later, her eyes lit up. I saw how happy I'd made her.

And that made me happy, too.

BRENDA CHAPMAN

Brenda Chapman is an Ottawa crime fiction author with over twenty published novels. In addition to short stories and standalones, she has written the lauded Stonechild and Rouleau police procedural series, the Anna Sweet mystery novellas, and the Jennifer Bannon mysteries for middle grade. Her work has been shortlisted for several awards including four Crime Writers of Canada Awards of Excellence. Her latest book, *Blind Date* is the first in the Hunter and Tate Mystery series (2022). Brenda's website is www.brendachapman.ca

THE FINAL HIT

BRENDA CHAPMAN

THE MORNING SUNLIGHT caught Billy full in the eyes like a splitting headache. He rolled onto his side and squinted at the woman lying next to him. He vaguely remembered her from the night before. Soft mouth. Long legs. Flaming red hair that tumbled past her shoulders after she shook it free.

"So, are you going to do it?" she asked, twirling a long strand around and around in her slender fingers. She'd propped herself up on an elbow and reached her free hand to rub her lacquered fingernails over the green eagle spreading its wings across his chest.

He wanted to ask her name but thought she might not appreciate the question. "Do what?" he asked instead.

"Wesley's off shift in an hour. He goes to Milo's bar for a couple of beers before heading home to sleep. You could do him before he gets into his car."

Billy took a moment to absorb what she was asking of him. The pain behind his eyes made it hard to concentrate. "And Wesley is...."

"My husband, silly. We already talked about this." Her fingers tiptoed across his skin. "You said...no, you promised that you could help me solve my problem." Her voice rose with every word until she was sitting straight up looking down at him. "Fifteen thousand in cash. You agreed it was more than generous. You promised you could help me." The pout on her face seemed practised, but still he felt trapped by her need.

He focused on the curtains blowing like white sails into the room while her fingers found their way to his thigh. His head felt like a hundred tiny hammers were pounding to get out. He tried to focus. Blacking out was becoming more and more of a problem. She'd been sitting at the bar when he walked into the Golden Dog to catch the start of the ballgame on the big screen. She was all right looking but not really his type. She'd slid her drink over to sit next to him after a whispered conversation with the bartender. *Lonnie.* Her name came to him out of the fog in his brain.

"That's not something I do anymore." He sat up and swung his legs over the side of the bed.

"But the bartender told me you were the man who solved problems for a price. I can't stand spending another minute living like this."

"Why don't you get a divorce? Walk out and not look back." He found his shirt on the floor and bent to retrieve it. He was going to have to have a chat with Joe and get him to stop giving out his name.

"Wesley won't let that happen." She leaned against the headboard with the sheet covering her legs. She hugged her chest into her bent knees, her long hair a veil covering her face. "He's not the forgiving kind." She raised her head and pushed aside a lank of hair. Her eyes were grey, cloudy pools of anguish. "Look, I understand if you're not certain about me. I'll give you a few days to decide if you want to help me out. I have a phone that can't be traced and I'll give you the number. The money's still on the table if you change your mind."

After she was in the shower, he went through her purse, found her driver's licence, and noted her name and address. Lonnie Murphy clocked in at five foot nine, one hundred and twenty-five pounds, thirty-four years old. He tucked her wallet back in her purse and left the motel room before she finished washing off his scent.

Billy had taken up walking since his last stint in jail. Today, he left his bachelor apartment after lunch and headed north toward the lakeshore. The route took him through residential streets, bypassing the busier thoroughfares that cut across St. Catharines. The city was poorly laid out, but he'd lived here his entire life and knew its peculiarities.

An hour later, he reached the entrance to the parkland trails and chose a path that took him through the thick woods with periodic glimpses of the Welland Canal on his right. After twenty minutes, he broke free of the trees to the full beauty of Sunset Beach, a long stretch of sand, lake, and sky that never failed to make him feel like a kid with nothing but long summer days ahead. His eyes were drawn to a lake freighter easing her way across the horizon. The day had clouded over and an autumn chill was keeping away the swimmers. He didn't like to think about the long, cold winter months ahead. He found a dry spot near the water and sat watching the waves roll in sheets onto the shore.

A day had passed since his encounter with the redhead. The entire episode had left him unmoored—like a dark beast was growing hungry in his belly. He was a forty-two-year-old alcoholic, working in a restaurant kitchen with no chance of going anywhere better. No adrenaline rushes that used to own him like a drug when he was part of the business. Fifteen thousand dollars would go a long way to easing his existence and was worth turning over in his mind. He occasionally felt the pull of his old life, but not because the work had given him any joy. Going straight had cost him his friendships and a lot of money. A hell of a lot of money.

Taking a new path through the woods, he thought about Lonnie. He had an image of her crying when she talked about the beatings, but the rest of what she said was foggy, maddeningly out of reach. He was drinking less than a month ago, but the blackouts came just the same once he got started into the hard stuff. His hands trembled and he shoved them into the pockets of his jacket. He'd left the bottle at home in a momentary burst of resolve, the only reason he wasn't chugging rye at the moment to get him through the walk home.

He took a new route through the city streets and ended up standing across the road from Milo's Sports Bar, knowing this had been his destination all along. He took a pair of glasses out of his pocket and adjusted his ball cap. He'd earlier put his long hair into a ponytail and safely tucked it under the hat. As disguises went, the changes would be enough to fool most people. It was amazing how few really looked at another person full on.

The brightness of the large room was a stark contrast to the Dog, his usual down-and-out tavern. He counted six television sets tuned to various sports events, a sound system pumping out top forty. This time of the afternoon was early for social drinkers, but a few couples were scattered amongst the booths. He crossed to the bar and took a stool with a view of the ballgame when he leaned back.

He'd done a search for Wesley Murphy and found a photo on LinkedIn. Wesley posing with his firefighting team at a charity football game. He was a bear of a man with black, curly hair and a wide grin that masked his dark underbelly. Billy scanned the bar but saw no sign of him. The bartender poured a draft beer and he hunkered down with a bowl of cashews.

Wesley arrived two hours and twenty minutes later and took a seat halfway down the bar. He chatted for a while with the bartender, who set a quart of beer in front of Wesley without being asked. They laughed and kidded each other until a server showed up with an order, drawing the bartender to the far end of the bar. Wesley raised his glass and glanced Billy's way. His eyes were friendly, his expression open to starting a conversation. Billy guessed this was providence shining on him. He'd been about to pay his tab and leave but had ordered one more pint for the road before Wesley showed up.

Wesley took a sip of beer. "Never seen you in here before."

"Just passing by and felt thirsty." He paused. "This your regular?"

"Could say. Who's winning?"

"Sorry? Oh, the ballgame. Jays by two runs. Sixth inning."

"Sweet."

The bartender returned and he and Wesley carried on their conversation. Billy bided his time, popped cashews into his mouth, one after the other. A different server set her tray on the counter and the bartender walked over to take the order. Wesley slid down a couple of seats toward him.

"Just got off shift. I come here on my way home to unwind."

"Oh yeah? What is it you do?"

"Firefighter."

Billy grinned. "Posed for any calendars lately?"

"Nope, too busy putting out blazes. What about you—live in St. Catharines?"

"Born and bred."

They were quiet for a bit, watching the game. The Jays' lead widened. They discussed the pitching. Billy couldn't think of anything to say outside of sports commentary that wouldn't tip his hand. He finished his beer and pushed the glass away from him. "Well, time to hit the road."

Wesley saluted. "Good meeting you, buddy. I should be kicking off myself. Time to see my little boy."

Billy hesitated. "You have a kid?"

"The reason I get up every day. Chad's turning three end of the month. You? Any kids?"

"A girl. She's ten now and lives with her mother." He never talked about his family, least of all with a guy he was sizing up to kill, but the fact Wesley and Lonnie had a kid gave him pause. Abusing your wife was one thing, but a child…the payoff from the hit dropped a slot in importance as he thought about the repercussions of his decision: a kid living in an abusive household or one growing up without a father. Neither choice left a good taste in his mouth having experienced both at different times. "See you around," he said, keeping the sudden surge of rage in check, taking one last look at the back of Wesley's head as he reached the front door and stepped outside into the falling darkness.

It took a week, but she was back in his bar, sitting at a table in the corner near the washrooms, this time with a glass of Sangria and a blouse so low cut he had to force his eyes up to her face. Man, he wished he could remember even ten minutes of that night he'd been in bed with her. She acknowledged him with a tilt of her glass where he stood leaning against the bar waiting for a beer.

He sauntered over and took the seat facing her with his back to the room. "I was waiting for you," she said. She turned her face toward him, and it was then that he saw the plum bruise running along her cheekbone and darkening the skin around her eye. She'd tried to hide the discolouration with makeup, but nothing could fully disguise the puffiness. "Have you reconsidered my offer?"

Billy touched under his own eye. "He do that to your face?"

"Who else?" She sounded weary. Defeated.

"I can help you solve your problem." The suggestion stilled the rage simmering at the back of his throat, and he accepted his decision to help her without further introspection. "This is the last time we meet in public."

"Agreed." Her eyes had lightened, and she rewarded him with a dazzling smile and a package slid under the table into his lap. "Half now. Half after. My cell number is on the envelope in case you lost it. I hope…we can see each other sometime later."

He felt a flicker of irritation for her presuming that he'd do the job, but he swallowed the feeling. He'd have to make contact with an old connection to buy a gun and a burner phone. Already, he was feeling more alive as he contemplated logistics. This was what his life had been missing. He tucked the money into his jacket and stood. "I'll be in touch."

You can't fight your nature, Billy thought, no matter how hard you try. He was walking down Ontario Street on his way to kill Wesley Murphy on this frosty, October evening. An eerie fog had settled on the city, making streetlights shimmer through the murk. He'd swallowed his second thoughts about the job, but the heavy feeling in his gut wasn't going away. Milo's neon-red sign wavered through the thick, damp air from the doorway where he stood in the shadows across the street.

The door to the bar opened and closed several times without any sign of Wesley. Billy wondered if he'd picked the wrong night. This could be one of Wesley's days off or he could be home sick. Lonnie could have got his schedule wrong. Life was filled with unforeseen circumstances, and he'd learned to roll with them. Go with the messages from the universe. If Wesley lived another day, so be it. There was always tomorrow.

Billy shivered inside his black leather jacket and thought about leaving. Before he exited the shadows, the bar door opened, spilling country and western music out into the night along with a blond woman and Wesley, holding a young boy in his arms. The three of them were laughing and the boy had his hands wrapped tightly around Wesley's neck. The woman called the boy Chad as she slid her hand up his sweater and tickled his ribs. Billy pulled back and followed them at a distance, curious about Wesley and the woman's open displays of affection, their obvious happiness with each other and the boy, who had the same colouring and eyes as the woman when they stood next to each other under a streetlight. She crouched to zipper his jacket and held his cheeks in both hands, the action so familiar that Billy knew instinctively that this was the kid's mother.

He followed them to a house four blocks over and watched them enter together. He waited until the lights went on in an upstairs bedroom before he slipped away on his route home.

He phoned Lonnie on his burner phone Saturday evening. "It's done," he said. "Check the news. They haven't named him yet, but they will."

He heard her nails clicking on keys and an intake of breath.

"Oh, thank God. Wesley didn't come home, and I was hoping against hope."

"The police will be there soon to inform you. Act surprised. About the rest of the money...." He didn't need to elaborate.

"Where and when do you want to meet?"

"We should hold off a couple of days. I'll be in the Lakeshore Road Metro parking lot on Wednesday at dusk, waiting for you."

"Perfect, and Billy...thank you. Thank you for giving me my life back."

"You and your son."

She took a moment to respond. "Yes, Chad and I don't have to live in fear anymore."

"That's as long as you pay me the rest of the money." He laughed to lighten the threat, but he wanted to make sure she knew.

Her voice was low and intense. "I always pay my debts."

The rest of the week went past in a blur. He worked a couple of shifts and spent his day off at Sunset Beach, trying to make peace with what he'd done. The rush of adrenaline was now a sick heaviness in his stomach. Every waking hour was a lead-up to Wednesday evening when he'd see her again. He was more than ready when the time to meet finally arrived.

He walked to the Metro and leaned against a corner of the building, watching the parking lot and trying not to look suspicious. It was fifteen minutes before closing time when she eased her black Hyundai into a spot at the far end of the lot as the shadows stretched wide fingers across the pavement. She took her time getting out of the car, her long legs bare under a short trench coat, platform heels making her rear end sway like an invitation as she crossed to the grocery store entrance. She stopped a couple of times to look around, but she couldn't see him from where he stood watching.

She was inside the store for ten minutes and emerged with a shopping bag tucked under one arm. By now, the shadows had merged into a band of black, and only a few cars were left in the lot. Closing time was minutes away. He pushed himself off the wall and met her at her car.

"You startled me," she said, grasping a hand to her chest.

"How did things go with the cops?"

"No problem. I'd imagined Wesley's death so many times that I could play the grieving widow in my sleep."

"This is your chance to ask any questions, because I won't be seeing you again."

She tilted her head to one side and studied him. Ran her tongue slowly across her top lip. "Yeah, probably not a good idea. Did he suffer or did you make it quick?"

"Quick. Wesley never knew what hit him."

"Pity. I would have liked him to feel some of the pain he inflicted on me all these years." She reached in her bag and withdrew another envelope. "I'll drop this on the ground and you can pick it up after I drive away."

"Have a good life, Lonnie. Don't marry any more assholes."

He bent and grabbed the money and lifted his head to watch her brake lights slam on before she reached the exit. Two unmarked police cars blocked her path and a third sidled up next to him.

"Well done." The woman detective rolled down the window, reached for the envelope with a gloved hand, and invited him into the back seat. Wesley slid across to the far side to give him space to climb in next to him.

"That went well," Billy said, turning sideways to look at Wesley. "She won't be stalking you for a good long time."

"And to think I was married to her once. We were kids, just out of high school. Not a life choice I'd recommend." Wesley reached over and shook Billy's hand. The wariness in his eyes was still there, but his grip was firm. "You have no idea the hell she's made my life."

"I could hazard a guess."

"My wife and I moved here from Mississauga when Chad was born, to get away from her. She was quiet this year and I let my guard down. Big, big mistake."

♥

Billy left the police station as sunlight was streaking the darkness in the east, refusing the offer of a lift home. He was doing a double shift at the restaurant starting in a few hours and needed the fresh air. He'd avoided being charged in exchange for his testimony. If the old crew could see him now, they'd never believe what he'd just done. They'd likely want to do something about it—something that involved a whole lot of hurt.

He whistled all the way down Lake Street on his way home to shower and change his clothes as the sun glinted off the weathered row of grey apartment buildings. He wasn't sure when exhaustion would set in, but knew its arrival was inevitable. He'd make the most of the day before then, hang onto the adrenaline pumping through his chest as long as he could.

Come the weekend, he'd catch the train to Toronto to finally see his kid. His ex said Stella had all but given up asking when he was coming to see her. He'd kept back a couple of thousand from Lonnie's advance for his troubles, nobody being the wiser, and he'd buy Stella something real nice to help her forget about all the times he hadn't shown up. Looking into his daughter's eyes after two years locked up might help lay some ghosts to rest.

He reached his low rise and stared up at his apartment window and the Canada flag draped across the glass to keep out the morning sun. He stood for a moment longer, surveying the low-income building with a critical eye as he tried to make sense of the last twenty-four hours. He pulled open the door and punched in the code to let him inside. The lobby smelled of curry and urine and a heaping load of despair. He thought it might be time change things up—stop searching for the meaning of life at the bottom of another whisky bottle, get a real job, and move out of this hellhole. Maybe go live in Mississauga to be closer to Stella. Who'd have believed that *not* killing somebody would give his own sorry existence a reason to keep going? He shook his head and smiled at the irony as he hit the up button on his way to the third floor.

ACKNOWLEDGEMENTS

Cold Canadian Crime was first conceptualized in the spring of 2021, although we didn't have a name for it then. We did, however, know that it would be written and compiled by members of Crime Writers of Canada to honour CWC's 40th Anniversary.

Deepest appreciation goes to our Managing Editor, Ludvica Boota, and the rest of the Anthology Committee: Alice Bienia, Susan Daly, Zana Gordon, Winona Kent, and Lorna Poplak.

But even the best teams do not work alone. Many thanks to the following people, without whose contributions, general assistance, and commitment this anthology would not have been possible:

The judges, Allison Dore, Lori McMulkin, and Katrin Szymanski, for their time, energy, and collaborative efforts.

Karen Abrahamson, Alison Bruce, Tuhin Giri, Taija Morgan, and Alexandra Zych, for their invaluable administrative, creative, and technical expertise.

William Deverell and Linwood Barclay, for their wise and witty words to lead off this collection.

And, of course, to all the authors who submitted their stories for consideration in *Cold Canadian Crime*. We couldn't have done it without you, and we wouldn't want to.

Last, but certainly not least, a huge vote of thanks to our readers. Thank you for reading Canadian crime and supporting Canadian authors. You are the reason we write.

Judy Penz Sheluk
Chair, Crime Writers of Canada 2020-22
Chair, 40th Anniversary Anthology Committee

FIND THE AUTHOR

K.L. Abrahamson
www.karenlabrahamson.com

Pam Barnsley
www.pambarnsley.com

Thom Bennett
www.thombennett.com

Susan Calder
www.susancalder.com

Melodie Campbell
www.melodiecampbell.com

Brenda Chapman
www.brendachapman.ca

Lisa de Nikolits
www.lisawriter.com

Elizabeth Elwood
www.elihuentertainment.com

Alice Fitzpatrick
www.alicefitzpatrick.com

Delee Fromm
www.linkedin.com/in/deleefromm

R.M. Greenaway
www.rmgreenaway.com

Blair Keetch
www.blairkeetch.com

Sylvia Maultash Warsh
www.sylviawarsh.com

Rosemary McCracken
www.rosemarymccracken.com

donalee Moulton
@donaleeMoulton

Lynne Murphy
www.lynnemurphy.ca

C.S. O'Cinneide
www.shekillslit.com

Lorna Poplak
www.lornapoplak.com

David A. Poulsen
www.facebook.com/david.poulsen.71

Gabrielle St. George
www.gabriellestgeorge.com

Hope Thompson
www.hopethompson.net

www.ingramcontent.com/pod-product-compliance
Lightning Source LLC
Chambersburg PA
CBHW070058120726
47909CB00002B/430